THE PATH OF DECISIONS

THE CREMELINO PROPHECY
BOOK II

MIKE SHELTON

Acknowledgements

First and foremost I thank my wife Melissa for all her patience as I have worked through multiple versions of manuscripts in this trilogy over many years. Her support of my dreams has always meant so much to me. I thank my children Danielle, Emily, and Ryan, my parents and my siblings for their continued interest, support, and encouragement of my writing.

This book would not have been accomplished without the work and help of Heather Moore and others at Precision Editing Group, as well as my beta readers. I really appreciate all the feedback and support they have given me.

Bringing my book to life visually was Brooke Gillette. She took a few notes and directions from me and expanded it into a colorful, awesome, and detailed cover. Her work is really amazing. Robert Altbauer also did an incredible job on the map.

The Path of Decisions is a work of fiction. Names, characters, places and incidents are the products of my imagination and are used fictitiously. Any resemblance to actual events, locales, or persons, living or dead, is entirely coincidental. I alone take full responsibility for any errors or omissions in this book.

-Mike-

Books by Mike Shelton

WESTERN CONTINENT BOOKS:
The Realm:
The Cremelino Prophecy:
The Path Of Destiny
The Path Of Decisions
The Path Of Peace
The Blade and the Bow (A prequel novella to The Cremelino Prophecy)

Dragon Riders:
The Alaris Chronicles:
The Dragon Orb
The Dragon Rider
The Dragon King
Prophecy Of The Dragon (A prequel novella to The Alaris Chronicles)

The Dragon Artifacts:
The Golden Dragon
The Golden Scepter
The Golden Empire

GEMSTONE OF WAYLAND BOOKS:
The TruthSeer Archives:
TruthStone
TruthSpell
TruthSeer
The Stones of Power (A prequel novella to The TruthSeer Archives)

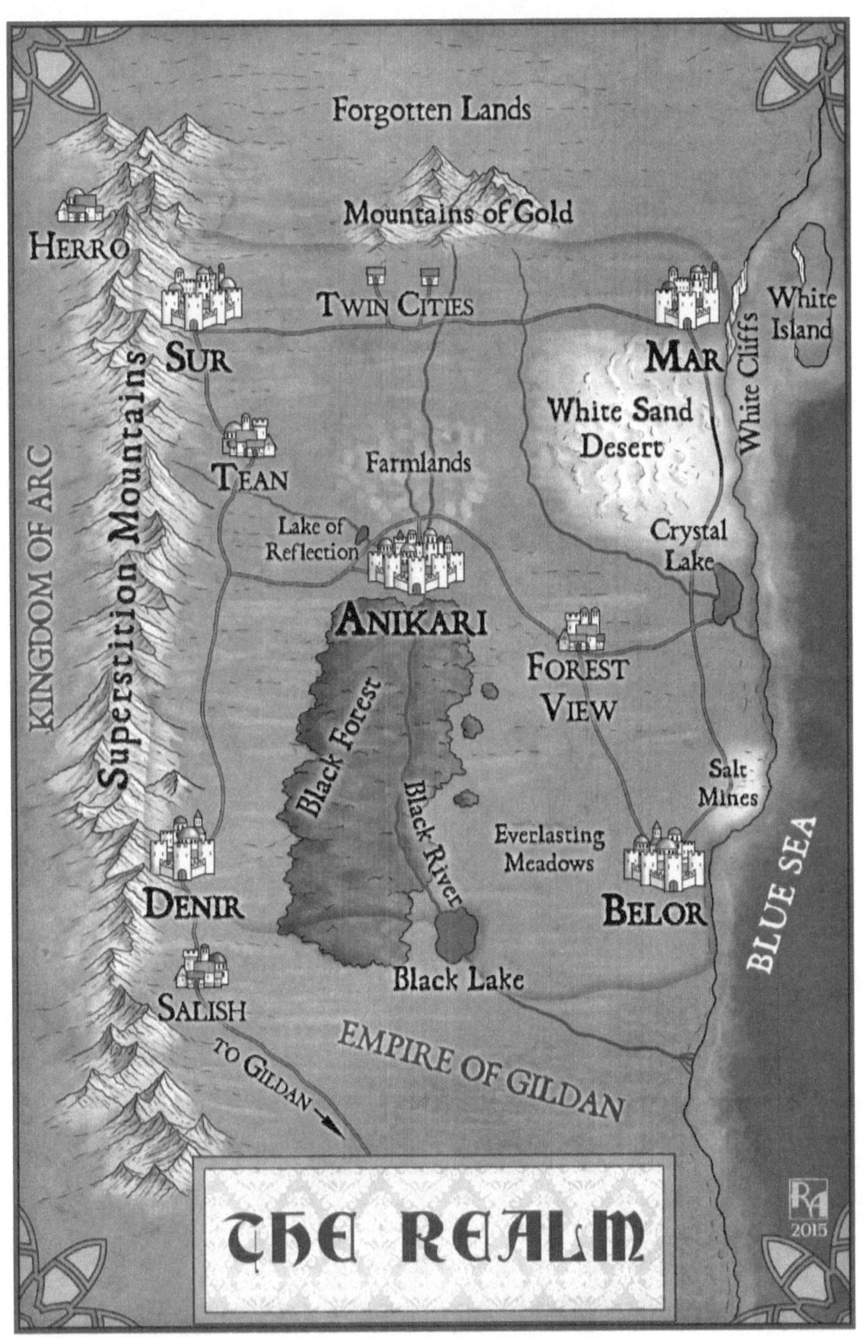

See Color map at www.MichaelSheltonBooks.com

Chapter One

Darius San Williams stood by himself, looking down from atop a small hill at one of the large estates in Denir. He admired the white stone structure, so unlike the buildings in Anikari, the capital city of the Realm. A city that he had lived in for all of his sixteen years—up until five months before.

The sound of horse hooves approaching at a fast gallop had him turning and looking back the way he had come.

Finally the King's messenger returns.

Walking back toward the growing crowd, Darius met the rider just as he dismounted off his swift brown quarter horse. He saluted Darius—an act that Darius found slightly amusing. He was at least ten years the man's junior.

Darius saluted back, "What's the news from the King?"

"King Edward wants you to bring most of your army and any of Gildan's commanders to Anikari." The messenger spoke even as he handed Darius a parchment. "Then march south to Belor. Let the rest of the Gildanian battalion here be escorted back to Salish on their side of the border. The King will send a battalion from the Anikari garrison to settle any continued disputes with the Gildanians."

Darius smiled inwardly. He was proud of what his army had accomplished under his leadership on this first assignment. He had, through somewhat unconventional means, captured a large battalion of Gildanian soldiers who had invaded the southern end of the Realm through the city of Denir. This he had done with only twenty-five men, a small portion of the entire Elite Army.

"Sir?" The messenger brought Darius out of his inner thoughts.

"Belor, hmmm," Darius said still running the instructions of the king over in his mind.

Before leaving Anikari his father had told him about a man who only went by the name of the Preacher. He had taken control of Belor and wanted to separate that region from the rest of the Realm. It was rumored that the man had the powers of a wizard, which as of late presented a special interest to Darius.

Although he had vehemently denied to Kelln, his best friend back in Anikari, as well as to Mezar, the captured Gildanian captain, that he was a wizard, his growing powers made him wonder what he was becoming. His control was getting better, but he lacked vital knowledge of what his powers could do. It seemed they only manifested themselves in the moment he needed to do something with them. During times of 'great need' as Kelln had said.

"Go and get yourself a hot meal," Darius told the messenger. Although the early spring weather was warmer in Denir than further north the air still had a coolness to it. "I will let you know my response soon."

As soon as he stepped away from the messenger, a few of his men tried to approach him, but a small group of women swarmed in around him instead and began congratulating him on his victory. Not one for the limelight in the past, he found himself beginning to enjoy the attention of others, rather than having to live under the shadow of his father, Richard, the Senior Councilor to King Edward.

He saw something colorful out of the corner of his eyes and turned his head. Through the early morning haze of lazy camp smoke in the cool, gray air, Leandra marched up to him. Fire seemed to blaze from her brown eyes, and her mouth turned down in a teeth-gritted scowl. Her short brown hair flew around her normally soft face. Darius knew that look and would have to do his best to smooth it over. It wouldn't do for him to be seen in front of others arguing with her.

Darius did his best to politely squeeze away from the other women who had cornered him. He reached out his hand to Leandra.

"What are you doing, Darius?" She motioned her arms around at the group of young women he had just stepped away from. "Aren't you the commander here?"

"They just wanted to congratulate me for saving the city." Darius puffed out his chest. "It's only natural."

Leandra continued to glare at Darius. He thought back to when they had met, months before, up in the Superstition Mountains. She was one of the camp cooks and seamstresses for King Edward's new Elite Army. Darius had found himself in those mountains newly recruited by the King, whisked away from his home with little warning. Leandra had befriended him and had been a good distraction for the anger and loneliness he felt at being away from Anikari and his friends. She had snuck away with his men when they had left to confront the

Gildanian battalion. At first Darius had been angry at her stowing away; afraid she would distract him. But lately, he was happy she had come along.

Darius put his arm around her and pulled her closer. His body was firm and well-toned now, after training for over six months. "A commander must be seen to be in charge, and the people have to feel safe, Leandra. I am only acting the part."

"So you don't care for those women giggling around you?"

"No. I only care for you, Leandra." He smoothed things over.

And Christine.

Darius cringed and felt some guilt at the unbidden thought. He had cared deeply for Christine Anderssn before leaving Anikari, even loved her. She was from the farmlands surrounding the capital city of the Realm. Six months ago he'd left that city behind him. The pain of not being able to tell her goodbye in person, due to the abruptness of his leaving, had receded through the months, mostly because he tucked it away deep inside.

He couldn't bear the pain, so he ignored it. He tried to talk himself into the fact that Christine had probably moved on without him, and with his growing powers and role in the Elite Army, maybe she was better without him. He may not return to the capital city for a long time, and when he did, she may not like who he had become.

"Now what did you want to see me about?" Darius asked Leandra as he walked back toward his camp. A few of his men tried to get answers from him regarding their next move. He shrugged them off and told them he would let them know when he was ready to move on and what would happen next. He had always wanted to be a commander of an army. His goal in life was to fight for the glory of the Realm, to keep her borders safe, and to make sure her people were at peace. It was only in the last year or so that he realized there was as much danger to that peace and glory from within the Realm as outside her borders.

"They are anxious to do something, Darius," Leandra said. "It's been two weeks already."

Darius had to admit part of the delay was that he wasn't very anxious to see the King or his father. They would only lord over him and tell him what to do. But with his new command and growing powers, he was ready to make some of his own decisions now.

Darius leaned down and gave Leandra a small kiss on the cheek. His dark hair had grown shaggier since being in the mountains. He was clean shaven, unlike many of the other nobles his age, who were wearing goatees these days. He looked at Leandra with his gray eyes and wondered what she really meant to him.

"I will see you later." He broke contact with her hand.

"When?" she asked, appearing afraid to let him out of her sight.

He smiled at her apparent jealously and appeased her. "We will have dinner together."

As Darius returned to his tent, he stole a long glance at the tent next to his where his men held Mezar. The man wasn't such a bad sort and seemed to be only a few years older than

Darius himself—though the age of Gildanians, with their dark black hair and smooth brown skin, was hard to tell.

The Gildanians, under the command of Mezar, had taken 500 men over the border and seemed poised to attack further. Darius and his men, working throughout the night setting traps for the enemy, had secured a quick and decisive victory. The use of his growing magical powers had aided in their success, but Darius wasn't secure enough in his position to admit that openly, yet.

I am not a wizard. The words echoed in his head. He had said them enough to himself that he should believe it by now, but did he?

He could hear the sounds of the men in the camp. Apparently they had seen him talking to the messenger, and conjecture stirred among the tents. Their first victory had aroused their ambitions for more excitement. Darius issued a call for his junior commanders to join in a conference with him in his tent.

An hour later, after meeting with his five commanders, he stood on a crate in front of his entire battalion of almost two hundred men.

"Some of us will be leaving soon." Darius raised his voice so all could see and hear him. Without even thinking about it he found himself using his growing powers to amplify his voice also. "I will need two units to stay and escort the Gildanian soldiers back to their side of the border. Two other units will return to Anikari with the Gildanian lieutenants in tow and wait for my further orders. I, with the remaining unit and the

Gildanian captain Mezar, will go to Belor first and deal with the trouble there in person."

A few confused whispers floated through the crowd of soldiers. Mezar, who stood with two guards at a short distance from Darius, lifted his head in Darius' directions. Only the tilt of his brown eyes hinted at surprise.

"I thought we were all supposed to return to Anikari now," said one of his men. "That's what we heard the messenger say."

"The King needs a group of soldiers in Belor as soon as possible," announced Darius to the group. "So I am going there first."

"But the King said to go to Anikari and then Belor," reiterated another voice from the back. Darius could not tell who it was, but it was the same arguments his own commanders had given him. "The King is not in charge of this army. I am." Darius let some anger show. "Commanders out in the field need to make decisions many times depending on the circumstances. I will send a missive back with the messenger with my reasoning on the issue at hand. We have been trained for events like this. If there is a problem in Belor, why go to Anikari first? I am sure the trouble in Belor is nothing a small number of us can't deal with. We will then return to Anikari and meet up with the rest of the army."

Neither protestor said anything more.

"Do you not want to fight for the King and protect his honor in Belor?" Darius knew they couldn't answer in the negative. "We will surprise those there who are causing the Realm trouble, capture their leader, then return to Anikari in victory and glory. Two battles will have been won. The King and our people will shower you all with their praises."

A few of the men reluctantly cheered, then others joined in. Darius smiled. These men were trained to follow the chain of command. He still had not finalized his plans for what would happen when he eventually arrived back in Anikari. He admitted to himself part of what he was doing was just because he could. Nobility, like the King, always thought they knew best, without consulting the facts or those in the trenches.

The King and his father's desire to control him grated on his nerves, and this maneuver would make a statement. But he knew that something had to be done with the nobility to change their attitudes and restore everlasting peace and glory to the Realm.

And why shouldn't I be the one to do it?

"But how will we go to Belor if not through Anikari?" asked a third man. "That is where the road leads."

"We will go across land, through the southern part of the Black Forest," answered Darius, "and we leave in three days, so go and start getting ready!"

The men chattered and whispered throughout the evening, arguing for and against what Darius had decided. No one much liked the forest, named as it was because of the rumors surrounding it. Yet, three days later the men Darius had chosen to accompany him stood ready to leave. There were forty men; a full command unit. They would travel lightly and live off the land.

The spirit of adventure seemed to take control as Darius marched them out of the city. The new uniforms that Darius had made for them in Denir looked sharp and ready for battle. His own silver armor and blue uniform stood out from his men.

Darius looked forward to crossing through the forest and seeing the Everlasting Meadows on the far side. He calculated they could be in Belor within a month.

Chapter Two

Christine Anderssn sat on her Cremelino horse, Lightning, at the edge of a meadow she and Darius had named the Field of Diamonds. With a long sigh, she gazed across the Lake of Reflection toward the Superstition Mountains and wondered for the thousandth time in the last seven months if she would ever see Darius again. Her long blonde hair, untied for now, blew around her shoulders in the breeze. Her green eyes, once soft, now hardened, stared off into the distance, as if she was willing herself to find Darius.

Her young life, all of fifteen years, had been in turmoil since Darius had left the city. A petition to the King regarding the condition of the farmers had been denied, and recently her father had passed away due to smoke and wounds sustained in a fire that had burned their barns and fields. The fire was set most assuredly by someone from the city who didn't care for the *outsiders*, as the farmers were commonly referred to.

Darius had been one of the few nobles who accepted Christine and her family.

A silent tear now dripped down Christine's face as she tried to find something to hold on to in her tumultuous life.

Stroking the brilliant white mane of her horse, she felt thoughts of comfort in return. The special Cremelino had been a gift from Darius. It was a breed of large horse usually only allowing one rider. The horse and rider developed a special bond with each other.

Christine had become used to the Cremelino's voice in the back of her mind by now. More than just closeness, she found out she could communicate with the horse through their thoughts. She didn't know if it was normal or not, but surmised that other nobles with Cremelinos were not able to communicate like she did. Maybe it was a remnant of the lesser wizards' blood that was rumored to still flow through some of those who lived in the farmlands.

Thinking of Darius left her heart feeling empty once again. She still hoped he thought of her with fondness and wished he would return soon.

Be at peace, Christine, he will return.

Through the tears, Christine smiled at Lightning's attempt at comfort. The horse was so named due to her speed.

"How can you be so sure?" she answered back.

The Prophecy. Darius has much to do with the prophecy:
Forgotten lines of ancient magic
* and the power of the throne.*
One will make them both his own
* if his heart sees the true power.*
He will bring light to fight darkness
and love to fight hate
if he reaches into the power of his heart . . .

"But how can prophecy help our plight?" Christine said out loud. "There is no excuse for the treatment we receive. My father is dead!" Christine held the tears in and replaced them with anger. If she couldn't feel joy, then anger would suffice as an emotion to hold on to. "Can prophecy bring *him* back?"

Let go of your anger, the Cremelino chastened her softly. *It will destroy you.*

Kicking the flanks of her horse, rather than sending the normal silent command, Christine rode out of the meadow. "My anger is all I have right now. Darius is gone. My father is gone. Will you leave me, too?" she asked the Cremelino.

Never, my child. I am here for you. This is the way things are meant to be.

Life should not be meant to be so cruel! Christine lashed back.

Weaving in and out of the budding, but still leafless, oaks and maples sprinkled with green pines, they flew over the early spring ground until they emerged onto the dirt road leading from the farm lands to the city. The road was ill maintained, and pot holes from a recent storm dotted the dirt. A new storm brooded on the horizon, sending a cool wind across Christine's face.

Up ahead before a bend in the road she spotted movement behind some trees. Christine slowed down, peering forward to catch the movement again. Lightning stomped the ground and whinnied, eyes fixed on the same spot.

As the two neared the spot, suddenly three young men jumped out in front of her horse, forcing them to stop. The abrupt halt caught Christine by surprise and she was thrown off the horse and onto the wet dirt.

"What do we have here?" said one of the young men, stepping out in front of the others. The three looked around the same age as Christine. Their wool pants tucked into their high black boots and thick black cloaks marked them from inside the walls of Anikari. The apparent leader had a goatee, while the others did not appear old enough yet to grow one.

Christine stood up and tried to ignore them, not even brushing herself off in her hurry to mount Lightning again. Her heart began to pound.

"Nice horse you have here," said the leader. "Looks way too rich for an outsider to own. Who do you think she stole it from, Nash?"

"Someone who would pay us a lot to have it returned, I bet," said Nash, shorter and stockier than the rest of them.

"She was a gift." Christine hoped only she heard the tremble in her voice. She grabbed a fistful of Lightning's mane to pull herself up.

The three young men laughed. Nash moved next to the horse, shoved Christine away, and reached his hand out to the mare's mane. "No one could afford to give you a gift like this."

With the touch of the man's hand, Lightning snorted and stepped back a pace.

"Watch out, Ridley," yelled the third man to the leader of the group.

With an angry neigh, Lightning reared up and kicked Ridley hard in the chest. A bag he had been holding smashed to the ground, and its contents scattered across the road as he crumpled beside it. The other two backed up a couple of steps, eyes suddenly hard.

Something caught Christine's eye, and she reached down and picked up a small packet from the scattered pack. It held flint, steel, and tinder, wrapped with a string. Sudden anger took the trembling from her limbs, and she turned to face the three men.

"What's this for?" she yelled at Ridley, who was scrambling backwards to get off of the ground.

He reached toward her to take back his belongings. "None of your business. Now give it back to me."

All three of the young men moved closer. Lightning moved between them and Christine.

"Stupid horse," said the third man, Christine hadn't caught his name. He was tall and thin and reminded Christine physically of her friend, Thomas. He tried to push the Cremelino away, but the horse pushed him back with her head.

"Leave the horse alone, Tad, and get the girl," Ridley said. "And get my things from the ground."

The three instigators moved closer to Christine again. Her heart pounded in her chest and ears. How was she going to fight three young men off? She still held the flint and steel. "Have you been starting the fires on our land?"

"What if we did? What are you going to do about it?" Nash said, grabbing for Christine's hand. He caught her wrist and held tight, yanking her forward and away from Lightning's protection.

"Let go of me! You have no right!" Christine yelled. The grip was strong, and her wrist throbbed with sudden pain.

Nash reached his other hand toward Christine's hand that held their belongings. She put the pack behind her back and Tad moved behind Christine and grabbed for it. She kicked back at him but couldn't get far enough with Nash holding on to her wrist.

The other two moved in closer around her, Ridley having grabbed a large stick to beat Lightning off with. Tad reached in and slapped Christine hard across the face, sending a sting of pain. The similarities to her friend Thomas ended with his tall physical build. The man's temperament was cruel, quite opposite of her friend.

"Her face looks as red as the fire did," said Nash, still holding her wrist.

"Shut up," said Ridley. "You talk too much."

Christine straightened up at the talk of the fire. Her anger from earlier resurfaced. "You started those fires? Why?"

Ridley stepped up in front of her face. "Because we heard about your pathetic petition. You need to stay out of our business and our city."

"We've done nothing to you." Christine's face reddened further, and her jaw clenched. She had never been so angry in her life. Her green eyes flashed hot. "We grow your food and raise your cattle. You would die without us!"

"That's your job, outsider." Ridley moved closer in front of her. She could smell his putrid breath. "You grow the food, and we eat it. You live in the farms, and we live in the city. You do what we say, and we live a happy life."

Christine tried to squirm out of the man's hold. "You killed my father!" Her mind flashed with her father lying in their home with burns and scrapes, trying to breathe, giving his final sentiments to their family. Christine and Lightning had rescued him from the fire, but the smoke and burns were too much to overcome his already weakened body. In his dying words, he revealed to his family his upbringing in the city and his suffering at the hands of his city-born ancestors. The same city these young men were from.

Ridley stroked his goatee and faltered for a moment at Christine's accusation, but quickly recovered and reached for her other hand. Nash backed away now, giving control of the situation to their leader. Grabbing the flint and steel pack, he pulled Christine's arm around her and held her tight. "Now what do we do with her, boys?"

The gang of tormentors laughed.

Christine, fall to the ground. The Cremelino's command came swift and fast to her mind.

Christine let her legs go limp. Her captor's hand slipped partially away. In that moment Lightning struck, wheeling around the group out of reach of the sticks and rearing down hard on the back of the leader who still had a slight grasp on her hand.

Bones snapped, and the man screamed out in pain. The other two moved to help him. Lightning reared again with her strong hooves pounding against Nash, leaving only Tad still standing. He moved around Lightning and grabbed Christine's long hair. She shrieked and jumped up on her feet in one quick motion. Her head slammed up under the Tad's chin. Following a loud crack, he screamed and held his jaw.

Christine reached down and picked up the flint and steel pack the men had dropped. She swung up onto Lightning and steadied herself. The horse barely waited for Christine to find a safe hold before speeding her away in a blur of unbelievable quickness. One last glance showed the three young men trying to get up. Ridley could barely stand.

Heart pounding with rage, Christine hardly felt the pain in her wrist. Adrenaline flowed freely through her terrified body. It felt good to fight back. It felt good to hurt those who had hurt her. There were no more tears, only a new, unyielding resolve to continue fighting.

Chapter Three

"Where are we going?" whispered Kelln, trying not to stumble in the darkness. It had been three weeks since the interrogators had last beaten him. Three long weeks since the Preacher had invaded his mind with his foul and evil magic and ripped memories from him. Memories that betrayed thoughts that his best friend, Darius, had the powers of a wizard. His body had been so weakened during the interrogation that his legs were just now strong enough to hold him up.

"Just keep hold of my hand," said Alessandra. She paused a moment and looked around, as if deciding which way to go. Her long auburn hair was died black again, the way it always was when she worked in secret.

Kelln remembered the first time they met, back in Anikari at the beginning of last summer, almost seven months ago. She was slightly older than his sixteen years and wore many disguises as she had helped others come into the Preacher's fold. It was hard to know what she really looked like.

It had been seven long months in Belor, and now winter was on the cusp of ending. Once again Alessandra led him out of a city. Kelln had left Anikari with her soon after his graduation from the academy. His father, the city's swordmaker, had defected to Belor to help the Preacher in his rebellion against King Edward. Kelln had wanted to find out for himself what was happening in Belor, so after consulting with Darius, he had consented to following Alessandra here.

Kelln squinted his eyes and tried to see Alessandra in the musty darkness, but no matter how hard he tried all he could distinguish was black. Pitch black. The kind he could smell and feel. He tried to keep from breathing too hard, as the smell reminded him of something rotten and left behind years ago. Off in the distance Kelln strained to listen to small trickles of water dripping on rock. The soft echoes grew louder as they walked in the dark caverns. He knew they were somewhere deep under the Belorian royal palace, deeper even than the dungeons he had been held and beaten in. It seemed like hours since Alessandra had offered him escape from the dungeon prison where he had been held unfairly for treason and murder.

He didn't know why she was helping him escape, though he hoped it had to do with feelings she might have for him. She supported the Preacher by helping the oppressed escape throughout the Realm and come to Belor to help the Preacher fight. The fight that, in Kelln's mind, was ridiculous and had little basis in fact or reason. The Preacher taught that the people in Belor were being burdened by King Edward and the Realm, that they had their own right to rule themselves, and that the Preacher should be their ruler. Kelln saw it as just another way for the Preacher to get more power. He hadn't seen any strong proof of anything to support the Preacher's claims of any real type of oppression.

Kelln felt rather than saw Alessandra slow down and turn in another direction. Something scattered off in front of him.

Something actually lives down here?

"I hope you know where you're going."

Even in the dark, Kelln knew the penetrating look Alessandra gave to him with her almond-shaped brown eyes. He was meant to be quiet and do what she told him. That was the deal she offered him when she came down early this morning into his cell. His heartbeat seemed to echo throughout the never-ending, narrowing cavern. He bumped into the cool, rough walls more often now. He didn't know if it was his weakening strength or the narrowing of the walls.

Kelln still wasn't sure he should trust Alessandra. He wondered if it was a trap, but the alternative was to die in the dungeon cells below Belor. His trial was a week away, and he was sure it would be a mockery of any justice. It would be a time for the Preacher to show his followers that he would not tolerate weakness or worse yet, rebellion in his ranks. In Belor's fight with the Realm, Kelln had disobeyed orders to kill a Realm soldier. The Preacher was using him as a means to keep others in control—a message and warning.

Kelln stumbled, and Alessandra waited for him. His breathing was ragged, and with limbs still recovering from the dungeon he barely stayed upright.

In all the months in prison, she had been the only one to see him. Well, the only one besides those who beat him. He still had a hard time sleeping at night. The horrors he went through would be a long time leaving. He had hoped so many times that his father or family would come see him, but they didn't. He couldn't understand how his father had been duped by the Preacher.

They stopped again.

Alessandra turned him yet again, through another hall. Off in the distance, Kelln thought he could make out a faint light. His heart seemed to lift out of the gloom toward a new sensation of hope. In the growing excitement he began to move more quickly, almost knocking Alessandra down.

"Just a minute," Alessandra said in a stern voice. "You have to go slowly."

"Why? I can see the opening." Kelln tried to move quicker.

Alessandra stopped and turned. She twisted Kelln's hand around. The outline of her tense face in the dim light made him stop. She had been entrusted with much under the Preacher's regime. Smuggling people out of Anikari was one of them. Being of Belorian blood himself, and with his father being a swordmaker, he guessed their family had been a logical choice to recruit.

"Why did you stop?" He tried to push past her slim but toned body.

Kelln tried following her pointing finger toward the ground about three feet in front of where they stood. It took a few seconds for the light to let him realize what was there. What he saw made his face rigid and his hands tighten; a three foot wide hole in the rock pathway.

"I didn't know." His voice quieted down.

"That's why I told you to follow me," she said with a smile he couldn't tell was wicked or congenial.

One by one they jumped across the large hole in the rock pathway. The sound of rushing water hit against the thick walls deep below. Alessandra made the jump in one quick motion.

Kelln however had to rest a moment to regain strength in his legs. With one false start, he jumped across the hole, falling to the ground on the other side. He maneuvered his pack on his back in order to stand back up. His weakened muscles were sore. He had never been tall or very strong, but had been agile and active enough to keep up with most of the stronger boys growing up.

Sudden light poured into Kelln's eyes as they emerged from the cave. He brought his hand up to shield the worst of it away while blinking a few times. His bright red hair reflected the western sun, and he soaked in the light and warmth he hadn't felt in months. He looked over at Alessandra and smiled.

"Where are we?"

"West of the city. About three hundred yards outside the walls."

Kelln looked down at a small stream moving a few feet from where they stood. Looking west, he viewed the Everlasting Meadows. Doing so brought back the memory of when he had first come to Belor with Alessandra. It seemed so long ago. Being at the southeast corner of the Realm, it would take some time to get back to Anikari. He needed to find Darius and talk to his friend's father, the King's councilor. They would know what to do. The Preacher needed to be stopped.

"I have to get back," said Alessandra.

"No! Stay with me!" Kelln blurted out without thinking. "Don't you understand what they are doing, Alessandra?"

Alessandra looked to the ground. He could tell that at least part of her wanted to stay. She paused as if considering. "I can't, Kelln. Not now."

Kelln walked over to her and held her face in his hands. "Why not? I don't understand you. Why save me, but not save yourself? I can tell you have doubts about what is going on. If you stay you might die."

Tears gathered in the corners of Alessandra's eyes. She tried to brush them away. She wrapped her arms around herself to keep the wind from blowing her clothes around. "You just don't understand."

"What don't I understand? Tell me," he pleaded. She was right, he didn't understand. He had watched how the Preacher not only intimidated people with his size, but with his evil powers. He was charismatic to the people, but he didn't care one bit about anyone other than himself.

Alessandra looked across the meadows and took a few moments to compose herself. Kelln's heart lifted. He hoped she would change her mind. She would be better off away from Belor.

She turned around and walked back toward the hidden cave they had emerged from moments before. "I have to go. It will take me a while to get back. I don't want them to be suspicious of me."

"How did you know the way out?" asked Kelln, knowing he wouldn't get an answer. She made him so angry sometimes. She was so beautiful, he couldn't stand it, yet she hid herself so much that Kelln didn't know who she really was.

"You'd better hurry away from the city. They will be searching for you soon." She brought a black cap out of a small pack she carried and tossed it to him. "And cover up that unruly red hair. You will be seen for miles if you don't."

"Sure." He smiled. "I don't understand, but I do appreciate you helping me."

"I'm not a monster." Her voice was tight with emotion. "I do care about you. I couldn't bear it if you were killed."

"Are you sure you won't come with me?"

Kelln thought he heard a whispered "yes" as Alessandra moved back behind two rocks toward the cave. He stood looking out across the meadows. A barely discernible spring green was starting to show through the winter brown. The wind blew across the blades of grass like the waves of an ocean bringing in a storm.

With careful, painful steps he descended the rocks into the Everlasting Meadows. His short legs shook from the exertion of the escape. However, he felt alive again. The wind grew slightly warmer as he descended into the grassy plain, and his spirits lifted.

He smiled to himself as he remembered how he and Darius had talked of wanting adventure. Well, this qualified as an adventure. It felt good to be free again. There were dangers, and ever since he had arrived in Belor his energy and free will seemed sapped from him. Now once again he was free and in control, and it felt fantastic.

The escape had come upon him so suddenly; he hadn't had time to think. He decided to head toward the Black Forest and then across the Black River. From there he would head north. He would not be able to hide long in the open meadows.

After leaving to Belor last year, Kelln was sure Darius would have tried to visit him. Maybe he tried and couldn't get into Belor. Darius's father would be keeping him busy in learning the politics of the Realm. Darius despised it, but Kelln wondered if his best friend would be able to get away from it all or not.

Looking around him, Kelln kept an eye out for anyone following or any other dangers. As adventuresome as he used to dream of being, he realized he had never actually been out alone very often. The quiet bothered him. He started whistling a silly tune and tried to keep his pace up.

With multiple stops to rest, it took him a grueling four days to reach the Black River. Kelln dropped exhausted onto the sandy banks of the swollen river. The recent rains had widened the river up the bank. A few trees stood inside the edge of the water. He caught some fish and cooked them over a small fire, not even waiting until they cooled down to devour the tasty meat.

"This is fantastic," he said out loud. He couldn't remember the last time he'd had a meal with meat. It wouldn't take long for his small frame to regain the strength he needed.

He spread the blanket in his pack across the ground and lay down. But he couldn't sleep. In the darkness, his memory ran wild with the whips, kicks, and inhumane treatment he had received in the black Belorian dungeons. He tried to block it all away and turned his thoughts to earlier in his life. He went back to that one time in the library with Darius when they had accidently been locked in the dark basement. It was then that Darius had first discovered his powers. Their great need to find their way out must have unlocked Darius's mind to his magical abilities. It seemed like a lifetime ago, but in reality it was only the previous spring.

Kelln smiled at the happy memory and wondered if Darius still had the sword he had taken out of the room. Thoughts of the sword made Kelln wonder about Darius's new magical abilities. He had seemed so reluctant to use them. Kelln would have embraced the power and strengthened it until he became the most powerful wizard in the Realm. He laughed out loud. It was easy to be tough when no one was around.

He wanted to return to Anikari and find Darius. The men in Belor would be looking for him, though. If he headed west for a few miles farther and then headed north he would circle around to the backside of Anikari, even though it meant passing deeper into the Black Forest. Looking around in the dark, he shivered slightly at treading deeper into the trees. He was aware of all the rumors and magical stories, but how could a bunch of trees and small animals hurt him?

The next day, Kelln crossed the river. He had taken most of the morning to find the narrowest stretch of river and gather some large rocks, which he threw in the water to make a place to step. Gathering some long branches, he tied them together with some roots to help him cross the rocks to the other side of the swift-moving water. Once over, he continued walking along the opposite bank of the river.

The thousand-year-old evergreens, each the circumference of many men, were dense and blocked most of the sunlight overhead. The modest light that did make it all the way to the ground gave little light to brushes and grasses, leaving the forest floor mostly bare and easy to walk through. By now, Kelln thought, he must be north of the Gildan Swamp and would be safe to head north towards Anikari.

He camped again that night, finding a small grove that let in the moonlight. Sometime during the night, a southeastern wind howling through the trees woke him. The wind seemed to be speaking a language of its own, warning Kelln of an upcoming dangerous storm. The moisture began to thicken the air and the temperature plummeted. Storms from the Eastern Sea could travel fast across the meadows. The starlit sky seemed to disappear as a dark fog moved in.

Kelln got up and tried to look around for some type of shelter. He gathered up his belongings and moved quickly. As he stood behind one of the larger trees he noticed a small mound of leaf-covered dirt a few yards in front of him. Something came to his mind from a book he had read years ago. Men in the Black Forest used to dig small holes to hide in. The mound he saw didn't look natural, and hope soared to his mind. He got down on all fours and started digging with his hands. The dirt was soft and moved easily.

He was still digging when the first drops of spring rain began to pelt his back. He would need to find shelter soon. He turned back toward the trees in abandonment of his search only to catch his foot on something. He fell to the ground and wet dirt splattered his clothes. He rolled over to see what he had tripped on. It was a large root.

He brought himself up off the ground and pulled on the root to see where it would lead. The movement seemed to sift away a small portion of dirt a few feet away from him.

The rain began to soak through him now as he dug around the spot with his fingers. A small hole opened up and gave him additional determination to dig. The dirt turned into mud as the brunt of the storm reached him. Cold, wet rain soaked him within minutes. He tried not to shiver, but he couldn't stop.

Finally, he hit a large slab of rock. With muddy hands he pried the stone up with a nearby moss-covered branch. A dark hole opened in the ground underneath him. He grabbed his pack and jumped into the darkness. He fell through empty blackness, dropping onto dry, hard ground below. The slab of rock had fallen back down over part of the hole, but rain cascaded down through the open portion. He used the stick he had brought down with him to reach up and push the stone back over to cover the opening.

Kelln sat down, breathing hard and listening to the muffled clatter of the ferocious storm beating on the ground above. His face dripped with a mixture of sweat and rain. He wiped his face off with his hand. His muscles ached and his body felt weak, but it was dry in the small cave. As he laid his head on his pack to rest for a few minutes, the faint echoes of the storm above receded from his conscious mind.

Chapter Four

An unexpected sound jolted Kelln awake. He sat up and tried to orient himself in the darkness of the cave. Instinctively he reached to his side for his sword, only to remember that Alessandra had only given him a small knife.

"Hello, my friend," a voice echoed in the cavernous hole.

Kelln jumped and crashed into the wall of the cave. He brought his knife out in front of him. "Who are you?"

An odd and wild laugh sounded close by him.

"Who?... What are you... doing here?" Kelln said as he backed away from the sound, knowing he didn't have much room if he needed to fight.

Without warning a bright flame flared up in front of him. His eyes, accustomed to the darkness, blinked in rapid response. In front of him stood a wild-looking older man, his gray hair and beard uncombed and disheveled. The old man limped toward him. His hands were gnarled and his clothes torn. Kelln tried to think through his options.

In the palm of one of the old man's hands appeared a small ball of light, not unlike the one Darius had produced in the library basement a year before.

"Don't worry. I won't hurt you." The old man moved closer. Kelln began to smell the man's woodsy breath. It was then he noticed the man's eyes. A solid milky color. Kelln let his breath out in a deep rush. The man was blind. That was all. Nothing to be afraid of.

"How did you get in here?" he finally got the nerve to ask.

"How did I get in here?" repeated the old man. "I should be asking *you* that question, my young friend. This is the back of my home. I was trying to rest when I began to hear a lot of noise in here."

"You live here? Out in the forest? But, you can't see!"

The man laughed a loud crackle. "The eyes are only one way to see."

Kelln was definitely confused. The man in front of him was crazy!

The man stepped closer to Kelln.. "You thought striking your flint to steel would be the only way to light a fire?"

"I guess so." Kelln answered, not knowing what else to say.

"Then how do you explain this?" The man waved his hand around the ball of light. "There are many ways to accomplish the same task."

"So you are a wizard?" Kelln surmised.

"That's a title people give those who do things in a different way than they understand. I'm no different from you. We both see—you with your eyes, I with an inner power. We both make fire—you with a flint, I with the wave of my hand." The old man stopped and smiled. His wrinkled face looked friendlier now. "But here I am lecturing you when you probably want to get warm and dry. Come with me, and we'll get you all fixed up."

The old man motioned Kelln forward. Kelln picked up his pack and stuck his knife back in his belt. They walked for a minute through a few turns in a small tunnel.

"You can really see without your eyes down here?" Kelln asked.

"When I am using the power I can sense auras and physical objects around me. It suits me just fine here in my cave."

"I didn't expect anyone."

"No, I guess you didn't." The old man laughed again.

"Sorry about the eyes." Kelln felt like he had to say something although it sounded foolish.

"I don't need to see now. I have seen enough in my lifetime. All there is to watch now is wickedness and foolishness."

They came to an open door in the rock and entered into a small furnished cave. The old man motioned Kelln to sit down on a small wooden chair. Before doing so, Kelln remembered his manners.

"My name is Kelln. I was looking for a way to keep dry in the storm."

"You were lucky to find this place. The storm sounded like a serious one."

"What is your name, sir?"

"My name is Alastair." The man turned to start fixing a warm meal for them.

Kelln looked around the remarkable room. A small stove made of rocks blackened by use sat as the centerpiece of the crowded room. A metal flue rose above it into the rocks. A few shelves stood against one wall next to a table made from fallen trees and branches. A lone sword stood against the opposite wall. Straight ahead, Kelln spotted a stack of books with loose papers crammed between the pages. Kelln wondered what a blind man did with books. Yet another corner held a few skins bundled together to sleep on.

"How long have you been here?" asked Kelln.

"It's hard to tell." The old man seemed to be thinking. "Spring is coming once again, so I would say about five years."

"That's fantastic." Kelln could get into an adventure like this. Living in a cave in the woods could be fun for a while, though he would need someone around to talk to, he guessed. When Kelln asked about the books, the old man shrugged and said he hadn't always been blind. He didn't seem to want to discuss anything more on the subject, so Kelln dropped it.

The old man finished preparing a meal of fried vegetables. Kelln was hungrier than he had first thought. They ate in silence, with Kelln wondering how Alastair survived out here in the forest all alone.

After finishing the meal Kelln titled his head back and enjoyed the final lingering flavor of the meal. "Where do you get your food from?"

Alastair stood and began rinsing the plates in a bowl of water. "I have a few friends in Belor that bring me items now and again."

Kelln stood up and helped Alastair finish cleaning then returned back to the two chairs in front of the rock stove.

"Tell me what troubles bring you here, young friend."

"How do you know I have troubles?" Kelln asked with defensive suspicion.

Alastair smiled. "Not too many people travel the Black Forest alone in the middle of a storm."

Kelln smiled back and relaxed. Why should he be suspicious of this old man? He thought about the flame and wondered how much power the man actually had. He started by telling Alastair he had come from Anikari but had lived in Belor for the past eight months, three of them in prison. The old man sat with patience and listened to Kelln's long story. He didn't ask any questions or offer any comment. Kelln thought he saw a sadness settle into the old man's face.

Kelln told Alastair about the Preacher and his teachings. He related his capture, imprisonment, torture, and recent escape. All the while Alastair sat with hands clasped and head down. When Kelln finished, the old man looked up, and Kelln glimpsed tears in his eyes.

"Would you like to hear the beginning of the story?" asked Alastair.

Kelln was a little confused. "What story?"

"Of the Preacher."

"You know of the Preacher?"

"Only too well," Alastair sighed, then began. "Years ago, Belor had grown into a beautiful city with wonderful people. They worked hard and trusted one another. It was a jewel of the Realm; people came from all over the Western Continent to vacation there so close to the sea. Belorians had peace with the rest of the Realm and were secure. One day, about fifteen years ago, a man came into Belor. He brought with him darkness and anger. He stirred the people up against one another. He prospered on prejudice and pride. His name I cannot even say. I only call him the dark one. He had foreign magic and used it for his gain and evil purposes. For five years this man ruled the underground in Belor. He influenced many important men, spiritually, economically, and politically. Families were ruined, and Belor became corrupt."

Kelln opened his mouth to ask a question, but the old man held his bony hand up in the air to stop him.

"Let me tell the whole story, young man. Then you may ask questions. One man stood up to this dark one. One man felt a spiritual enlightenment and taught that God would protect the righteous from outside evil influences. He was a mighty man who had a lot of influence, especially over the older people in Belor; he had taught them for years. He, too, had the old magic in him. He wasn't necessarily strong in its use, but he used the power for healing and help. Many joined with him to fight against the dark one and his evil. They fought not with weapons, but with words. They did not want to increase the violence."

Kelln shifted in his seat as Alastair paused to put some more wood on the stove. It was dry and started popping and snapping. Kelln's clothes began drying out with the increased heat.

"This man had a son who also had a beautiful daughter. The wise man sent his son to Mar and then across the sea to be taught by the wise ones in the eastern kingdoms. He hoped his son would one day return with the knowledge and strength that would help to save the city and carry on in peace after the old man died. For five years the man, with less and less support, fought against the growing evil, waiting for his son to return.

"His son returned with fire and determination to set right that which had gone wrong in Belor. He had pride in Belor and taught this to the people. He was tall, powerful, and charismatic. Many people began to follow him, and with the help of his father, they began to turn the tide of evil. But the dark one held strong power over many of the city's organizations. The father thought that as the people returned to righteousness and peace, this man of evil would lose his power and leave. His son, however, became preoccupied with the dark one and vowed to destroy him himself. This son forgot all other things in his quest against this evil one.

"One day the son came to his father with a gleam in his eye and told him the dark one would bother them no more. Hours later a servant found the evil man dead in his bed, a pure-silver knife stabbed through his heart. The son took personal pride in the killing. His father, of course, was saddened. His son, his joy and the hope of the people, had committed a grievous sin."

"But he had rid the world of an evil man," interrupted Kelln for the first time in the long telling.

"Yes, but at what price? No matter how evil the man was, it is not our decision to take his life in cold blood. The son continued his preaching against evil, the people joined him, and the city began to prosper once again. However, as prosperity increased, the son took more and more power upon himself. He began preaching against everyone who had influence with Belor but was not Belorian."

"The Preacher," whispered Kelln.

"Yes, he became known as the Preacher, a mockery of what he claimed to be. He became even worse than the dark one in many ways. The dark one taught evil as evil. The

Preacher taught evil but disguised it as good. His pride knew no limits, and he claimed Belorians were a special people and needed to rid themselves of all but the true Belorian blood. People from other cities and backgrounds began to disappear. The Preacher forgot the original teachings of his father; the things of fairness, peace, and love… the things of human decency."

"What happened to his father?" Kelln interrupted.

Alastair paused. "He tried to reason with his son. He tried to turn his heart around, but the son wouldn't listen. The Preacher and his father fought. Their argument turned from words to magic. You see, the Preacher had become obsessed with the magic the dark one possessed and had begun to study it himself. He couldn't control it yet, and in the midst of their fight he lashed out in anger against his father and struck him down, hurting him terribly."

Tears rolled down the old man's wrinkled face and Kelln was sorry to have opened up old wounds. He knew all too well the length the Preacher would go to keep his power and control the people. Absently he rubbed his forehead with his hand, pushing back the memories of when the Preacher had invaded his mind and stolen his thoughts.

After a few deep breaths, Alastair continued. "The Preacher's father was weak in the power and couldn't fight back. Some friends of the father begged the Preacher to let him live. So, instead of killing him, the son banished his father from Belor and exiled him with a promise that he would not go to any other cities of the Realm but live as a vagabond for the rest of his life."

"Where did he go?" asked Kelln. "Is he still alive?"

Alastair stood, turned and wiped his eyes, then faced Kelln again. "Oh, yes, he is still very much alive, though many days he wonders if it would have been better to die. He now lives in a small cave in the Black Forest."

Silence sat thick in the small room. Kelln took a few moments to consider the story. His hands sweated with the heat of the stove. What could he say? Then it dawned on him. "The Preacher is your son?"

The old man nodded his head. A heavy sadness filled the air.

"And your eyes?" Kelln touched his own eyes absently and realized his own torture could have been worse. "It was the Preacher that did this to you. This is how he hurt you?"

"Yes." Alastair sat down and gathered his emotions.

Kelln gazed down into the fire and stirred the coals around with a stick. "What stopped you from going and getting help? Why would you promise to stay silent?"

"My granddaughter. She cared for me when he was in Mar. We became very close. He vowed if I told anyone about his growing powers and what he had done, he would destroy her. I couldn't risk it. I found this cave a few weeks after I left Belor and have used it ever since, waiting to die. But God has spared me for some reason."

"But why would God do this to you?"

"Oh, Kelln. God did not do this to me. Man did. God gave me life and a family, but men took it away. God gave Belor beauty, but men took it away."

"How do you stand it? Everything you have has been taken from you." Kelln was bewildered. He had never met such a man like this before.

"Remember, young friend," Alastair continued. "Don't ever let others determine your worth. That is what brings pride. Always remember what you have inside is only determined by you. Evil men can change your circumstances and surroundings. They can belittle and hurt you. They can take your money, property, and loved ones, but they can never take away what is inside. That is how I live. That is how I survive." A glow surrounded the exiled man as he talked in a gruff voice.

"The power," Kelln said, remembering Darius's abilities. "You are glowing."

Alastair's laugh filled the cave. "So you say. I cannot see it. Isn't that ironic?"

Kelln told Alastair about Darius and his newfound abilities. Alastair listened in silence and seemed strengthened by the news. He explained to Kelln the responsibility of those born with the gift of power and that Darius would face many hard decisions as he learned to deal with it.

"It has been a long day for both of us, my new friend. There are some extra blankets and skins in the corner behind the table. You are welcome to find a place to rest." Alastair walked slowly toward his own bedding.

Kelln sat dazed at what had just transpired. Life and its meaning were starting to change before his eyes. The truth seemed to radiate from this tired, gnarled old man—a truth he had never expected but needed to understand more about. The words Alastair had shared felt much more alive in him than the words the Preacher and Alessandra spoke. They made sense, and they felt good. Especially in contrast to his suffering, this new idea of personal hope lifted his soul closer to where his upbeat attitude used to be before he went to Belor.

He had to reach Darius and share with him the things Alastair had taught him. He needed to help his friend learn about and accept the responsibilities of his emerging powers. That would be his purpose now.

As Kelln sat and thought, the warmth of the fire and ordeal of the day overcame him, and he drifted off to sleep himself. It was a deep and dreamless slumber.

A few hours later, a sweet aroma filled Kelln's nostrils. Sausage and a hint of potatoes. He savored it a moment before opening his eyes. Alastair was pouring a warm drink from a pot on the stove.

The sound of the storm had abated during the night, and all was quiet for a while with two relative strangers enjoying their meal together. After finishing, they talked for hours of Anikari and the Realm. Alastair seemed to be a river of fresh information that Kelln soaked in. He retired that next evening mentally and emotionally exhausted, and this time he did dream. He dreamed of faraway places he wasn't sure existed.

He woke in the morning feeling fresh and alive again. The world was a brighter place. His scars from the Preacher—both mental and physical—had receded to the back of his mind.

"You rested well?" asked Alastair, with a smile.

"Oh yes. It was fantastic!" exclaimed Kelln. Then he paused. "I found God."

"Where did you find Him?" asked Alastair with a small smile across his face.

"I know many people seem to search for God. Someone said I would find him in Belor. Others try to find him in the mountains or in the cities. But from what you said about the things people couldn't take from you, I would say that I found God in here." Kelln pointed to his chest. "He was always here. I found him in my heart. I now have a purpose I believe in."

The old man smiled for a moment, his eyes buried in a mass of age-old wrinkles. He walked to where a small door made from branches and vines wedged into one of the cave walls and pushed it open. Sunlight streamed in, almost blinding Kelln. He blinked a few times, then shadowed his eyes with his hand and walked to the door. It exited onto the back of a small hill.

Kelln found the view breathless. He stood amazed that the dark, foreboding clouds, piercing wind, and monstrous thunder did not leave any scars on the land. Instead, he saw deep blue skies, brilliant sunlight, and a rare light feathery blanket of pure-white spring snow. The world seemed new and refreshed. It seemed as if all evil and darkness had been washed away. Light green buds filled most of the trees and stood out in dark contrast to the late spring snow.

Kelln walked out for a few minutes on his own, catching a rabbit with a bow that Alastair had in his cave. Alastair took the animal, dressed it and cooked it. It tasted good to fill Kelln's stomach with a heavy meal. His strength seemed to multiply, and he felt inside, as well as outside, that nothing would control him again.

Alastair didn't ask Kelln when he would go, so Kelln took a few weeks to fully rebuild his strength. Each day he went out of the cave, walking farther and farther. Small leaves were beginning to show on the early blooming aspens. One day Kelln returned from walking around the forested area with a clean-shaven face and half a dozen fish. His strength had grown, and though he still showed some outward signs of bruises, he felt strong and healthy once again.

"Alastair, I must be going soon."

"I know, my friend. I can tell you are getting restless. Eat with me tonight, and then leave tomorrow. You must get out of the forest before another spring storm hits. It was a dry winter, but spring brings some awful thunderstorms. The river will swell its banks soon."

Later that day while eating, Alastair looked up with a jolt and moved towards the door.

"What is it?" asked Kelln.

"There's someone out there. We must put the fire out. They'll notice the smoke."

Kelln helped Alastair cover the fire in a way so as to not let any new smoke rise up out of the cave. They peered out of the door. Off in the distance of the setting sun, Kelln followed the outline of five men, looking as if they were searching for something. They walked with a purpose, dressed in Belorian uniforms and carrying heavy swords at their sides. They approached closer.

Kelln felt terror rise again at visions of being held in the dungeons, but his newfound faith gave him a reassuring calm. "I'm going out to investigate," he said. "I don't want you to get hurt." He grabbed the sword from Alastair's shelf and wrapped his cloak around him.

The old man nodded. Kelln slipped out to some trees and peered into the lowering sun, shielding his eyes. Out of the stillness of the evening he heard a scream off to his right. A girl! The men looked up also but didn't seem to care. With swift movements Kelln moved from tree to tree. The ground had dried from the storms but was still soft and easy to move on.

He heard the scream again, this time yelling for help. The painful cry sounded familiar. *Alessandra! How could it be?*

Kelln's heart pounded, and his face and palms sweated with nervousness even in the cool evening air. The sun dropped behind the trees, readying itself for another night's sleep.

Kelln thought he made out something moving behind a tree. A man running away, appearing like a shadow in the failing sunlight. The scream pierced the air once again. It was from the direction the man had just come from. Kelln forgot to take cover now and darted out across the sparse ground toward the sound. His soft shoes crushed decomposing leaves and fallen pine needles. He came to a small rise in the land and spotted someone a few feet below rubbing her leg. Her dark hair covered her face in front and flowed down over a dark brown coat in back. The person turned around and Kelln gasped.

"Alessandra," he whispered, not moving.

With guilt she glanced up at him with tears in her reddened eyes. She looked so lost and alone. So hurt.

"I'm sorry," was all she whispered.

Kelln took a step forward and was shoved from behind. He rolled down the small hill and tried to regain his footing, slipping on the slick, mud-covered ground instead. In an instant three men grabbed him with rough hands. They shoved him into the dirt with no concern for his safety and took his bow, arrows, and knife away. Kelln struggled against one and kicked out at another. He might be small, but he had learned to defend himself a long time ago. He tried to wiggle out of their arms.

One of the larger men brought his arm back and struck the side of Kelln's head hard. Stars exploded around Kelln, and he reeled to the side. One of the other men grabbed his hands roughly, tied them together, and pushed him up against a tree.

As a trickle of blood rolled down his face, he looked over at Alessandra, who sobbed into her hands. One of the men walked over to her and yanked her up off of the ground.

"You did a fine job, Alessandra. Your father would be proud of you," said the man.

Kelln was confused, trying to figure out what happened. He didn't think he had ever met Alessandra's father. Had she turned him over to the Belorians again?

"If it wasn't for her," said one of the other men to Kelln, "we would have never found you, traitor."

"We knew you would come running to help her," said another. "She has that effect on people."

Kelln couldn't believe what he heard. He looked at Alessandra and opened his mouth as if to say something but couldn't figure out what to say. She continued to look back at him with red and swollen eyes, then looked over to where three other men walked down the embankment, holding Alastair between them. He looked weak and helpless.

"No, not him!" Alessandra blurted out.

Alastair turned towards her sound. "Alessandra," he whispered, throat raw with emotion. "It's been such a long time."

"You know each other?" asked Kelln.

"Grandfather! I am so sorry. I didn't know," cried Alessandra. "I didn't know."

"Grandfather?" Kelln repeated, paused, and looked stunned. He gazed from Alastair to Alessandra, realization dawning, "The... Preacher's... daughter?"

Chapter Five

The Black Forest became dark and dreary. Evergreen pines and towering firs kept the sky hidden most of the time. The undergrowth was thin this time of year. The leafed plants were just beginning to bud again with early spring rains. Darius could sense a deep presence in the trees, but nothing that affected him further than the far reaches of his mind.

Having discovered his magical abilities less than a year earlier, he was still trying to determine the extent of what he could do. One thing for certain he had learned was that his power responded to him in times of great need and when he felt threatened or angry. The power was hard to control and even harder to know how to work with. He knew the men talked about it behind his back, and he had not formally or verbally accepted the fact that he was a wizard, but he had to admit deep down inside that it was looking that way.

Magic was not looked on favorably in the Realm, especially in Anikari. Ever since the wizard rebellion centuries before, the Realm had been fairly successful in keeping magic outside of its borders. Darius knew the Empire of Gildan and the Kingdom of Arc had no such compunctions against magic, and it operated openly there, as well as in the smaller kingdoms to the south.

He pushed the senses of his mind outward around him now. The deep forest was rumored to be magical, and myths and stories were told of the old days when things happened in the Black Forest that were not explained. As he reached his mind out, he felt another presence—one he was sure was magic. He didn't know what it was, and afraid to alert another person of his own presence, he pulled back mentally until the power sat inside him once again.

Marching through the forest was hard. They had packed light, but still each night setting up camp and then dissolving it in the morning took more time that he would have liked. A strong storm had caught them a few weeks earlier, and the ensuing mud slowed the party dramatically.

Darius was anxious to get to Belor and see what the troubles there were about. He had heard about the Preacher from his father before last summer's training season in the Superstition Mountains. Belor was larger than Denir, but he couldn't imagine having any problem with his forty men securing the town and taking the Preacher in.

The men caught small game in the forest to eat and found a few small streams for fish to supplement the food they had brought with them from Denir. The nights were warming slightly, but the men still needed campfires for warmth.

One night, after many of the men had retired, Darius sat next to Mezar. He didn't feel a need to keep Mezar tied up, and the man didn't seem to want to go anywhere. Darius kept him by his side so when he returned to Anikari he would meet the King with his Gildanian prisoner in tow. Even so, something else seemed to keep Mezar close to Darius. It was something Darius hadn't been able to explain to himself.

Darius engaged his prisoner in conversation. "Have you ever seen the Everlasting Meadows, Mezar?"

"Yes. Once as a small boy my grandfather took me to Black Lake. We journeyed around the eastern edge until we stood on the edge of the meadows at the border of our two kingdoms. He told me to look out across the grasslands and remember that as the meadows are everlasting, so are we."

"What did he mean by that?"

"I'm not sure. But I think he believed we lived forever."

"He didn't acknowledge death?" asked Darius.

"I don't think that was it. He didn't suppose we lived again, as some of the Eastern Kingdoms believe. More so, he thought that our souls continued life after our body was laid to rest."

"Is your grandfather a religious man?" Darius was intrigued with such thoughts. He moved around on a large log, trying to get more comfortable.

The firelight made Mezar's brown skin, dark hair, and slightly upturned eyes seem more mysterious. "I wouldn't call him overly religious, though he does have strong views. He... uh... has had to be very strong in his position."

Switching subjects Mezar eyed the sword. "Do you believe your sword has power?"

Darius brought his hand to the pommel of his sword. Thoughts of when he had found it in the basement of the academy library flashed through Darius's mind. In sharp detail, he remembered the vision he had seen of when his sword had been forged. Wizards chanting around the forge had infused the weapon with power.

"I have seen the power in your sword, Commander." Mezar gave a small grin, "In fact, I remember the point of it touching my back when you captured me."

Darius laughed. It was hard to think of the man as his prisoner. "Are you any good with the sword?" Darius asked Mezar.

Mezar grinned. "Quite good. One of the best there is, I would dare say."

Darius relaxed again. "I still believe the bow to be the best weapon, but the sword is a close second."

"The bow!" Mezar exclaimed with a laugh. "It's too slow and inaccurate."

"But the sword cannot travel across distances," said Darius with a smile.

"You do realize the power in your sword is much more than a normal sword, or bow for that matter."

Darius nodded his agreement to Mezar's assessment of his weapon. He could feel the power coursing through him. It seemed to augment his own growing powers.

They talked late into the night of weapons, travels, and boyhood activities. Darius realized he was not much different than the Gildanian.

Eventually, Darius stood up and prepared to retire. He turned with one last question. "Why do you speak our language so well? Does everyone in the empire?"

"No. Not everyone. I was specially trained."

"Why? Since you are an officer in the army?"

"Yes. Something like that. My grandfather believes I should be educated well with all the workings of our neighboring kingdoms."

"You speak much of your grandfather. What about your father?"

Mezar frowned, the inner part of his brows almost touching. "He didn't spend much time with me as a boy. His work took him away from home often. We don't always see eye to eye on things."

Darius was surprised once again at their similarities. "Sounds like my father. He wants me to be a noble councilor like he is. To serve and bow to the King. I can't do that. I can't just sit around all day. All I have ever wanted was to help the Realm keep peace. The other councilors think if we are safe from the neighboring kingdoms all is fine, but I have seen so many injustices within our borders. The councilors sit in their meetings all day and do not see what is in front of them. What they are doing is destroying us from the inside."

Mezar raised his eyebrows, smiled, and stayed silent. As Darius walked back to his tent, a guard came up to Mezar to escort him to his own. Darius liked the man, but that didn't mean he trusted him without a guard.

A few days later a substantial storm hit the forest, the temperatures dropped, and the little army was left with a light layer of snow. The group stayed holed up for a few days in some small caves they had found along a worn-out river bank until the ground dried up. Once they started east again it was at a much slower pace. The forest became thicker the farther east they went. Leaves were budding on the trees, and small shoots of green reached out of the ground in sporadic patterns.

Two scouts Darius had sent up ahead came running back one morning. "There are a group of men a short distance away breaking camp. They seemed to be heading toward Belor."

"How many did you see?"

"About ten men with swords," answered the scout. "Two others seemed to be prisoners, and one other was a girl."

"A girl? Who would send a girl out in this forest?" Darius mumbled, looking around for Leandra. Coming out of her tent, she smiled at him. Her short dark hair bounced above her shoulders, and he found himself momentarily lost in her smile.

She walked over to him and Darius put his arm around her. He knew the men grumbled behind his back about her being there with him. He liked her well enough, but the main reason he brought her along was because he could. No one could tell him otherwise. He knew it was probably a petty thing to do, but it was something he could control.

"I will take half of the unit with me, and we will surround them. It shouldn't be hard. No killing unless you have to." Darius had been caught up in the glory of his victory in Denir but did not like the idea of killing. It seemed more powerful to him to control someone who was alive than someone who was dead. "The remaining men, break up camp and join us when you can."

A short time later, Darius and his twenty men had the group in sight. They were walking east with, as the scouts had said, what appeared to be two prisoners. Darius took five of his men with him, circled around in front of the party, and charged in.

"Put your weapons down," Darius ordered to a surprised group. He stood in his newly made blue uniform, covered on the shoulders and breast with armor. His hand rested on the hilt of his sword. He was ready for trouble.

They paused for a moment but took up a battle stance. They had uniforms and moved with trained precision. Leaping forward, they attacked Darius and his men. However, the other half of Darius's men came up behind them. Darius's sword glowed slightly with the thrill of battle, and the other men backed away. Darius rushed in and knocked a few swords out of men's hands. They scrambled to pick them up again, but Darius's men were too quick and held the Belorians at bay. With superior numbers and fighting skills, Darius and his men soon prevailed. The others surrendered and lowered their swords.

"Who are you?" asked one of the Belorians, who seemed to be in charge.

"We are the King's Elite Army." Darius still held his sword in his hand, but the glow had subsided. The men they had caught kept shifting eyes on it.

"What king?" the same man asked.

"What do you mean, what king?" said Darius, anger spilling out from him. "Your King! King Edward DarSan Montere. This is his forest. Now, who are you?" He pointed his sword at the leader. The power of the sword brightened the forest around them.

Many of the men flinched and backed up. One held his ground. "We are from Belor. We were sent to find these two traitors," said a man, pointing to the back of the group. "And the only commands we answer to are from the Preacher."

Darius walked toward them, his silver armor gleaming. His sword glowed brighter with his anger.

"Darius?" yelled a high-pitched voice from the back of the opposing group.

Darius stopped short. "Kelln?" He strode to the back of the men. "What are you doing here?"

Before Kelln could answer, Darius turned his attention to the men holding his friend. "Release him!"

"And him too," said Kelln, pointing at Alastair.

"They are our prisoners." One of the opposing soldiers pointed out to Darius.

"And you are ours now. So release them."

"I wouldn't want to make him angry," Kelln said with a huge smile.

Slow, but in compliance, the man untied the ropes binding Kelln and Alastair's wrists.

Behind the two, a girl stepped forward.

"Who is she?" asked Darius.

Kelln sneered at Alessandra. "A traitor. She turned me in after helping me escape."

"Escape from where?" Darius was so surprised to find his old friend out in the middle of the Black Forest that for a minute he forgot about the others.

Kelln looked around. "It's a long story, Darius. Maybe later."

Alastair turned to Kelln and put a hand on his shoulder. "Do not be angry with her, my new friend. Remember who her father is. The Preacher has had much longer to manipulate his own daughter than he has with the rest of the people."

Kelln growled in his throat but didn't say anything more to Alastair or Alessandra. After an uncomfortable moment of silence he motioned to Alastair. "Darius, this is a friend of mine."

Alastair looked at Darius and took a few steps so he was standing directly in front of him. Darius took a step back when he saw the old man's eyes. Alastair smiled and whispered softly. "You must be Kelln's friend. He was right. I can feel the power in you. You will have many decisions to make about this power, young man. Your choices will influence the destiny of many."

Darius furrowed his eyebrows at the old man. He was sure the other soldiers hadn't heard the soft speaking, but he didn't want to let on his discomfort at the man's words. So he turned back to Kelln, who stood grinning from ear to ear.

"It really is nice to see a friendly face, Kelln." Darius slapped his old friend on the back.

"This is fantastic!" Kelln still smiled. "Really fantastic. I was going to walk all the way to Anikari to find you, but here you are in the middle of the forest finding me." He grabbed Darius in a big hug, his head only reaching to Darius's chin. "Nice armor by the way."

Darius didn't know how fantastic it was or wasn't, but he could see that he had a lot to learn. He didn't like the things that Alastair had said to him. "I can see I don't understand everything going on here. We will make camp here and wait for my other men to rejoin us. They should be here within the hour."

The Belorians were gathered and guards set to watch them. Alessandra stood with Alastair, her grandfather, off to the side. They talked in whispered voices. Her eyes kept darting around, looking at Kelln.

Darius walked off with Kelln out of earshot of the other men. On their way to distance themselves, Leandra met them.

"Is this your friend, Darius?" asked Leandra.

"This is Kelln. We grew up together in the academy in Anikari." He introduced them.

Leandra drew closer and put her hands around Darius's arm. "Darius is a famous commander now."

Kelln raised his eyebrows but said nothing.

Darius leaned down and gave Leandra a kiss on the forehead. "Why don't you go and keep Mezar company, Leandra? Kelln and I need to catch up on some things."

Leandra pushed out her bottom lip in a mock pout. Squeezing his arm tightly once more before letting go, she said her goodbyes.

Darius didn't know where to start. The last time he had seen his old friend was in Anikari the night before Kelln had left with some mysterious girl to go to Belor and see what had happened to his father. It had only been a short time afterward that Darius himself had been scripted into the King's Elite Army. A lot had changed since then.

That had been over eight months before. He remembered the day well. With no warning at all, Darius and other men a few years older than him had been taken to the castle and informed by King Edward and his councilor, Richard—Darius's father—that they were now going to be part of a specially trained Elite Army. It was that day, upon the sudden news of being subscribed into the new army, and the inability to see Christine before they left, that made Darius fully realize his path in life: restoring glory again to the Realm, and fighting for the underprivileged people in its borders.

Kelln stood looking at Darius as if trying to figure out what to say himself. "Who was that? What about Christine?" His eyes followed Leandra as she walked away.

Darius frowned. "Christine is probably better off without me." He said it more gruffly than he intended.

Kelln stiffened. "Why do you say that? You're not saying this… this girl has replaced Christine as the love of your life? I haven't been gone that long, Darius. You two were in love. Real love." Kelln's hands waved around the air as he talked.

"Nobody has replaced anyone, Kelln, but people change. I have changed."

Kelln glanced over toward where Alessandra and Alastair stood talking.

Darius followed his eye movements. "So what is the story between you and her?"

Kelln sighed and began to tell Darius everything that had befallen him since he had arrived in Belor: the growing powers of the Preacher and his plans to defy the Realm, lead the city, and maybe take over the Realm; Kelln's own imprisonment and torture and finally his escape; meeting Alastair and eventually being recaptured.

Darius listened intently, especially about the Preacher. He gasped at Kelln's torture and wondered how he could now be so jovial.

"Well, we certainly aren't boys anymore, are we?" said Darius.

"No. I guess not. We have grown and discovered new things about ourselves." Kelln looked at Darius as if he hoped Darius would talk more about himself. Darius did not, so Kelln continued. "I have even found the peace of God."

"You found what?"

"I found out that what we are inside is what makes us who we are, Darius," Kelln continued in all seriousness. "That is the only way I can deal with everything that has happened to me."

"I'm not sure I'm following you, Kel. I have been trained in the King's Elite Army, become the first commander, won my first battle, and am leading men now to Belor to capture the Preacher. I am a commander now. A commander with power. That is what defines who I am. Someday I will be the general of the entire army."

"But you are more, Darius. Don't you understand? You don't have to be just a commander, or even a general, if you don't want to. Power is not what you wanted."

"But power is what I have now," Darius retorted. "You are the one who told me to embrace my powers, Kelln. You told me not to hide them."

Darius breathed deeply and looked around the campsite, making sure no one had heard his outburst. He was changing inside, and not even his best friend could understand that.

Kelln spoke more softly. "Remember you wanted to travel the Realm and do things differently than your father."

Darius frowned at the mention of his father. Anger began mounting again. Darius forced a laugh. "I thought that once, Kel. But events didn't seem to work out that way. Look at me now. I have become the mightiest leader in the King's army. He will revere me when I return victorious to Anikari. The Realm needs protection, not only from outside, but from within. I need to make the King and his councilor's see the people for who they are and understand that they can't control everyone. They sit in their meetings and make decisions without being out among the people and understanding them."

"Does he know about your power?"

"My power?" Darius glared down at his old friend. "I know how they all talk about me behind my back. My glowing sword, my ability to move quickly, knocking people over with a push of air, hearing things before anyone else does. The power is growing inside me, Kelln. I see things more clearly, and I feel things more. The anger drives the power and feeds it. That is when I am most powerful."

Kelln took a few steps back and opened his mouth, but nothing came out.

"You are welcome to stay with us," Darius informed his friend formally. "Tomorrow we finish our march toward Belor. You can go or stay, but this is what I must do now. I will confront the Preacher and see what his grievances are. Maybe he is not so far off the track as many believe."

Kelln tried to pat down his unruly red hair, but an evening wind blew it all around. "You need to watch out for the

Preacher, Darius. He is dangerous. He is more powerful than you think."

"He cannot be that strong," Darius sneered. "You can stay here or go with us, but I *am* going to Belor."

"Fine," Kelln mumbled. "Someone needs to watch over your ego."

In the blink of an eye, Darius was in front of Kelln's face with a warning. "Watch your step, Kelln."

With no more words, Kelln walked away from Darius and back to the campfire. Darius watched him go and felt guilty for being so harsh to his friend. Kelln had always been beside him in the past. If his friend could see reason, they could walk together again and accomplish anything they wanted to.

The next day the party resumed walking toward Belor, and by nightfall they reached the banks of the Black River. Darius stood at its side, looking into its swift currents. The early spring storms had swollen the river beyond its winter's bank. He watched his face reflecting in the dark moving water. His features would appear and disappear as the water hit rocks and turned into white foam. Two arms wrapped around him from the back. Leandra.

"We haven't spoken in a while," her soft, breathy voice whispered behind him.

"I've been busy," Darius said, hoping to make her leave. He wanted to be left alone.

"Remember when we first met and we were sitting around the old fire up in the Superstition Mountains camp?"

Darius smiled at the memory. He remembered how flustered he had been.

"Remember I said you would become a great leader for the King? Well, Darius, you are." Leandra shifted closer to him and put her head against his shoulder.

Darius sighed and continued looking at the rushing waters. "I know. Sometimes I feel so powerful when I am leading the men. I feel like I am unconquerable, that nothing can stand in my way. But when I am by myself looking into this raging river I think of how small and weak I am."

Leandra leaned into him further. He could feel her warm breath on his neck, forming a small swirl of steam in the cool night air. The sounds of campfires crackled in the camp. All was secure and peaceful.

"You cannot conquer everything at once," said Leandra as she looked at the river. "But someday, Darius, you will."

Darius brought his head back from hers, turned around, and put his hand on her face. He drew Leandra in close and kissed her. She always seemed to soften his anger. They stood holding each other in silence as it slipped into the cool peacefulness of the night air.

Something in the back of his mind tried to warn him, but he pushed it away and enjoyed the moment.

Chapter Six

Christine Anderssn sat with some of her friends arguing about an upcoming vote among the farmers. The petition they took to the King had been ignored, and discontent was moving toward action on both sides.

"We must make a plan." Thomas stood in front of his friends, skinny as a rail, flailing his arms around for emphasis. Having grown up only a few farms over from Christine, he had known Anya, Karel, and Christine for years, though he was two years older than any of them. Stephanie, the other in the group, stood silently to the side. Her family was fairly new to the area. "Soldiers have been sent to Belor and Denir to deal with trouble, but he ignores us here in his own backyard."

"I'm not going if she is going to be there," Anya said, pointing to Christine. "She's stirring up more trouble. Things were quiet until that boyfriend of hers from the city started hanging around. Ever since he left there has not been any peace around here."

"It doesn't have anything to do with that, Anya," said Thomas. He was always the first to stand up for Christine.

Christine had heard enough arguing and not enough doing. "Well, while you two sit here and argue, I'm going to go do something about this situation. I have some plans of my own to bring to the other farmers." Christine turned, making her long blonde hair swish around her head. She jumped on Lightning, her Cremelino horse, and raced away.

Nice touch, alienating your friends now.

Christine slammed her mind shut against Lightning. She watched Thomas and Anya over her shoulder in the fading distance.

Anya leaned close to Thomas, and Thomas stumbled backwards into a log. He was so clueless to Anya's advances. Of course, Anya advanced toward anything that was male and had two legs these days. She was obsessed with finding a husband. Christine faced forward again, gritted her teeth, and rode harder.

An hour later, Christine sat away from her friends on the front row of another gathering. They stood in one of the larger barns in the farmlands and had made room for people to sit on bales of hay. Spring planting was just around the corner, and sacks of seeds sat around the edges.

Nothing much was being decided on, so Christine stood and waited for the crowd to silence. The death of her father still gave her some respect and notice.

"I think we should boycott the city from getting any more food from us," she began. "Don't sell them any of our stored vegetables or any beef or pork. They can't go anywhere else at this time of year to get food. They make us store it all and then demand the price for which they will buy it from us. Maybe when they are starving they will listen to our demands."

"She is right," someone else argued. "The King doesn't care. I bet he has enough food for months stored in that castle of his. But if his people start to get hungry, maybe he will do something about the problem."

"I agree with Christine. Something harsh has to be done. They need to see we aren't just talking but that we are doing something," said another man from the back of the musty barn.

The air, still cool, caused Christine to wrap a wool cloak around her shoulders. "Everyone must agree, because if we don't they will see our weakness, and it will never work."

A lady stood up from the side shadows. "But if we don't sell them our food, we won't have any money. I am a widow with two children. I need to think of them, too."

A heated discussion erupted.

"Everyone is too afraid to stand up and do anything." Christine walked back and forth in front of the group. She removed her cloak and strode around to emphasize her point. "Think of us as a whole and what would be the best, not just for ourselves. The only way we hold any power is to be united. If we stop the food, they will be forced to listen or die."

"Let them all die!" shouted someone as others joined in.

"What about the children?" asked the same widow in a worn-out voice.

"Who invited you here, old lady?" asked one of the men. "I don't remember seeing you around here. Who are you?"

The widow answered that she was a poor farmer from up north of the farmlands. The man who had questioned her moved closer to her.

"I thought I knew everyone from up in that area. That is where my family is from. Why don't I know you?"

The lady shrunk back into the shadows a little further. The room had all turned toward her with their threatening looks.

"Let me see your hands!" demanded the man.

The old woman started to turn them over but then pulled out a knife from under her coat. She jumped onto a wooden fence in the barn and shouted for them to get away. Shouts erupted toward this imposter from the city. Her hands showed no signs of farming or even much age. She ran for an open window and dove through.

Christine's eyes went wild, and she jumped to follow the lady. The crowd seemed to freeze for a brief moment, as if all of them were deciding what to do. As Christine neared the barn door, someone stepped in front of her and grabbed her wrist.

"Christine, this has to stop." It was her brother, Jain. Though barely fourteen years old now, he held her in a strong grip.

"Let go of me, Jain. Let me get that woman." Christine's eyes darted toward where the woman had gone. She tried to pull away.

"Then what will you do... kill her?"

The room fell silent awaiting the answer.

"If that is what it takes." Eyes blazing and hair messed up, Christine's jaw tightened. Jain held her firm. "Whoever that lady was, she had a good point. What about the children in the city? What if they starve?"

"Jain, don't you remember how the children in the city treated you when you were a child? They teased you and beat you up. We need to get back at them. To teach them a lesson."

"By killing them?"

"If some die, maybe others will listen." She pulled her arm away from Jain and turned to the rest of the room. They stood in silence, watching the two siblings argue the points they all held inside of them. "Would you rather their children die or ours?" she asked.

"Why is death the only choice? Why is killing and fighting the only choice?" Jain raised his voice.

"Jain, you always wanted to fight. What happened? Ever since our father died you seem to have forgotten how to fight."

"No, Christine, you are wrong." His voice boomed in anger, and his neck muscles bulged. "I remember what we fight for. We fight for understanding, not revenge. That is what our father would want. Remember, Christine! Remember how peaceful he was. He would not agree to what you want to do. You used to believe in peace. You always told me to stop fighting when I was younger. I see that now. What happened?" Jain stood on the edge of tears.

"They killed our father!" Christine's eyes became moist as she stood in defiance of everything her brother said to her. Couldn't he understand that she wasn't the same person she was a year ago? A year ago, she had Darius by her side, her father still lived, and food was stored in the barns. She didn't like the violence either, but what was she to do? She couldn't stand idly by any longer and watch the city stomp on the farmlands. "That is what happened, Jain. They burned our farms and killed my father."

"I hate that they killed him, Christine. I still hope it was a bad dream. Hoping he will return. However, all of the hoping, praying, or killing won't bring him back. You need to accept that and just go on the best you can. Make things better for those younger than us, not worse." Jain walked closer to his sister and lowered his voice. "Look at the good our father did, the kind of man he was. What would he want? He would not want us to plan to kill with such openness and ease." He paused. "Against the army of Anikari, what can we do?"

Christine felt a pinprick of emotion welling up inside her, but she couldn't let it out. Not now. She had lost too much. She couldn't be swayed by her brother's words.

"Don't you understand what they have done to us and what we need to do to get back at them?" Christine said. "They can't get away with this. Jain, I am your sister. Listen to me!"

"You are not my sister, Christine. My sister is warm, understanding, kind, and fun." Jain held his dark, blond head low and started to walk out. "What happened to my sweet sister?"

As Jain left the barn all eyes turned back to Christine. She stood still for a moment, regained her composure, and asked, "Are we going to listen to him? He's still a boy." She walked toward the group. Silence filled the cold evening.

Thomas came forward. "I think we'd better end tonight. It's late." Others mumbled and echoed his words, and the crowd disbursed, leaving Christine standing alone.

* * *

Two days later a wagon of winter vegetables approached the city gate from the farmlands. Its wheels turned in slow rotations through the rain-soaked road. The driver felt and heard a loud bang on the back of his wagon. Turning back, he saw his vegetables rolling out of the back. Three hooded figures on horseback smashed them before the driver could stop and get off. As he ran to the back of his wagon, the three riders were already far down the road—two brown horses led by a large white horse of extreme speed.

The man surveyed his smashed food as the guard from the city gate came out to see what was happening. Few vegetables were salvageable. The farmer had lost most of his wagon and most of his monthly income.

Over the next few weeks similar disturbances happened more frequently at both the west and north gates. Grain stored in the large silos in the farmlands was not able to make it safely to the city. The wagons came less often. Only a few were fortunate enough to deliver to the city by going in the middle of the night.

People in the city began to take armed guards out to stop the bandits from spoiling their food, but they were not fast enough. The bandits started attacking farther and farther away from the city. Soon all wagons stopped, and the city had to pull out all of its food reserves in order to continue to feed the people.

* * *

Caroline, Christine's mother, approached her one day and reminded her of spring planting and that they would need help this year with Stefen gone.

"We don't need to plant so much food anymore," Christine said.

Her mother looked confused. "I don't understand."

"We only need to plant for the farmlands. The city will not be getting any more deliveries." Christine's hair was dirty and tied in a ponytail, her cotton dress hanging loosely on her thinning frame.

"Christine, what are you doing?" her mother's voice pleaded. "You need to eat. You are getting sick."

"I have to go, Mother." Christine walked to the back door. Lightning stood just outside the door, waiting for her. Jumping on top of Lightning, Christine barely acknowledged her mother.

Christine, you can't keep doing this.

"I am doing what needs to be done." She spoke out loud to her Cremelino. "Only a few help me now, but more will see the way soon. We stopped most of the food deliveries."

But the prophecy…

I don't understand your prophecies, she argued in her mind. *What do I have to do with them? I am a farm girl. No prophecy could include me. No prophecy could foresee or even care about us here in the farmlands.* They rode at a quick trot back toward the city gate. Christine had to make sure no other deliveries were made.

The prophecy is about Darius.

Christine tightened her lips, keeping the tears inside. Nine months without Darius. Nine months without his laughter, his strength, his comfort. She still remembered his arms wrapped around her. It seemed he had pulled fear and frustration right out of her, leaving her with a feeling of peace and contentment. Oh, how she wished she had him with her now.

She was doing all she could to make things right, but no one seemed to understand, least of all her family and friends. Was she doing what was right? She was terrified of losing more than she already had, but she couldn't sit still and do nothing.

So every day, with a few additional supporters, she would stop deliveries of food to the city. It was working. People in the city were starting to feel the pinch.

The King sent a few soldiers out to the farmlands to reason. Some of them started to negotiate, but Christine knew it wouldn't do any good. They needed to make the city hurt before they got some concessions. The King, with troops in Denir and Belor, couldn't spare many men to stop Christine and her band of crusaders. Many of the farmers did not agree with her methods, but when pressed for names from the guards, the other farmers held their tongue and protected their fellow farmers.

* * *

Thomas sat with Karel, Anya, and Stephanie together one evening discussing Christine and what they knew she was doing. Anya leaned against Thomas, who leaned against a wall next to the stone fireplace in his small farm home. Stephanie and Karel sat in two wooden chairs next to the hearth. They held their hands toward the small fire, warming them from the early spring chill hanging in the evening air. No one spoke at the moment. The fire seemed to consume their attention. A loud pop sent a spark onto the floor, jarring Thomas from his thoughts.

"We need to stop her. That's all there is to it. I know she was our friend. But this has gone on too long. Someone could get hurt. She could get hurt."

"We've been through this over and over, Thomas," said Karel. "What can we do?"

"Remember when she used to talk about freedom through peace?" reminisced Stephanie. "Now she won't have anything to do with anything peaceful. She is making things worse for the farmlands."

"She even looks sick," Karel continued. "I think Jain was right when he said it's just not Christine anymore. Something snapped in her."

"She won't even talk to me," added Anya. "We used to be best friends. I've known her most of my life. I want to help her." Anya put her face into her hands. "But I can't stand being around her right now."

The talk continued, going over and over what they had already discussed time and time again. Thomas knew something had to be done, but didn't know what. When it came down to it, she was still their friend, but she wouldn't listen to them or anything reasonable. Finally, Thomas stood up.

"I don't care if she is our friend. This has gotten out of control. The King's army will, in all certainty, march into the farmlands and take what they want as soon as they return from the other cities. As her friends, it's up to us to stop her. I have a plan, but we will need Jain's help too."

The group of friends moved closer together as Thomas started explaining his idea. As he did so, one by one, frowns covered the faces of everyone in the small room.

Chapter Seven

The sun shone the day after Darius and Kelln's reunion, promising warmer weather. Darius and his unit of the Elite Army, along with the captured Belorian soldiers, faced the task of trying to cross the Black River. It had swollen with the recent storm, and the water raged with small white caps as it bounced off rocks and fallen trees. A group of soldiers spent the first part of the morning scouting up and down the river for the best spot to cross. A few miles downriver, closer to the Gildanian swamp that bordered the Realm's southern neighbor, they found a place where the river seemed to be narrower and less rough.

Darius had two men take a rope across on horseback to the other bank. The men struggled but were able to cross with the help of the Belorians' strong horses. The men tied the rope to a sturdy pine on each side of the river. This would give something for them to hold on to as they crossed through the chilling water.

The water was a numbing cold and would send them into hypothermia if they did not get warm on the other side. The first soldiers to cross had the task of starting a fire and setting up the tents. One by one they crossed—Darius waiting until the last. The prisoners were escorted across first; then two of the captains helped Leandra and Alastair. Only Alessandra, Kelln, Mezar, and Darius were left. Alessandra and Kelln began to walk across the waist-high water.

In front of Kelln, Darius watched Alessandra stumble. One arm came off the rope as the raging current pulled at her body like a leaf in a windstorm. Instinct caused Kelln to reach for her, but in doing so he lost his own footing. The rushing river swept one foot up out of the water, one hand remaining on the rope, the other flailing around for something to grab on to. Mezar, who stood behind Kelln, had only begun walking across. He reached out a sure hand for Kelln and steadied him.

Alessandra's eyes glazed over in helplessness. Her feet were being pulled by the river, and one hand slipped off the rope. She screamed as the strong fingers of her remaining hand continued to slip off of the slick rope.

"Help," she continued shouting. Her cries were lost in the roar of the river to all but the few around her. Men watched from the other side with helpless stares. She hadn't been able to regain her hold, and her face shivered white in the bitter, rushing water.

Alessandra kicked wildly, trying to get upright. Kelln reached for her once again, but he was too late. Her last fingers slipped from the rope, and she disappeared beneath the powerful current. The others caught a glimpse of her head for only a second before the water swallowed it up.

Kelln shouted to the other side for some men to ride down river and find her. They looked to Darius, and he reiterated Kelln's command.

Alastair looked about wildly, not seeing what was happening. "Kelln, where is she?" He roared over the din of the river.

Kelln felt dazed and only looked downriver until he realized that Alastair couldn't see where he was looking. "She fell into the river. Darius's guards will find her."

Alastair sat down hard onto the ground, his weathered face crushed.

Darius reached for the rope and started to cross as fast as he could. As he did so, he felt the rope begin to sag and unravel.

"Hold the rope!" he commanded. He looked ahead and saw Mezar pushing Kelln forward. Kelln seemed to stagger in a daze as he looked downriver.

The rope slipped from his hand again as Darius's foot slipped on a rock. One leg kicked out into the water. But he held on, not wanting to end up like Alessandra. Kelln had reached the other side, and Mezar was halfway between Darius and the eastern bank of the river.

"Hurry, Mezar!" yelled Darius. "The rope cannot hold both of us much longer. It's too wet."

The rope was splitting right between them. Darius's mind reached out without him realizing it. The power in him surged, but before he could do anything, he became aware of the touch of another power. This was the first time he had ever felt someone else's magic so directly, but he recognized it for what it was. The power held the rope together. Darius didn't have time to think but grabbed ahead on the rope as fast as he could. He slipped once and hit his knee on a rock, propelling himself toward the other side.

Darius saw Mezar fall onto the other bank in front of him and the soldiers reached up and pulled him to safety. He felt the other power leave, so he pulled upon his as much as he could to keep the rope stable. He tugged hard on the rope and thrust himself out of the water, falling on the bank where two men caught him. He looked back at the rope and let the power go. The rope split in two, its two ends dangling back into the current of the river.

He fell over on the ground and fought to stay conscious. Using the power had drained him. His head hurt, his knee was swollen, and his strength was failing. A few of his men picked him up and brought him to the fire. He propped himself up against a log and was given something warm to drink. Soon he stood up.

"Sir, you need to rest," said his medical officer.

Leandra came over to him to comfort him. Darius tried to stand on his own, but his knee started to buckle. He locked it and stood firm.

"This is a test of our strength." Darius spoke to his men. "These are the things we were trained to do. We will rest tonight and then go forward into Belor tomorrow."

"Not everyone made it, Darius," Kelln pointed out.

Darius looked from Kelln to his soldiers. They shook their heads in silent acknowledgement of Kelln's statement.

"You tried, Kelln," whispered Alastair.

Kelln's face grew hard. "I don't know why I did. She betrayed me!"

Alastair winced and looked like he had been physically hit by the remark. "You must forgive her, Kelln."

"How? Why?"

"Remember who her father is. He has manipulated a whole city. She doesn't understand what she did. She was a sweet girl," Alastair said sadly, as if remembering past times.

"I don't know. It's one thing to turn someone in. But I thought she liked me, really liked me. She helped me escape and then turned me in again!" His temper flared.

"Kelln, remember who her grandfather is also. Try to forgive her for my sake."

Kelln looked into the old man's blind eyes and breathed out a deep puff of air. "I am sorry, Alastair." He turned his face away in shame. "My pain is not half what yours must be. Your son's betrayal and now your granddaughter is gone."

"They are not lost yet."

"But..." started Kelln.

"Alessandra is tough, Kelln. You know that. She has had to survive many things."

Darius limped over to Kelln. "We'll find her. I will keep my men looking."

Kelln rounded on him, his anger flaring up once again. "And you, you could have saved her."

"What? We all tried, Kelln."

"No, you didn't. You could have used your power."

Darius looked around to see if anyone was listening. He grabbed Kelln by the arm and pulled him away from prying ears. "Kelln, I don't know what you think I am or what you think I can do. We were all on the edge of life and death back there. We all did what we could."

"I saw the rope fraying, Darius. I'm not stupid. Then all of a sudden the threads came back together. I don't know what you have learned since I've been gone, but you alluded to the fact that you have grown in your power." Kelln stood close to Darius and looked up, wet red hair plastered to his head.

"Kelln, listen. It wasn't me using power on the rope. Someone else here has some kind of power also. I sensed it."

"Don't give me excuses." Kelln picked up a stick and threw it toward the river. "Now you are just passing blame around. No one else here has…" Kelln stopped mid-sentence.

"Has what?" Darius asked when Kelln stopped.

"Alastair," he whispered.

"What?"

"Alastair. Alastair has the power. I've seen him use it. He won't deny it."

Darius tried to ask more questions, but Kelln was set about getting back to the camp and didn't want to talk about it anymore.

Later that night, Darius found himself sitting around the fire with Kelln, Alastair, Leandra, Mezar, and his captains. The other soldiers sat at another fire nearby but out of earshot. At Darius's fire they discussed how to get into Belor. Kelln mentioned how Alessandra had helped him escape under the walls of the castle and the city. He didn't know, though, if he could retrace his steps.

"I can," said Alastair.

"What? You? But you can't see, old man," said one of the captains under Darius.

"I can see with my hands and my ears. I will remember."

"What are you talking about, Alastair?" Kelln asked.

"Remember, I used to live in Belor. I used to live in the palace."

"Your son is this Preacher, right?" asked Darius. "He sounds like an interesting man. I look forward to meeting with him."

"He most likely will meet you first, or one of his guards will, unless we get into the city unseen," said Kelln.

"Where are these tunnels?" asked Darius.

"They begin at the southeast corner of the city," Kelln said. "They lead through a hill under the city wall and up into the castle dungeon where I was imprisoned, and where, high above in the more lavish suites of the palace, the Preacher resides."

"Kelln can be my eyes. He can guide me, and I will guide you with what I know," said Alastair.

"I don't know..." hesitated Darius.

"Darius, the Preacher has an army there. You can't just walk up to the front door, knock and be invited in to the party," said Kelln.

"I have before," Darius laughed, remembering back to Denir. "I captured Mezar and his men without too much work."

Mezar raised his eyebrows and smiled, his white teeth contrasting against his brown skin. The foreigner made no attempt to escape and didn't join in many of the group conversations but seemed to always be listening. Darius still wondered what the man's motive was. He was looking forward to bringing him, along with the Preacher, into Anikari and showing the King what he had accomplished on his own. For now, however, Mezar seemed content to stay by Darius's side.

"But maybe you are right, Kelln," Darius continued after a short pause. "Being cautious will help us to maintain our surprise arrival."

The group lingered a while longer, planning and discussing the entrance into Belor. Darius sent two scouts ahead to look for any Belorians.

Then he stood up and walked back to his tent. The difficult river crossing had been harder on his body than he admitted to the others. His knee and muscles ached. Bringing his arms back behind him, he stretched, longing for a normal bed once again. As he opened the flap to his tent, Alastair came up behind him.

"Commander, could I have a minute of your time?"

Darius turned around and raised his eyebrows at the question. It was still unnerving to look at a man who was blind but seemed to see things anyways.

Alastair reached over and touched Darius's arm. His power stirred within him. Who was this man? Had it been his power at the river? Darius didn't think so.

"You must be careful commander," Alastair said in a loud whisper. "There are many forces at play here and not only those you can see with your eyes."

Darius moved his arm away from Alastair's hand. The power receded again. "I have heard of this Preacher. I will be careful of him and his men, but I have an army at my disposal also."

"That's not what I mean. You must be careful of what is inside you." His wrinkled, bony finger landed hard against Darius's chest. Darius felt a burning and backed away.

"What are you? How did you do that?"

"It is your power recognizing someone else with the power."

"Was it you at the river today who kept the rope from breaking?"

"No. My power is weak and only good for a few things. I felt another with more power than mine." Alastair stood close to Darius.

"Another? Who?" Darius was excited at the increased help it might mean, but also afraid of someone with that kind of power in his party.

"I don't know, Commander," admitted Alastair. "It is different from what I have felt before."

"But this Preacher of Belor, he has powers, too?" Darius asked.

"Ah, yes. But his powers were only partially inherited; the rest were learned. And what he learned was bad—an evil side to the power. Do not underestimate him."

"I will be fine." Darius smiled down at the old man and moved to enter his tent again.

"You are a foolish young man. You might have power, but no common sense. You don't understand what is at play here."

Darius whipped around and grabbed the old man's tunic. "Right now, old man, you are in my care. I am a commander of the King's Elite Army, with power to decide your fate as well as that of those around me. Be careful what you say."

A guard came up by Darius's tent. "Is everything all right, sir?"

Darius felt foolish holding the blind man's tunic in his hands. He let go. "Yes. All is fine. I was just retiring to bed. It's been a long day."

The guard walked away. Alastair turned to go also. Over his shoulder he asked one more question of Darius. "Are you a wizard of the heart, mind, or earth?"

Darius froze but said nothing. He didn't know what the old man was talking about. He was not ready to have this discussion right now. "I am not a wizard, just a commander with some minor powers that I am just beginning to learn how to use."

"From where did you inherit your power?"

Darius frowned in dismissal. "I am not in the mood to discuss my personal life with you."

"Power is either learned or inherited," Alastair continued, despite the warning in Darius's voice to stop. "Since you don't seem to understand yours yet, I assume yours is inherited and not learned."

"You go too far in pushing me, Alastair. For Kelln's sake, I will keep you safe until we reach Belor. Then you are on your own. If you interfere in my business again I won't be so tolerant." With that, Darius entered his tent.

Darius tried to lie down and sleep, but he couldn't get the day's events from his mind. Mostly, he was bothered by who else in his small group had power and how much power they might hold. Was there a traitor in their midst? But why would a traitor save his life? It didn't make sense. And what right did the old man have to ask him personal questions about his abilities? He didn't know what branch of magic he had. He hadn't even known there were differing types of the power.

And as for inheritance, he knew his father didn't possess any sort of magic. But he had to admit, he did have powers of some type or another and those powers gave him an advantage. He needed to learn to use that advantage more. His first test would be with the Preacher.

At last tiredness overcame his thoughts, and he slipped into a comfortable sleep.

Chapter Eight

Every fifth man held a torch as the group walked with slow and deliberate steps through the century-old tunnels under Belor. It had been three days since the forging of the Black River. As they came to each fork in the tunnels, Kelln described the surroundings, and Alastair would turn one way or another, leading the party forward. He was going on memory of years before. They lost all track of time in the dark labyrinth. For Darius the trek was taking much too long, and he became short-tempered and irritated. The tunnels made a perfect trap. The power in him wanted to jump out and strike someone, but he kept it in check.

Soon Darius would face the infamous Preacher. He would find out where his powers came from and bring him to heel for his crimes against the Realm.

Leandra echoed Darius's growing fears. "Are you sure we aren't lost?" The darkness, distant echoing of water, and occasional scamper of something across the floor had them all jumpy.

"We are close," was all the old man said.

A few moments later Alastair stopped and informed Darius they were about to enter the lower dungeon of the palace, and he knew of a room they could enter that he surmised was rarely used. They moved through a doorway leading into a hallway under the palace walls. Darius felt the presence of a power and shuddered at its strength. Darius ordered their Belorian prisoners into one of the cells. He closed and locked the door and told them to exchange clothes with some of his men.

"There used to be six men. Now I only count five," Darius said to his men. "Where is the other?"

The Elite soldiers spread out and looked everywhere, but the missing man couldn't be found.

"Do you want us to backtrack and look for him?" asked one of Darius's men.

"No, that will take too long, and we could lose what element of surprise we have left." Darius and four of his men put on the uniforms of the Belorian guards; then they went to find the Preacher. Alastair told Kelln the way, then remained below the palace with Mezar and the rest of Darius's Elite soldiers.

The small group of impostors climbed the numerous stone stairs bringing them out of the eerie dungeons and into the main palace grounds. The palace courtyard seemed to be clean and well kept. Darius noticed others dressed like them in the red Belorian uniforms. He touched Kelln's arm. Kelln jumped and frowned. After asking directions, they continued toward the Preacher's sitting rooms. It was early evening now, and they hoped the Preacher would be in his chambers.

Guards stood stationed outside of the Preacher's room. Dressed in a Belorian uniform, Darius asked to see the Preacher.

"What is your purpose?" asked one of the guards.

"We have captured the escaped prisoner."

Darius looked at Kelln without emotion. Kelln looked like he might reach out and try to kill him.

"Give him to us, and we will bring him in," one of the guards insisted.

"He is dangerous. The Preacher ordered us to deliver him in person," continued Darius.

"Just a moment," said the guard as he went inside the room.

"This is your plan?" whispered Kelln in anger. "You had no right to drag me into this. I shouldn't even be here."

"Then why are you?" Darius's mouth held tight, and his eyebrows furrowed.

"To help you," Kelln shot back.

Darius was about to argue when the guard returned and motioned them in. Kelln was pushed in front of Darius and his soldiers, who all had their hands on the hilt of their swords.

As the imposters entered the ornate and lush room, the Preacher stood looking out of a window. His back was toward the visitors. The man was dressed all in black, from his boots to a cape that almost seemed to float around him. The only color was a yellow band around his arm, and his short-cropped red hair, marking him Belorian by birth. The opulence of the room showed Darius the Preacher's weakness. This man was motivated by greed and excess; he wanted others to see his power through his wealth.

The room was warm, with a large fire in the corner stone fireplace. Gold artifacts and books covered one wall and a large tapestry the other. Oversized red velvet chairs with cushions stood in each corner. The lavish room was as much a royal suite as some of the rooms in the castle in Anikari. The guards left and the six of them seemed alone in the room with the Preacher.

Darius smiled at the stroke of luck. This would be easier than capturing Mezar and his battalion.

"Sir, we have returned with the prisoner." Darius kept his voice even. He felt power crackling through the walls.

"Very good," said the Preacher without turning around. "He will be executed in two days."

Kelln gulped and turned pale as the Preacher continued.

"Right before you!" The Preacher spun around with fire in his eyes. "How dare you come in here. Darius, isn't it?"

The sound of Darius's sword being pulled from his sheath filled the air. The power surged in him, and the sword glowed. The rest of the group followed, and the hiss of swords against scabbards filled the air. Before Darius had taken two steps, men began to pour into the room from behind the tapestry and from a doorway in the opposite corner. The Elite men's training was far superior to the Belorians', Darius guessed, but could not match what seemed like dozens of men surrounding them at once in the large room. Their swords were drawn and their teeth clenched. They were ready to fight to the death, but he thought he could even the odds.

Darius let himself get angry, then filled himself with power and pushed out a force of air toward the Preacher. It was easier every time. As suddenly as Darius had acted, the Preacher reacted and sent his own answer of fire toward Darius. Bright power hit Darius on the arm, and he fell onto a soft carpet. A horrible taint of magic spread through his body. It was all he could do to summon his own power and to feel clean and calm again. The stench of the Preacher's magic filled his nostrils with a vile scent, and his mouth tasted unnatural.

"How...?" Darius whispered. His eyes went wide.

A portion of the group cleared as someone walked through and into the center of the room next to the Preacher.

"Alessandra!" exclaimed Kelln.

"My daughter warned me of your coming. She seemed to have a change of heart from last week." The Preacher's wicked smile moved from Alessandra to Kelln. The Preacher's guards took away all of Darius's men, leaving only Darius and Kelln in the room with him and Alessandra. Two guards remained standing next to either side of the door.

Alessandra stood alone by the window. Tears stained her green riding shirt. She walked with a limp, and her arms were bandaged. Kelln's face twisted in a grimace.

The Preacher took two steps forward with incredible speed. It brought him face to face with Darius. "As for your little puny power, you might want to learn something about it before you attack a master wizard."

"A master?" Darius still stood dazed at the amount of power he had felt hit him. He realized at that moment this man called simply the Preacher was not simple at all.

The Preacher's grin went from ear to ear. "I could have killed you. I surmise you know that now. But that would not solve anything. I am sure, like others, you have been told lies about me and about the power we both share. Now you can see for yourself how powerful I am. I am a master wizard in the ways of the power that you cannot even comprehend. I can feel great potential in you. I am very interested in getting to know you better, Darius."

Two guards stood by the door, and Kelln stood a few paces from Darius, glaring at Alessandra.

"Bring him in," ordered the Preacher in answer to a knock on the door. In walked Alastair. Armored guards held him on each side. The Preacher turned toward Kelln. "Do not think you were so special to her, Kelln. She wanted so much more to keep her grandfather alive."

"Is he so strong you need two guards to hold him?" asked Kelln.

Alastair stood in silence. Kelln watched Alessandra looking at him. Tears dripped from the corner of her eyes.

"Father." The Preacher looked into Alastair's face. "It has been a long time. I thought you had died by now."

"You are no son of mine."

Annoyance flashed across the Preacher's face. "Take them all away! Except for Darius. I would like to visit with this commander of whom I have heard so much."

In an instant the guards removed them from the Preacher's rooms.

After all were gone, the Preacher turned to Darius. "Well, I have heard a lot about you, Darius, Commander of the King's Elite Army." He smiled and motioned Darius to sit down. The Preacher's chair sat slightly higher than his own. Maybe the man wasn't so confident after all.

"Where did you get that sword?" the Preacher asked.

"I found it." Darius was not ready to relay too much information too quickly. He had to work this situation to his advantage before the Preacher locked him away.

Darius remembered the day he had first learned he had power inside him. He and Kelln had been stuck in the dark in a room under the old library. Willing himself to see through the fear of darkness, he had found a spark of flame forming in his hands. His life had never been the same since then. That was the day he had also found the sword lying in an old cupboard in the room. At first touch, he had been given a vision of how the sword had been forged, with magic.

"Found it?" the Preacher walked over to where the rare sword sat against a wall and picked it up. "Do you know what the writing says?"

"No." Darius wondered why the sword held the Preacher's attention so much.

"It is the sword of a master. The inscription names its maker. A very powerful wizard." The Preacher's fingers trembled as he held the hilt. "I can feel its power." The Preacher closed his eyes for a brief moment, as if soaking in the power of the sword.

"How do you know about this?"

"I know a great many things, Darius. I have been in Mar's underground, where many secrets can be found, and I have learned things at the feet of the sorcerers and wizards far away across the Eastern Sea. They are respected in that continent. I have power you could only dream of. I would be a powerful ally for you."

Darius smiled and leaned his tired body back in the soft red chair. His mind raced with possibilities as he felt the Preacher's power wash over him. Powerful feelings drew him closer to the man in front of him. Maybe this preacher wasn't so bad. He felt a kinship with him already. When the Preacher looked at him he felt confident and was sure they could work things out. Maybe the Preacher could help Darius cleanse the Realm from apathy and complacency among its noble elite.

"Did the sword awaken your power?" asked the Preacher.

"Yes. How did you know?" Darius sat up straight in the chair.

"That is often the case. A magical talisman or relic reaches deep inside you and brings to the forefront your potential to use the power."

Darius soaked the words of the Preacher in. If this Preacher understood him and the power, then he might be able to instruct Darius in its use.

Finally someone to teach and train me.

The Preacher pulled down a long cord with his jeweled fingers, and a bell rang off in the distance. A beautiful servant girl with dark tilted eyes and black hair entered the room. Her skin was a soft brown, not unlike Mezar's, but her build was smaller. She appeared to be not much younger than Darius. She smiled at Darius and curtsied as she left.

"You are admiring my servants? She is from one of the eastern kingdoms. They are raised there to respect our powers."

"I am admiring the way your servants treat you," Darius smiled. He lifted his goblet and drank in deep gulps. The juice was a cool blend of apple and pear.

Something deep inside Darius warned him that what he was feeling wasn't real. The Preacher was somehow manipulating his feelings and thoughts. The drain on his body from the trek through the Black Forest and his confrontation with the Preacher's power was too much to fight the deep compulsion. Darius stopped fighting it and relaxed. He began asking the Preacher about his powers. They talked and laughed and discussed strategies deep into the night.

The Preacher eventually stood. "You and I are a lot alike Darius. You can see that can't you?"

Darius stood up from his chair and stood a few feet from the Preacher. The man was a few inches taller than Darius, but he felt awed in his presence. So much power and wealth and poise.

"We both have been treated unfairly." Darius agreed almost without thought. "I would like to learn more about you and your powers."

"And you will," the preacher added. "Stay with me for a while, and I will teach you."

Darius smiled. This was going much better than planned. He looked at the Preacher again and something in the back of his mind set off an alarm. There was something else he should be doing here in Belor, but he couldn't seem to remember what it was. He thought he heard someone calling his name—far, far away in the back of his mind. He shook his head to clear it. "I am tired. Can we continue this conversation tomorrow?"

The Preacher smiled and called for a servant to lead Darius to his guest rooms. Darius told the Preacher about Mezar and Leandra, his two friends, and the Preacher provided rooms for them lower in the palace. The Elite Army soldiers, however, stayed in the barracks and were watched closely.

The room Darius was led to had all the comforts imaginable, including running water and eastern-born servants. Before retiring to bed, he looked out of the high window. A full moon and stars made the domed roofs of most of the buildings stand in a soft glow. Belor was a beautiful city. He could understand why the Preacher wanted to defend it. His eyes glazed over as he stood, trying to remember something important, but all he felt was a deep tiredness.

With little more than a thought, Darius put out the flames of the many candles around the room. He smiled at the small task. He was already getting better at controlling his powers. That night, as the castle cooled down, he lay on the soft down bed and thought about the day. The longer he was away from the Preacher's presence the more he realized that maybe he wasn't thinking clearly. Just at the verge of falling asleep something pricked his mind again. A warning. But it was slippery and slid away into dreams of being a great wielder of magic and having servants do his bidding.

* * *

Kelln awoke the next day on a hard, rocky floor. It took him a few minutes to remember what had happened. He had been taken to a small room. It wasn't in the dungeon, for which he was grateful for. However, just being held again in the building where he had undergone so much torture sent new pain coursing through his mind. The only furnishings of the room were a small table, one chair, and a blanket. A washbasin and a pitcher of water sat in the corner. Kelln washed his face and looked out of the small square window, which seemed to be at least twenty feet from the ground. People were scurrying and running around below him as if something important had occurred. He heard a guard outside of his room talking. He leaned his ear against the door to hear.

Kelln yelled for the guard to bring him some food. When the guard came to check on Kelln he asked him about what was going on. It seemed that Darius was the talk of Belor. He and the Preacher had been seen walking around and chatting amicably that morning. Rumors were flying around about a union of the two.

Kelln saw Darius coming up a long curved stairway. His old friend was dressed all in black, in apparent facsimile of the Preacher. Kelln pushed the guard aside, spilling his food everywhere. He ran toward Darius.

"What do you think you are doing, Darius? You're a traitor to the Realm!"

The guard jumped up and ran toward Kelln. He grabbed him from behind and forced him to the ground, splitting his lip on the corner of a broken stone.

"Bring him to his room and leave him with me," Darius ordered the guard. Kelln couldn't believe how the guard obeyed.

The door closed, leaving Kelln slumped in his chair rubbing his lip. Darius brought him some water and a cloth.

"Tell me this is some kind of trick," Kelln said.

"What do you mean, Kelln?" asked Darius with a smug face.

"Come on, Darius. I am your best friend. You can tell me what the truth is. Tell me your real plan."

"My best friend? Where were you when I was sent away suddenly from Anikari?"

Kelln couldn't believe his ears. "You can't be serious. I couldn't leave here. You know that. The Preacher had me under lock and key, and now he's done something to your mind."

"You asked my plan. The Preacher and I have been discussing plans all morning. He is teaching me to use my powers. He is a great visionary, Kelln. Changes need to be made in the Realm. Together we will demand that those changes be made. It's what we need, Kelln. Don't you see? There is so much more glory for the Realm if we fix things. It's a perfect plan and a perfect time."

"You're crazy." Kelln stood up. "The Preacher is crazy. You can't fight against King Edward and the Realm. He got to you, Darius. The Preacher did this to me too. He messes with people's minds. Listen to yourself."

Darius paused and shook his head for a moment. "Kelln, I feel different when I am around him. I feel confident, and I have a clear vision of what to do."

"That's what he wants you to think. He is manipulating you just like everyone else."

"I don't expect you to understand, Kelln," said Darius. "You're not a military person. You don't see all of the injustice occurring. We are all being manipulated by the same king."

"Darius, I lived in Anikari with you. Sure there are problems, but things are not that bad. The Preacher is trying to get power for himself. That's all it is. He is taking your frustrations with your father and the King and making them seem bigger than they really are. You just can't march in and..."

"I can, and I will. The Realm has caused too much trouble for everyone. These people here in Belor suffer, the farmers back around Anikari suffer, and you and I have suffered because of the politics of the Realm."

"It's not because of the Realm. It's because of men in the Realm. Don't fight against them. If you want to change things, fight from within. You will die in a war, Darius."

Darius laughed. "I will not die. Don't you see the loyalty in my men and the men of the Preacher? They will protect us so we can save them."

"You aren't doing this for them. I understand now." Kelln walked closer to Darius, his voice rising louder. "You want the power."

"You're right, I want power, Kelln. Have you ever felt the power of an army behind you? Of winning a victory?"

"Darius!" Kelln couldn't believe what he was hearing. How could he make his friend see how the Preacher was manipulating his insecurities? He thought back to all the years they attended the Academy together. Darius was always the one to smooth things over for Kelln when he got into trouble. Darius was always careful in what he said and how he treated others. Darius always wanted to keep the Realm peaceful, not destroy it for his own power and glory. Darius always was the one to get Kelln out of trouble. Now it was Kelln's turn to help Darius.

"And most of all, Kelln, the power I have inside. It's amazing. The Preacher can teach me how to use it to its full potential."

"No. Alastair told me the Preacher uses his power for evil."

"He's just jealous. You all are jealous," Darius yelled, his eyes going out of focus.

Kelln couldn't believe his best friend had turned against him. They had ridden horses together, played ball together, studied together, and shared their innermost secrets with each other. What had the Preacher done to him? What power had he used?

"Darius, do you remember when we got caught down under the library? Remember when we found out about your powers and were talking about what we wanted to do in life?"

Darius nodded, and his eyes seemed to refocus for a moment.

"You talked about how you couldn't understand how your father seemed to crave the power and glory of politics and that you missed him being away from you and your mother."

Darius nodded again. "That is true. No one should have the power he and the King have to control other's lives."

"But don't you see, Darius? You are doing the same thing. You are caught up in power and glory."

"This is who I am now, Kelln. I have been given the ability to change things. You'll see." A new fire of madness glowed in Darius's eyes.

It scared Kelln and frustrated him to see his friend this way. He had to try and break the spell. "Look at yourself,

Darius." Kelln paused, then in anger yelled out, "you are no better than you think your father is!"

With one flick of his wrist, Darius sent the power at Kelln, pushing him away. Kelln flew across the room and smacked into a small table. His weight broke two of the table's legs into splinters. Darius made the chair fly across the room, breaking into pieces against the stone wall above Kelln. Kelln covered his head. He felt blood in his hair and winced at the pain. He wanted so much to get up and hit Darius back, but somehow conversations with Alastair came flooding into his head. He tried instead to hold back the tears and find peace.

"You have changed, Darius," was all Kelln whispered. He sat crumpled on the floor, bruised and bleeding.

"I am the same, Kelln." Darius headed towards the door.

"You are looking on the outside. Look on the inside. It has grown cold. Look into your heart. Please, Darius, don't do this."

Kelln looked at Darius's back and thought again about charging him. It would not do any good. Not with the kind of power Darius now had.

Darius opened the door.

"What will happen to me?" asked Kelln.

"That is up to the Preacher." Darius walked out holding his back straight. "You are his prisoner."

After Darius left, Kelln tried to rinse his face off in the water basin, but the water hadn't been changed from earlier, and it seemed to smear the dirt over his face. What was Darius saying? Surely he wouldn't sacrifice his old friend like this.

Maybe no one was strong enough to resist the Preacher's power.

He sat down on the floor and leaned back against the rough brick wall. His lip and eye were swelling, making his face ache with pain. He closed his eyes and found himself dreaming of Anikari. A pleasant dream. Kelln knew it to be a dream, but it helped him relax. He saw old friends in his dream. His heart jumped as he remembered his family. He wondered what had become of them here in Belor. It had been months since he had seen them.

Chapter Nine

Richard San Williams sat in a chair opposite King Edward DarSan Montere. He had been King of the Realm for many years and his reign had been mostly peaceful. Lately, however, too many events were getting out of hand. Today he sat slumped in his tall, cushioned chair. The dark velvet drapes were pulled shut, and despite the numerous lamps, the room seemed dark and depressing. Edward's once-large frame seemed to have shrunken in recent weeks. His face seemed older, and his thoughts were not always clear.

"One of your messengers came in from Belor this morning, your Highness. It seems my son, Darius, has been there for a few days. He crossed through the Black Forest directly to Belor. I have sent a messenger requesting him to return once again."

"Good, Richard. It won't be long now. It won't be long."

"But Sire, he has already disobeyed your orders, and there are rumors of him becoming cocky and boastful. And now we find him in Belor consorting with the Preacher."

"He is young, Richard. Remember at that age what we all wanted? We wanted to be noticed, to have people look at us, to have power." The King stopped and placed his hand against his head.

"What has happened, Edward? You were fine a few weeks ago." Richard stood up and paced the floor of the King's private chamber. His dark brown hair was similar in color to his son's, but unlike his son, he kept a trimmed mustache and goatee. He had noticed recently that his beard was showing more gray.

"The doctor is convinced I was somehow poisoned. There is no other explanation. He thought it would pass. However, I'm not so sure. It's still working deep within me. I can feel it. I think it started with those headaches months ago. It must have been planned back then. A slow process that would not attract any suspicion on anyone. It might be my time."

"What do you mean, your time? You are still young. You could rule the Realm for another twenty years. We will find an antidote."

"We are all given a role to play, Richard. I kept the peace the best I knew how. I realize I may have been too harsh at times, but I felt I had no other choice. My purpose is gone. I wasn't the rightful heir, anyway. Maybe that is why my family has all passed on before me. Once my wife and daughter died in the plague, I decided to do what was right and bring the throne back to its rightful line. I was just bridging the gap until it was time for another… your son… to take the next step."

The King coughed and took a deep breath. "I recognize the look in your eyes, Richard. You think he is too young and too brash. Maybe he is. But strength and wisdom brought on by age are not always what is needed. Youth many times brings the vision and energy that is better in certain circumstances. It's not always our choice. We are directed by one higher than us."

"Who is higher than you, my King?" Richard felt helpless. Edward must get better. Darius wasn't ready. He may never be ready. What was all this rambling from the King about a higher power? He was getting delirious. Richard walked over to open the drapes and let some light in.

"I don't know him well. Alas, maybe that is also why I must give away my kingdom now. But there is someone out there, Richard. Someone that directs us toward good. I have felt him before, when I am doing the right thing."

Richard remembered the time after an archery contest that Darius had won. Richard was cross at his son for showing bad sportsmanship and letting his anger control him. They had both said things to each other that were hurtful. Richard had taken a walk around an old field, trying to decide what to do about his son. He had felt something inside of him at that time also, but had been too afraid to rely on it, and so he buried it back inside. It happened to be the same day he found out about his son being in line to be the next king.

Richard walked back toward Edward and dropped down on a chair next to him. The lightened room made him feel better. It would be evening soon, but the last rays of light cascaded across the walls opposite where they sat. He still could not come to grips with his son being the next king. Oh, King Edward had explained it to him numerous times. Richard's father, at one time the heir to the throne, had been disowned by his father, King Charles. That line had then shifted to Edward, a younger son who was born a year after the banishment. As a small child at the time, Richard was also included in the banishment with his father, but his son, Darius, was not.

Darius still didn't know. It was the worst of many secrets Richard had kept through the years. Darius and he had not gotten along well the last few years. Darius didn't want to settle down and take on the role of a councilor; he wanted freedom and adventure. His foray into the farmlands and friendship with them had emboldened the farmers. Along with the recent troubles in Denir and Belor, the farmers were revolting and stopping food from coming into the city. No one was happy.

"Edward, we have been friends for a long time, so I must ask you: why did your father disown my father? What did he do to deserve being dismissed so cruelly from the royal line? What could have been so bad?"

The King sat up straighter and looked out the large glass window across from him. Richard let him be for a moment. He knew it was uncomfortable now for the King to move around much, but he grew restless after not receiving an answer.

"Edward?" asked Richard again, when no answer came. "I have to know."

"Yes, I guess you do." Edward smiled a reassuring smile.

Richard awaited the knowledge he had craved to understand ever since he found out his father and he should have been the next Kings of the Realm.

"Richard, your father married a... girl from outside of nobility."

Richard thought for a moment. "It has been done before. I can't believe the King would disown him for that. I..."

The King interrupted him with a cough, then continued. "She was… from the farmlands, and he had a child with her. That child was you."

Richard stood up without even thinking and stumbled to the window ledge. Grasping it hard, he looked straight down at the castle grounds. He distinguished his own house a short distance away. Then his head lifted toward the city walls and out into the distant farmlands. His hands clenched the ledge so tightly that the ancient rock almost crumbled. Thoughts of his boyhood played out in small sketches across his mind. He visualized his father and mother. They had loved each other so much, but his father had given up the kingdom for her.

"My mother was an outsider?" he screamed at the King. He couldn't believe he was a descendant of those who tried to take over the Realm through rebellion. "That is who I am? One of them?" Spittle flew from his lips. He had never been so livid in his entire life, and he knew it wasn't an altogether rational response.

Richard opened his mouth to continue the retort but closed it before saying anything else. Why was it so bad? He had never paused to wonder why the city people detested the outsiders. It was just the way it was. He thought back to his boyhood and realized that he had never learned such disgust from his parents. They were open and friendly to all. It was his own drive to be something more than his father, to be a noble and to have the best things in life that drove him to those attitudes.

Whatever the reason for his hatred, this information should not have been withheld from him. Rage filled his frame as he approached the King's chair. He stood over the King like a hawk looking at his prey. "Why didn't you tell me before? There is no excuse for this, Edward. You had no right."

The King's face reddened at Richard's accusations. "I had all the right, Richard. Do not forget who I am. I *am* King of this Realm. It is my responsibility to protect it and provide for it the best way I know how. I must act for the good and benefit of the whole. Do not lecture me on what is my right. You serve at *my* whim." He began to cough hard.

Richard brought a goblet of water for Edward and helped him drink. The King rested his head back down on his pillow and continued speaking, though in a softer manner.

"We all have struggles to face, Richard. And there is a time for each struggle."

"You are becoming quite the philosopher as you die, Edward." Richard still felt betrayed and perturbed. "Don't you remember who the farmers are? They were people kicked out of the city generations ago because of disregard for the nobility and the rules of the Realm. They protected and intermarried with insurgent wizards who disregarded the law and tried to rise up against the true rulers. They were criminals and rebels. They are outsiders! I can't be one of them!"

"I agree some rebelled against the rule of the Realm. Maybe the King's rule was too harsh against the wizards of that time and they felt they had no other choice. Other kingdoms have wizards. Why did we not want them? I don't know all the answers, Richard, but maybe they were justified in what they did."

"Justified? Never. It is never justified in fighting those who rightly rule. They disgraced themselves. Those who didn't die deserved to be kicked out of the city."

"Richard, that was so long ago. Why do we continue to call them outsiders? All they are now is really farmers. Those lesser wizards originally banished have melded in with the farmers for generations." The King took another sip from his cup and laid his head back. "They raise and grow food for us. Why is that so bad?"

Richard plopped back in his chair. His whole life was unraveling before his eyes. Why did this hurt him so much? It wasn't that he was part outsider—that did hurt, but it was more that there was information and secrets about himself that he didn't know.

"I have had to carry this burden with me. It has not been easy." King Edward's voice trailed off.

Richard took a deep breath and tried to regain a calmness he didn't feel. "And my burden is?"

"Richard, I have had to try and make the kinds of decisions I thought your father would make. I never remarried because I wanted to restore the line back to your family. It is not easy being the King."

"Nor a king's councilor," Richard muttered under his breath.

Chapter Ten

Kelln had been moved down to the dungeon again. The days had passed with no visitors and little food. He tried not to despair. At least he wasn't being beaten and tortured this time. He surmised that the Preacher had been too busy with Darius to think about him.

One morning, shortly after being given a few scraps of bread and overripe fruit, Alessandra entered his cell. Kelln was lying on a thin blanket in the corner of the stone floor. Upon seeing her, he turned his face away and closed his eyes against the hurt and pain.

"Kelln," she whispered, "we need to talk."

Kelln remained silent as Alessandra opened the cell door and walked over to him. She tried to turn his head toward her. He tried to ignore her soft hands and cringed inside when he couldn't. He opened his eyes and looked at her. She was inches away. Her mysterious dark eyes were red and watery and filled with fear. Her arm was bandaged still, and fading bruises covered part of her face.

He suddenly felt self-conscious and reached his hand up to smooth down his red curls, only to find himself wincing at his own bruises and cuts.

"What happened to you?" she whispered.

"Your father's newest ally, my old friend Darius, seems to now have a temper."

"My father is planning on having you executed soon."

"So I've been told. Does it matter now? I have no friends!" He spat the words out.

"I will help you escape."

Kelln shook his head as if trying to make sure he was fully awake. He couldn't trust her again. But if there was any hope at all of surviving, he had to at least listen to her. "How did you survive the river? We looked everywhere."

"I hit my head and floated up unconscious next to some logs far down river. One of the scouts out guarding the city found me and brought me back."

"Some trick you pulled to get away." Kelln turned his body to sit up. He didn't like looking up at her and feeling inferior.

"It was no trick, Kelln. Believe me. I almost died," Alessandra pled, tears rolling down her cheeks.

Kelln only grunted a reply. He didn't know what to believe. But he would do anything to get away from the Preacher. He would take poison himself before allowing that man to enter his mind again. "Who let you into my cell?"

"I gave the guard some drink... it made him sleepy," she said with little emotion. "Did you hear what I said about helping you?"

"You want to help me escape. I've heard that before, Alessandra, a couple of days before you turned me back in. I won't let your father torture me more!"

Alessandra looked hurt, but Kelln didn't really care at the moment. He hurt inside and out and was on the verge of losing his life.

"It wasn't my fault. It was my... father." She seemed to hesitate on the last word. "I realize now what he has done. Being away from the castle for a few days helped me clear my head and really see what you have seen all along—he is using everyone for his own gain. Now, he is even influencing your friend Darius. He has him under some kind of spell or something. You must warn Anikari. If those two join forces like they are now saying and march against the King, it will be bloody." She lowered her head and whispered, "I don't know if I believe in his cause anymore."

"You don't sound convinced."

"You just don't understand, Kelln." Alessandra barely held back the tears. "You didn't grow up here, around him. He is so powerful. It's hard not to listen to him and be filled with pride and righteous anger. But..."

"But what, Alessandra? He might have started out with good ideas, but now, look around you. Belor is only one city compared to what the King has at his disposal. Your father is crazy to fight the Realm. He is so hungry for power he doesn't care what is right and wrong anymore. Darius, too."

"He was a good friend, wasn't he?" Alessandra asked with sympathy.

"Yes, he was." Kelln hung his head low. "And still is! I must help him."

"Then you must get out and warn the King." Alessandra's large brown eyes flashed with excitement. "That's the only way."

"You come with me, then." Kelln wasn't going to let her turn him in again. He needed to keep her close.

"I... don't know."

"Alessandra." He said her name softly, but with emotion. "Either you come this time, or I don't go. It's that simple. You stay, and I stay and die. If somehow you have a plan to help me escape, you escape with me. Leave his influence behind. It is the only way."

Alessandra headed for the door. "Be ready early tomorrow morning. I will be here before the sun is up."

Kelln looked hard at her. His heart was in turmoil. He loved the way her hair fell over her shoulders, and even in redness, her eyes captivated him. Yet he couldn't trust her. At least not yet. "So are we leaving together?"

"Do I have a choice?" Alessandra grimaced a small smile. "You are right. I need to leave."

"Alessandra, can you find out about my family for me? Just let me know how they are doing."

"I will try." She reached for the door. "Just be ready tomorrow morning."

* * *

The next morning, as promised, Alessandra came back to Kelln's cell, slipping in between guard shifts. Her hair had changed once again. It was tucked under a shirt in the back, colored dark brown, and covered with a hat. She even took on the walk of someone different. She led him out of the room and down some narrow winding servant stairs into a small storage closet.

"Here, change into these," she said.

Kelln lifted the clothes up out of a bag and almost laughed. "These are women's clothes! I'm not going to—"

"Do you want to escape?" Alessandra said as she put some other clothes over her shirt and pants. After they changed, she brought out some kind of powder, mixed it with water, and spread it over Kelln's arms, neck, and face.

"What's this for? It smells disgusting." Kelln's nostrils flared.

"As it dries, it will wrinkle and make you look diseased," smiled Alessandra. Kelln hoped they wouldn't pass a mirror. He didn't think he could bear to look.

They cracked open the door to the closet to check their escape route. All seemed to be clear. The two escapees walked into another corridor and out through a garden exit into the early morning air. The stars were beginning to fade as a slight yellow light grew out of the eastern sky. It would be a clear day. The warmth of spring was in the air. They snuck up around a tall stone column and up behind a lone guard. Alessandra whispered for Kelln to stay, and she walked with careful steps toward the guard. She drew out a sword from her baggy clothes and hit him over the head with the hilt. Kelln gasped for a moment as Alessandra motioned him forward.

"He'll be all right," she whispered to him in answer to his questioning eyes. Sometimes he wondered if he was safe with her. He wasn't made for all this fighting.

They spotted a few other people. Kelln figured it was the bakers and those who worked the markets. One of the city cleanup patrols was just leaving through a small gate to dump the prior day's waste. Swiftly the two "women" moved toward the north gate. As they neared, they met up with other women who were dressed as they were and were preparing to bring the morning meal to the soldiers outside the gate.

Alessandra and Kelln followed two of them toward the gate, but before they got far, Alessandra came up and told them they would take the food instead. They began to argue.

"This woman's son is out on the battle field," Alessandra began, pointing to Kelln. "As you can see, she has a horrible disease and wants to talk to her son before she dies."

The other women looked at Kelln, grimaced, and backed away as if afraid of the disease. Kelln just smiled back at them without opening his mouth. He couldn't believe they thought he was a woman. He hoped no one he knew ever found out about this. He had a covering on his head along with a baggy shirt and long skirt. His small height added to the effect that he was an old diseased woman. The other women gave Kelln and Alessandra their food and walked away.

Alessandra turned and whispered to Kelln that all they had to do was get past the guards now. The gate stood under heavy guard. As they approached, they were stopped and looked at with suspicion.

"Aren't you a little old for a server?" one of them asked Kelln.

"She is sick and wants to see her son," repeated Alessandra.

"What kind of disease do you have?" another guard asked Kelln as he continued staring at the ground.

"She can't hear you. The disease has made her deaf," said Alessandra. The guards remained suspicious, but after looking at Kelln's skin they let the two through the gates. What harm could two ugly women do? The guards continued to watch the pair until they were out of sight. Kelln and Alessandra spotted some soldiers a distance from the gate and started moving in their direction. The guards behind them soon lost interest and went back to their posts.

"Now how do we get out of here without being noticed?" Kelln asked Alessandra.

"When we get close to the soldiers, start to cough and act like you are sick. I will leave the food with them and walk you over to the edge of the road. We will have to make it up from there."

Kelln did as he was told, still doubting the results. The soldiers took one look at Kelln and wanted nothing to do with him. He couldn't resist a little wave of his fingers to them. He almost laughed at their stunned reaction.

When he started coughing and wheezing they almost fell over themselves backing away. Alessandra came to Kelln's rescue, and they walked off together. Off the road a little way, they watched the soldiers devouring their food. They were not interested in two unattractive serving women.

"Why don't you sit down?" motioned Alessandra to Kelln.

"What?" his eyes narrowed, as he whispered, "The ground is cold."

"Just do it!" she barked softly, looking back toward the soldiers. A new group seemed to be coming their way up the road. "We must hurry."

Kelln nodded. He saw a soldier glance over at them, but when Kelln starting coughing again, the soldier turned away. Alessandra bent over to help him, and they moved, disappearing from the soldiers' view behind some bushes. As fast as they could they crawled away from the road, their clothes dragging on the hard ground. Kelln's hands began to feel raw and sore as they crawled over bushes, rocks, and sticks. The spring grass was just starting to fill in. The sun warmed their backs as it rose into the day.

They reached a group of short trees with new green leaves, stood behind one and peeled the outer layers of their clothes off. They stuffed them into a hole in the trunk of an old maple tree, then began running in a northwesterly direction toward Anikari.

Kelln hoped they didn't meet up with anyone until he could find a stream to wash in. He could hardly stand the smell that he carried. And he didn't make a very pretty old woman either.

"This is just fantastic," he whispered with sarcasm dripping from his lips.

Chapter Eleven

"Hey, get back here!" shouted the aged farmer as the three city boys ran off. "That's my family's food for the winter."

"Well, here is some of it back then, outsider." One of the boys turned around and, with a laugh, sent two potatoes hurling through the air, barely missing the man.

"Again?" asked the man's wife as she came out to see what all the yelling was about.

"Yes. The second time this week. But they only found a little food from the barn this time. They didn't go into the cellar."

"Things are desperate for everyone, it seems."

The weary old man dropped his tired frame to the ground. Wet from the recent rainstorm, the ground soaked through his sturdy work pants. But the old man didn't care.

"Come on, Grandpa," his wife said with a small smile. "Get up. We've been through this before."

"I know we can make it; it's been like this our whole lives. But the younger generation of farmers doesn't seem to want to stand for it anymore. Can't say I blame them. It's been five generations since the wizard rebellion. The farmers took pity on their families and took them in, and it has been trouble for us ever since. The power of those wizards is now long gone. Something's going to happen soon. Something dangerous, if this keeps up. There will be all-out war, and the farmers won't have a chance."

He reached up and grabbed his wife's hand and walked into their small warm cottage, looking back once as he shut the door. As he did, he watched three horses racing from the farmlands toward the boys who had tried to steal their food. The old man knew they would head to the city gates to once again fight against those delivering food. As always they were led by a beautiful, large white horse.

Fighting had erupted all around the outskirts of Anikari. People needed food, and the fear of not surviving drove people to do things they wouldn't have ordinarily done. Many on both sides of the turmoil had been wounded, though no one had been killed yet.

* * *

Christine, hidden under a mask and cloak, hung back with other raiders until food wagons from other Realm cities came into view. Now they stopped all wagons from entering or leaving the city gates. Some of the city men had hired private guards to surround their wagon trains and keep the thieves away. Sometimes they succeeded; other times they didn't.

Everyone in the farmlands knew of Christine and her vigilante war. Convincing a few other farmers to help from time to time, she and her followers stayed masked so as to not be caught and turned in by the city guard.

Later that day Christine sat once again on her white Cremelino and watched another wagon filled with food come around a corner. Its gray colors signified the food was from Sur, a large city to the northwest of Anikari. A lot of the wheat, oats, and other grains were grown and stored in that city. Workers there were now shipping the end of last year's harvest. The covered cart seemed to be alone, without an armed escort. This one would be easy. The wagon was an old one, the sides nailed together numerous times to keep it together on the road. The canopy was faded and full of colorful patched-up holes. A lone man sat in front, driving the scrawny horses.

"Now!" Christine yelled, and she and the other raiders drove their horses full speed toward the rickety wagon. One rider jumped onto the back to pull its wares out. Instead, a fist from under the canvas struck him in the jaw and a couple of pairs of hands pulled him down.

Another raider jumped on top of the canvas, falling into the apparently empty wagon. He, too, was restrained from getting up as the wagon continued moving.

Christine had seen this enough times in the past few weeks. Some of the city people sent decoys out to attract their attention, while other wagons rode on by without being touched. She looked around but saw no other wagons. In fact, the air grew oddly quiet.

Riding up alongside of the wagon, Christine decided that if things had to be done right she would have to do them herself. She jumped off her white horse onto the seat next to the driver. She went to grab the reins and drive the horses away, but she gasped at the man beside her. It was someone she knew. It was Karel, her cousin.

Someone else grabbed her from behind. She struggled against being held, her feet knocking the reins out of the driver's hands.

Help! she sent the message out to her horse in her mind. She heard her horse bump into the wagon. The horses pulling the wagon veered off the side of the road, making the wagon tilt. Christine fell onto the driver, and the rickety wagon rolled to a stop. She scrambled to get up, but hands from behind had secured her. She couldn't move. All she could do was yell.

"What are you doing? Let—" They gagged her mouth and then turned her around. *Thomas!* Her head screamed. *And Jain! And Karel!* She couldn't believe this. What was happening? Was her own brother kidnapping her?

Lightning reached out to her. *There are too many of them. I will follow you, and then we will find a way out. They cannot catch me.*

Christine felt a sense of frantic worry from her Cremelino. Lightning seemed to reach out to someone else for help. Someone farther away.

The horses were set loose and the wagon was left on the side of the road. The kidnappers removed Christine's mask but placed a covering over her eyes so she couldn't see where she was going. Her long riding skirt was ripped, her face dirty, and her long blonde hair mixed with dust and sweat. She was so angry that thinking became difficult for her.

After stopping momentarily, the kidnappers lifted her up onto another horse. She rode for a short time and then, by the smell of her surroundings, guessed they had entered one of the local barns. Her nose twitched at the stench as someone helped her dismount. They had her sit down in silence for what seemed like hours, her hands still tied. Her mind thought frantically of ways to escape.

Eventually she heard footsteps, and someone removed her eye wrap. She blinked a few times in the musty light. All she could see was a small corner of the barn and... Thomas. She wished they would ungag her. She hated the feeling of not being able to move her mouth.

Thomas brought some food over.

"Christine, I am going to take the gag off and untie your hands so you can eat. But if you start screaming, we will put it back on."

She felt like lashing out and hitting him, but her hunger kept her emotions under control, so she nodded yes, and Thomas took the gag off and untied her hands. Just because she wasn't supposed to yell, didn't mean she couldn't give him dirty looks… and she did.

"I'm sorry, Christine." Thomas hung his head down. "We didn't know what else to do."

The food, a vegetable stew, smelled wonderful. She tried to eat, but her stomach felt nauseated, and the food wasn't helping. Christine had never felt anger like this before, except for maybe when her father had died.

"Too many people are being hurt by your raids. We have to think of another way." Thomas continued, "The King is sending out more patrols, and soon you are going to get yourself killed."

Christine finally spoke. "You, Karel, Jain... Who else?"

"Many of the farmers want you to stop. They backed you at first, but now you won't listen to reason."

"And where is Jain now? Can't he face me?" She was bitter and furious.

"He's talking to your mother. Karel and Anya are outside keeping watch. Do you feel all right... I mean we didn't hurt you did we?"

Thomas, poor Thomas, Christine thought. Then she laughed inside. *It serves him right!* He deserved to worry. Maybe she wouldn't answer him. Make him suffer some more. Thomas heard a sound and turned around. Christine kicked the plate of food up at the back of him and started to get up. She forgot that one of her feet was tied down. She tripped and fell hard onto an old wooden crate, sprawling all over the sharp edges. She felt a sliver slide deeply into the palm of one of her hands. Karel, who had heard the noise from outside, came rushing over and picked her up. He wouldn't look her in the eyes though.

"Tied down like an animal!" she hissed, "What comes next?"

"Please, Christine—" started Karel.

"Don't 'please' me, Karel. My own cousin."

"I... we... just give us some time, Christine. Things are getting complicated. Rumors are the King is dying and will name a new king soon. The city is in a panic since Edward has no heirs. Unless someone strong takes the throne, civil war will erupt, with many of the councilors vying for the position of King. We have been approached separately by multiple factions asking for our help... in trade for protection."

"You trust them?" asked Christine. "They are all the same. They'll use us to get their own king elected, then they will turn against us."

"I admit it may be a small chance, but this is better than no chance at all, Christine. You just can't go around raiding forever. We need our money. And everyone needs food," continued Karel. "You don't understand how your actions are hurting all of us. We are worse now than before."

"Money... that's all they think about; and now is it all we think about too?"

Anya had just walked in. Her jaw was tight and her eyes watery. "No, we think about lives also, Christine. You don't care who gets hurt or killed, farmer or city dweller."

Christine felt the sting of the statement. Had she become so callused she hadn't noticed? But there had been no other way. Had there? She looked at the splinter in her palm and tried to dig the piece of wood out, giving her something to do while they spoke.

Anya continued speaking, turning to Thomas and Karel. "Thomas, you stand guard for the next three hours; then Jain is supposed to be back. I am going to get some more food for us. It may be a long night."

Karel turned to go with Anya, then turned back to Christine. "Things will be all right."

"For whom?" Christine was still frustrated, but some of her anger had been taken away by Anya's stinging statement.

"For all of us, I hope, Christine."

Chapter Twelve

Jain Anderssn was trying to explain to their mother where Christine was. Caroline couldn't believe what Jain and his friends had done to her daughter. He argued their point, and she conceded that something had to be done. Jain knew it upset his mother to say so, but she agreed it wouldn't hurt to keep Christine in the barn until morning.

Emily, Jain, and Christine's younger sister, walked into the room asking what was going on. Caroline didn't feel it fair to hide anything from her, so she nodded to Jain to tell her what was happening.

Emily smiled and laughed nervously. "Maybe Christine will settle down a bit now."

"I should have stepped in earlier, but with your father gone..." Caroline had tried to be strong for her children, but tears filled the corners of her eyes.

Jain knew his mother missed their father horribly. They all did. His death had brought the three of them closer, but Christine had pushed away from them.

In the midst of their conversation, a knock came at the door. Caroline wiped her eyes while Jain opened the door. The three of them only stared at who was there. Jain had never seen him up close, but he knew who it was. There was too much resemblance to Darius for him to be anyone other than Darius's father, Senior Councilor Richard San Williams himself.

"Councilor… uh… come in," said Caroline as she motioned for him to enter.

"I am sorry to bother you, but I need to talk to your daughter."

"My daughter?" Caroline wondered if they would arrest her.

"Christine. Is she here?" Richard asked.

"No. Not right now."

"What's going on? Is she in trouble?" Jain jumped in. Even though he had just tied her up, he was still ready to defend her against any city men, especially the Senior Councilor.

"I have to talk to her. It's very important. She's not in trouble. I promise I won't hurt her. I just need to talk, please." His voice almost cracked.

Jain stood, looking at Richard suspiciously. He was about to speak when his mother jumped in.

"Why do you want to see her, Councilor?" Caroline glanced around him, seeing if anyone else was outside with him.

Richard sighed deeply and looked at each of them before answering. "It's hard to say. I just need to ask her something."

Jain still didn't trust him, but he noticed that the councilor seemed more subdued than he would have thought, given the circumstances.

"I know what she has been doing, but I promise that I just want to talk to her. Will you take me to where she is?"

"Will you go blindfolded?" Jain asked Richard before his mother could say anything.

"What? Don't you know who I am?" Richard straightened himself up to his full height. "How dare you!" He couldn't believe these farmers. He was trying to understand them—now that he was one of them by birth. But they were going too far.

"Then, I guess you can't see her." Jain jutted out his chin in defiance.

"Jain!" Caroline admonished. "If the Councilor wants to try and help this situation, we should let him."

"I don't trust him. In order to prove himself, he must go blindfolded."

Richard took a deep breath and sighed deeply. He nodded his head slowly. "I will do as you say, young man, but no tricks. This is a very serious situation, more than you know."

Caroline stepped forward and bowed her head to him in deference to his position. "Thank you for coming out here, Councilor. I know it may have been uncomfortable for you. But if there is anything you can do to help my daughter and this whole situation, I welcome it."

Richard smiled a genuine smile and nodded his head. "I just hope it's not too late." Caroline watched Jain blindfold the councilor and then help him onto a horse. They rode off together deeper into the farmlands.

* * *

Christine heard a horse and the voices of more people, one of which was Jain. Her back was to the barn door, but to the side she could see Karel and Thomas offer an awkward bow.

"Got them bowing to you now, huh, Jain? Is that what this is all about?" Christine almost spat the words out. She wouldn't dignify her brother's appearance by turning around.

"Christine, someone's here to see you," was all Jain said.

She heard footsteps approach.

"Christine," said a deep voice that had a tint of familiarity to it.

Christine turned around slowly and then almost fell off the old wooden crate that she sat on. She didn't know what to say. She thought about the last time she had talked to Richard San Williams. She had tried to sneak through the castle in disguise, and he had caught her. What did he want now? Did he know it was her destroying so many carts of food? Was she going to the castle dungeons?

"May we talk alone?" Richard turned to Jain and Thomas. "I promise nothing will happen."

Jain eyed him carefully, and the young men walked away to the other side of the barn.

Christine and Richard sat in silence a few moments. Richard gazed out toward the middle of the barn as if gathering his thoughts. Christine took the time to look at the Councilor's profile. She saw a resemblance to Darius in his father and all of a sudden felt self-conscious of how she must look. Embarrassment at what she had been doing flicked through her mind. What would Darius have said? Suddenly she wondered if something had happened to him. Was that why Richard had come? Nine months had passed without her hearing from him.

Finally Richard turned back to Christine. He paused a moment longer and then spoke, "Christine... I know you don't trust me, but you must listen to what I have to say. It was an extremely difficult decision for me to come to you."

Christine furrowed her eyebrows. At least it didn't sound like Richard was bringing bad news about Darius. Instinctively she reached up and smoothed her hair.

"I have come to ask you to stop the fighting," he continued.

"You came out here to ask me that?" Christine laughed.

"Just listen. I am only asking the fighting to cease for a few days; a truce. As you have most likely heard, there is trouble within the city. The King..."

"Your problems are not mine." Christine couldn't believe he was trying to do this. "We have already been approached by others."

"Others?" Richard seemed surprised. "Who?"

"It is no secret that the King doesn't have an heir to the throne. There are other groups who may treat us better than you."

Richard looked surprised. "And you believe that?"

Christine thought a moment. "No, actually, I don't believe that any of you will treat us better. Why do you ask me?"

"I know it's you riding around on the Cremelino."

It was Christine's turn to look surprised.

"There are not many farmers who have an expensive Cremelino." The councilor stood up from the crate he had been sitting on. "Listen to me, Christine. An announcement will be made in the next few days. Please stop the fighting until then."

"It must be an important announcement for you to lower yourself to our level and to come out to the farmlands. Is it about an heir to the throne?"

Richard looked down. Beads of sweat began to appear on his face. "You must keep this confidential, Christine. There is much more at stake than you or even I could believe at this moment. I am only telling you to show you that I really want to resolve this now."

"Who?" she asked, not really expecting an answer.

"I can't say." He did not look her in the eyes.

"What difference does a new king make? There will still be fighting."

"Maybe not." Richard's voice lowered.

"What are you saying? That the new king is a benevolent man who loves the farmers? Or, is he going to be a farmer, perhaps?"

Richard did not smile at her sarcasm. "Will you call off the fighting?"

"I don't know if I can. As you can see, my so-called friends and brother have limited whatever power I had. What if we are attacked?"

"I will stop that. Will you do your part?" Richard looked her directly in the eyes. His eyes held a pleading she had never seen before. They reminded her of Darius so much she had to hold back a gasp. *Oh, Darius.* It was hard to hold back the tears, but she couldn't let the councilor see her weaken. She bit the inside of her check to buy time to think.

What isn't Richard telling me? He is hiding something. She projected her thoughts out to her Cremelino.

Trust him this once, Christine, came the reply. *The power of the prophecy is building. Soon you will know all!*

Lightning's reply surprised her. "Give me one good reason to stop the fighting."

Richard stopped pacing and looked at the ground. Then he looked back at her. After a few long seconds he said softly, "because my mother was from the farmlands."

Christine's eyes widened in disbelief, and a small laugh escaped her chapped lips. For a moment she just watched him, looking for any sign of deception.

"I just found out two days ago," the Councilor said. "I didn't know before."

Christine was still speechless. Maybe that's why Darius had been so nice to her, even though he didn't know about his parentage.

"I'm confused, Christine. I don't know what to do." The Councilor's shoulders slumped. He looked exhausted.

She knew that had been hard for the man to admit. She would not have expected it of him. Darius always said he was a hard man—someone who fiercely protected the Realm, but from the seat of his castle chair.

"Will you stop the fighting?" he asked once again.

Christine's voice came out very quiet. "I will try. But it may take a few days."

Richard smiled nervously. "A few days are all we have."

Christine just nodded.

"I had better leave now," Richard said. "Please keep this information to yourself for a few days. It might be pivotal information in the naming of the new king."

She thought he meant it could start unnecessary fighting before the naming of the King. She wondered if it was someone who had approached them already. "Can you talk to my brother?"

He nodded and began to walk away.

"The son of a farmer, huh?" she whispered toward his back with a smile on her lips, "Maybe there is hope for you yet."

Richard turned and looked over his shoulder at her.

"And, Councilor, I have a secret for you." She paused as he took a few steps back toward her. "Something I just recently found out also. My father's father was from the city. We're not so unlike each other as you had thought."

Richards's eyes widened with shock. Fear, exasperation, and surprise all crossed his face in a matter of seconds. He turned away, shoulders slumped. "Does anyone actually know who they really are?" he muttered the words while turning toward Jain.

A few minutes later, Jain took Richard back on his horse. Before leaving, he gave instructions to the others to let Christine out of the barn.

Christine sat on Lightning and watched the backs of Jain and the Councilor in the far distance. She thought of how Darius had been pushing away from his father's rule before he left. He had felt forced and manipulated into doing his father's will, and Christine now wondered if that had just happened to her.

Soon, my child, soon, came the familiar voice of Lightning. *Soon you will have all the answers.*

Giving her horse a soft loving tap, she vowed to never block the horse out again. Lightning whinnied with delight, and they galloped off to her home.

Chapter Thirteen

Darius walked around Belor with Leandra and Mezar on either side of him. Trailing a dozen yards behind was a contingent of guards, half of them Elite soldiers and half belonging to the Preacher. He had talked the Preacher into letting him have some of his own guards around him. Taking a tour of the city had been Leandra's idea, and Darius had readily agreed.

He and the Preacher had been conferencing for the past week, and Darius was intrigued with the man on multiple levels. The man's control of magic beckoned him strongly, and Darius had a sudden urge to learn more about his own hidden powers. The Preacher's ability to stand up to the King and the rule of the Realm also interested him.

"The domes here in Belor are similar to those at my home in Gildan, though ours are filled with lights." Mezar interrupted Darius's thoughts.

"Lights?" Darius looked at Mezar.

"Some are candles, some magic, but many of our domes reflect different colors at night. It is beautiful."

"Do you miss it?" asked Leandra. She had been more subdued and quiet recently and paying more attention to Mezar than Darius.

"Ahh." Mezar looked wistful. "I do miss certain things. Though I am having quite the adventure here, don't you think?" He winked at Leandra.

Darius frowned at the exchange. "You don't act like a prisoner, Mezar. I don't quite understand you."

Mezar's eyes almost seemed to close as he smiled. "You might not understand me yet, but we are not unlike each other."

Darius shook his head. He really didn't understand how Mezar, being a prisoner, could be so content with what was going on. He was obviously very intelligent and had been a young commander of a Gildan Battalion, but he was still hiding something. But Darius liked the man well enough. He had not tried to escape and had actually been friendly toward Darius.

"It's different here than in Anikari," Darius responded. "Angled roofs are normal there. The nobles seem to crave stone houses, while merchants have brick, and others out in the farmlands have smaller wooden homes."

"And what do you like, Commander Darius?" Mezar asked.

The question gave pause to Darius. Most of his growing-up years were had in a large stone house close to the castle. He knew that when he was younger they lived farther out by the walls of the city in a smaller home. None of them were overly comfortable. He wasn't really sure what he liked.

"I like wood. It is warm and inviting and can be painted different colors," added Leandra.

Mezar smiled again. "I would like very much to see a home like that. Maybe I could visit your home someday."

Leandra blushed at Mezar's statement. Darius thought he should feel jealous, but for some reason he felt relief. He wondered though at Mezar's boldness.

"Personally, I don't think it is the materials that make a home, but the people in it," Darius said in thoughtful contemplation.

Both Mezar and Leandra stopped and looked at Darius with surprised looks.

"What? Don't you think I can have thoughts of comfort and home? I have not always been a commander." Darius felt slightly perturbed at their assuming looks.

Suddenly they came up on the backside of the palace. Spring gardens were being tended by gardeners, and other servants were cleaning the sides of the great smooth stone walls. Daffodils and tulips bloomed, and the air held their fragrance. As they neared the palace once again Darius felt a tug inside of him, pulling him toward the Preacher. Concern must have shown on his face.

"Darius, what is wrong?" asked Leandra from the side of him.

"The Preacher." Darius stopped and looked up toward the top of the palace. A huge dome sat atop of three smaller domes.

"Commander." Mezar put his hand on Darius arm. "May I speak freely?"

Darius turned to him and nodded.

"This Preacher. His powers are not good. He has cowed and manipulated his people. What are you doing with him?"

The question surprised Darius. "I don't have to explain myself to you," he retorted.

Mezar stepped back. "I meant no affront to you, Commander."

Darius knew he had reacted poorly. He realized that he had felt much more relaxed walking around the city, but Mezar was right. The people were quiet and subdued. The normal markets that should exist in a city this size were too contrived and orderly. The Preacher definitely had a hold on the people of Belor. Did the man have a hold on him also? "The Preacher wants to be my ally."

"And what do you want?" Mezar asked.

That was a question Darius had been asking himself all day. When he was with the Preacher he felt connected to him and wanted to be around him. He accepted the Preacher's plight as his own. But when he was away from him, the feeling faded. He was left to wonder what he really wanted.

The three of them entered a smaller door in the back of the building. Apprehension filled Darius at the thought of meeting with the Preacher again. His jaw clenched as he thought about how he was always being manipulated to do someone else's bidding. His father, King Edward, and now the Preacher.

Darius fought the tug of power pulling him forward and chose to walk at his own pace. Soon they heard a commotion around a corner and stopped to see what it was. They stood behind a large granite column and witnessed the Preacher's interaction with some men.

"What is the status of my army?" asked the Preacher.

A nervous-looking man in a dark red uniform highlighted with a yellow sash stepped forward. "Sire, as I have told you before, we do not have an army. We have a thousand men who have been told to fight. They…"

Whatever the man was going to say next was interrupted by a flash of power from the Preacher's hands. A blue light surrounded the man's neck, and choking sounds followed. In less than a minute he dropped to the ground.

The Preacher turned to the other three men. "Anyone else want to make excuses for why more men are not ready to fight?"

The three men looked at the ground silently. One of them, a thin, older-looking gentleman, looked up as if to say something, but apparently changed his mind.

"Good," the Preacher continued. "You will have my army ready in two days. I will join with this Darius boy and his men to finalize my hold on Belor and then march to Anikari for formal recognition of my position."

Behind the column, Darius stiffened at being referred to as a boy.

One of the men spoke to the Preacher. "Can we trust him, Sire? He is one of them."

The Preacher bellowed a loud laugh. "Leave him to me. He cannot resist my power. He hardly even knows who he really is or what he can do." The Preacher turned to look toward where Darius and his friends stood.

Darius didn't think they were seen, but an abnormal feeling washed over him. He saw Mezar stiffen next to him and begin to back away, motioning for Darius and Leandra him.

Darius reluctantly followed. He would have rather confronted the Preacher but knew it wasn't the smartest thing to do.

Back outside, the three of them breathed the clean air. Staying quiet until they were away from the palace once again, the three strode at a pace to not attract attention.

They reached an empty street, and Darius stopped. "He called me a boy!"

Mezar smiled briefly and nodded his head. "I told you he is dangerous. You feel his power, don't you?"

Darius nodded. "How did you know?"

"I have had training in these types of things," Mezar said cryptically and shrugged.

Darius wondered again who this Gildanian really was. There were more layers and secrets in Mezar than in any man he had met.

"Darius, what are you going to do?" asked Leandra.

Darius didn't know how to answer. He had powers that were obviously inferior to the Preacher. He wished he knew more about them. He wondered if there was anyone else who could help him learn.

The three continued walking around the city, back to the front of the palace. Darius noticed more intensely the fear in people's eyes. After seeing the Preacher kill one of his men so carelessly he understood their feelings. A leader should look out for his men and protect them, not make them cower and be afraid. Thoughts of guilt ran through his mind.

"Mezar, am I a good leader?"

Mezar opened his slanted eyes wider in surprise. "Commander, you have always treated me well."

"I still don't understand why," Darius mumbled.

"You're a wonderful commander, Darius. You are the first commander of the King's Elite Army," Leandra added.

Darius looked annoyed. "I don't need your pandering, Leandra. I want real answers."

Leandra cowered back toward Mezar.

Mezar continued, "I think your men support you, but somewhat grudgingly. You are obviously a good tactician, great with the sword, and, may I add, have powers at your disposal that others don't."

Darius glanced at Leandra. He didn't know if she understood what Mezar was saying or not. "Leandra, go and get us some bread and meat in the market." He pointed up the street towards the vendors.

Leandra didn't look happy but glanced at Mezar first for assurance. He nodded, and she left. Darius didn't know what that look was all about. He would find out later. Right now he had to deal with Mezar alone.

He directed his answer to Mezar. "You must not talk about other powers I have."

"Then you will never be a great commander," Mezar said bluntly.

"How dare you!" Darius raised his voice.

"You asked for an answer, Commander. I gave it. You have everything most people want. You are young, strong, skilled, and powerful, but you hide who you are."

Darius's cheeks burned red, and his hands clenched. "You do not know who I am. You don't know anything about me."

"I know what you could be if you focused and learned from the right teacher. I know you feel it, Darius. You just need to learn how to control the power and use it wisely."

Darius opened his mouth to spit back a retort, but he took a deep breath instead and let some of the anger go. He knew Mezar was right, but it wasn't that easy. He looked around, making sure they were still alone. He could see the bright skirts of Leandra still in the marketplace.

"What you say is true, Mezar, but leaders in the Realm do not look as kindly on wizards as they do in your kingdom. There is no one to teach me." He hung his head a little lower. It was the first time he had admitted to anyone besides Kelln that he had powers. He felt guilty admitting it but also relieved.

"Ahh," Mezar said. "Yes. I forgot the Realm's aversion to those types of things. It is not so in Gildan."

"There is no law about magic specifically as far as I know." Darius tried to feel hopeful. "But I have heard my father's aversion to it mentioned numerous times."

"Maybe you can change your father's mind, along with others'. Make them see it isn't bad or evil, but just another tool to use—for good or bad, I suppose, but it is not evil in itself."

Darius was going to ask Mezar what else he knew about wizarding powers, when Leandra came back to them with a basketful of bread, meat, and cheeses. They ate as they continued their tour around the city. Darius had a hard time concentrating on anything he saw. His mind raced with questions and possibilities, but not a lot of answers or solutions.

He felt he was on the brink of making a decision that could change the entire course of his life and that of others around him. Could others accept him for who he was? Would his father or the King let him still lead the Elite Army if they knew he had magical abilities?

Darius grunted in frustration. Mezar looked over at him but didn't say anything else.

The three found themselves by the northern city gate when a commotion caught their eyes. A dozen guards crowded around a man on horseback. Darius felt for the familiar hilt of his sword but realized it wasn't there. The Preacher had convinced him to leave it in the castle. He ground his teeth in frustration once again and moved toward the group.

Some of the guards scowled while others parted for Darius. Looking up at the man on horseback, Darius saw that a large "A" covered the right breast of his red and purple uniform. A messenger from Anikari.

Noticing Darius's uniform also, the messenger dropped down off his horse and bowed his head slightly. "Commander Darius San Williams?"

Darius nodded in the affirmative and stepped closer. Belorian guards still stood next to the messenger.

"I have two messages for you."

"From whom?"

"One is from your mother, sir, and one is from the King."

Darius paused for a moment and told the guards to let him approach. "Give me the letters," he said to the messenger.

The messenger handed him the letters and bowed with appropriate deference. Darius was slightly annoyed that the

King had approached him so soon after arriving in Belor. But the letter from his mother had him more worried. He motioned for one of the guards to escort the messenger to get some food with a warning to not harm the man.

Before opening the letters, Darius walked back to the palace grounds. Mezar and Leandra walked away together to give him some room. He moved off into a corner of the gardens and opened and read the one from the King first. He could tell it was written by his father's hand.

"Why the scowl?" The Preacher spoke from in front of him.

Darius jumped. He had been so engrossed in the letter that he had let his guard down and hadn't felt the Preacher approach. The man was all smiles and cordiality, yet Darius felt a dirty, evil underpinning as he approached.

"The King is commanding me to return to Anikari at once," he said to the Preacher.

"Well, why don't we all go and meet him? My army will be ready to march in two days."

"He says I must come without my army and as quickly as I can." Darius tried to understand the tone of the letter. "It is a curious letter. I can tell it was written by my father's hand, but it has the King's seal at the bottom." Darius tilted the letter so the Preacher could read it himself. He felt the Preacher's warm breath, and his mind went back to what he had seen earlier that day. The Preacher killing one of his own men in cold blood. He shivered despite the warm spring morning, and suppressed a desire to run away from the man.

Darius excused himself and took a few steps away to open his mother's letter. She had written him once while he was in training. It was a very informational letter of day-to-day happenings around Anikari. This letter was different. It was written in obvious haste. She expressed her love for him and pleaded with him to follow the King's instructions. Darius was puzzled. His mother rarely became involved in the affairs of the kingdom, though any other woman in her position would have. She had always seemed content to stay at home and only attended state functions with his father when necessary. He felt a tugging in his chest he hadn't felt in a while.

"I must go at once," Darius stated to the Preacher. Leandra and Mezar had moved in closer.

"But why?" asked the Preacher. "Why not wait and take the army with you? We will be ready soon. It will be a perfect surprise. You and I striding into Anikari together. They will give us what we want then." The Preacher's voice boomed louder, and others in the area turned toward them.

A day before Darius might have gone along with the Preacher. Even now he felt the man's powerful pull on him. He grounded his thoughts with what he had seen of the city and the Preacher earlier that day. This joining together was not what he wanted. He had to make a decision on which path he wanted to be on.

Before he could answer, a guard rushed up to the Preacher. He bowed low and waited for the Preacher to acknowledge him.

"Sire, the prisoner has escaped. The boy from Anikari."

The Preacher's face turned scarlet. "How did this happen?"

The guard cowered back. "He must have had help. When we brought him his afternoon meal, he was no longer in his cell."

Darius took interest in the conversation. He cringed inside as he remembered how he had treated Kelln. It was inexcusable, he knew, and he hadn't had the courage yet to face him again. The fog on his mind had lifted partially—enough that he could see it was the Preacher's influence that had caused such rage in him. He shook his head as if trying to dismiss how he had left his friend sprawled on the ground.

"Find whomever helped him escape, and bring them to me. They must still be in the city." The Preacher's mouth tightened and he looked around as if seeing through the entire city. For all Darius knew, he could.

The guard looked like he wanted to say something, but swallowed hard and closed his mouth.

The Preacher looked back to the guard. "You have more to say?"

"It is rumored that your daughter was the last one to see him."

Rage flew from the Preacher's eyes, and the air filled with power. In an open display of the magic he held, the Preacher with a loud roar sent a line of fire from his fingers toward the guard's chest. "Don't bring my daughter into this, you coward. Find him now! I will deal with her."

Darius stepped back. Even Mezar, eyes wide, took a few paces back from where he stood, bringing Leandra with him.

The small crowd watched as the guard crumbled to the ground in a ball of flames. The Preacher turned to Darius with a fervor that kept anyone else from talking.

"Now, Commander Darius San Williams, when are we going to Anikari to confront the King?"

Darius had never known such fear before, but he kept his face still and used a soft but firm voice to calm the Preacher down. "I will go first to assess the situation. Then I will send for you. It is better to be prepared."

The Preacher stepped up only inches from Darius's face. Darius had to fight to keep from cowering before so much evil power. He felt a push against his mind but pushed back as hard as he could. He was rewarded with a slight grin from the Preacher.

"Good," the Preacher said. "You still have fight in you. I was worried you were going soft on me with the letter from your mother."

"I know what needs to be done." It was an ambiguous enough statement, Darius knew. In fact, he still wasn't entirely sure what he would do, but he did know how dangerous the man in front of him was.

"Are you afraid of me?" The Preacher stepped back, put his arms out wide, and let the wind blow his robes around.

Darius could not admit the fear he had or the loathing he was developing for this man. "I am afraid of what the King might do if I, his commander, do not answer his call to return."

"You are wiser than I first thought, Darius. It is good for you to go ahead and prepare. It will make my grand entry even more significant. But you must take someone with you."

"I will take Mezar with me to present to the King. We will leave at first light tomorrow."

The Preacher's anger had subsided from the earlier bout with his guard and he now seemed to be in a more congenial mood. "When should I meet you?"

"Come to Forest View in five days unless I send a message otherwise. By then I will have assessed the situation fully."

Darius turned away from the Preacher. Upon doing so, he felt a strong impression pleading for him to hurry. It was felt in the back of his mind, similar to what he had felt the day before when a similar command to return and help had been voiced in his mind.

The Preacher called after Darius. "Did you say something else, Commander? "

"No."

"Hmmm," the Preacher voiced his thoughts. "I felt a fleeting thought that I didn't recognize."

"However," Darius took a few steps forward, "I have decided to leave this afternoon instead."

"Why the sudden change in plans?" The Preacher seemed suspicious.

"If I ride hard all day, changing horses, I should be able to reach Forest View tomorrow night. Then I will find out what the King wants the next day. The earlier we know the better." Darius hoped the Preacher bought the story. He couldn't explain the sudden thoughts that had barraged his mind, or who had sent them.

Turning back to Mezar, Darius instructed him to go with a guard and collect his things. He wanted to leave as soon as he could.

Mezar smiled at him.

Darius couldn't believe Mezar's disposition. Did nothing faze him? "Don't you know that I am taking you to see the King of the Realm? You are a Gildanian commander who trespassed with an army on Realm soil. Aren't you afraid of what could happen to you?"

"I do not think you will let any harm come to me," Mezar said with a smile. "I am looking forward to seeing more of the Realm and some of your peculiar politics. This seems to be a time of change in your kingdom."

Darius shook his head and grunted. *Crazy Gildanian!*

In the corner of his eye he saw Leandra shrinking back toward the castle. She usually begged Darius to go with him. This time she didn't. Her behavior lately had been different. Almost as if she was biding her time for something. He would deal with her later, right now he had to get away from the Preacher and find out what was happening in Anikari.

Less than an hour later, upon two of the best thoroughbred horses in Belor, Darius and Mezar left for Anikari. Darius was glad to be away from the Preacher but was apprehensive about seeing the King and his father again. What did they want? How would they react to him disobeying orders and going to Belor? How would he react to their need to control him? He ground his teeth in frustration for the third time that day and vowed to make his own decisions.

Chapter Fourteen

It was exhilarating for Darius to be riding again. He loved the way the wind rushed against him as they flew northward in the cool, crisp, early spring air. The day had opened with sun, but clouds and fog blew in from the Blue Sea only a few miles to the east. Mezar pulled a scarf up around his neck.

Allowing his horse to rest for a few minutes, Darius slowed down. He sat with shoulders tensed and focused. He could see Mezar watching him from the side.

"Mezar, tell me about yourself. How did you get to be a commander at your age? What is your emperor trying to prove by sending you to invade the Realm?"

Mezar brought his horse closer and smiled. "It seems that you and I have much in common. From what I understand you were raised in nobility and given as much an education as possible. You were chosen out of many young men to lead this Elite Army for your king. I, too, was raised in nobility and have a father who wants me to understand what is going on. Not just in Gildan, but in all our neighboring countries. Politics is in my blood, I guess you could say, and I have no choice in it."

"There is always a choice," voiced Darius. Though he understood what Mezar meant.

"Ahh. I guess there is. However, there is one difference between you and me. You are looking for reasons to run from your upbringing and the opportunity for leadership. I, on the other hand, accept my role in life. Being in politics and being a leader is not always a manipulated situation; it's an opportunity to help others. A good leader makes others' lives better."

"But what if I don't want to be a leader?" asked Darius.

Mezar paused a moment while they rode in single file across a small stream. Once on the other side he resumed speaking. "Darius, you are a leader. I don't think that is the question. What you want is to be a leader who makes his own decisions. But I think you would be a leader whether you were in this army or not. You can't run from your destiny. You can choose, however, to be a good leader or a bad leader. That is your choice."

Darius frowned. "Are you saying I'm a bad leader?"

"Not a bad leader. You captured me, didn't you? But you rule through fear and uncertainty rather than respect. Your men cannot follow you freely if they don't know where your loyalties lie and what your purpose is."

"My loyalties lie with me!" Darius grew angry. "That is how I make my decisions."

"Then you are a very dangerous leader, Commander; more so with the power you wield."

"What do you know of my power, Gildanian?"

"More than you think," Mezar said with a knowing smile and kicked his horse forward in front of Darius.

"You're pushing it, Gildanian." Darius raised his voice. Mezar knew more than what he was saying. He acted more like Darius's superior than his prisoner at times. Darius snapped the reins on his horse and jumped back out in front of Mezar. The two of them then raced up the road as fast as their horses could carry them.

They stayed that night under some large and sheltering pine trees, with little conversation other than to discuss camp duties. The next day, after changing horses in a small village, they reached Forest View late in the evening and settled at an inn on the northern edge of town.

With a deep feeling of familiarity, the surroundings began to look like Anikari again. The buildings were more angular now, with straight sloping roofs, rather than the domes and clay construction of Belor. The way everyone was dressed, the setup of the market section of town, the language of the people; it was comfortable to him. Flowers bloomed in window sills, and grass grew in front of some of the larger estates. The scent of spring filled the air.

Darius sensed a general nervousness in the town. He couldn't place the trouble, and it bothered him. He had been gone almost nine months now and, except for news from Sean San Gant, the son of a minor noble who had been up in the mountains when he was training, had received hardly any information of the Realm during that time. He had been so focused on himself that he hadn't realized how cut off he'd been from the rest of the kingdom's doings. Darius realized again that the farther away from the Preacher he went, the lighter he felt—like a burden had been lifted from him. He was only now beginning to understand the source of the Preacher's power, how different it felt from his own power.

Mezar and Darius sat in the far end of the inn's common room. They engaged in light conversation, mainly about the food and the music. He was beginning to feel more relaxed and tried to enjoy the company. The exotic young man from their southern neighbor drew a lot of stares from around the room. His darker complexion, slender build, and slanted eyes seemed to draw people to him. Most of the serving ladies found at least one excuse to come to their table that evening.

Darius didn't advertise his presence but didn't hide the fact either. A few other patrons looked at his uniform and tried to place who he was. The music being played and sung by a trio of musicians made him homesick. One of the songs reminded him of a barn dance he had attended with Christine. He wondered what she thought of him now, after being gone so long.

The room began to get more crowded and warm, so Darius and Mezar went up to their own room. Because they traveled on the King's summons, they had been able to secure privacy. Other travelers had been put out of their room because of it. Darius would rather be alone, but he couldn't very well put Mezar in his own room, though something inside of him told him he could trust the man entirely.

He felt a closeness to Mezar that he couldn't explain. It seemed ridiculous, and he hadn't voiced it to others. It was like a long-lost friend returned, and Darius wondered if Mezar felt something similar. That is why Mezar's words the previous day had upset him so much, because it was a voice to some of his own doubts and inadequacies. Mezar understood him somehow as Kelln never did. It wasn't that Darius was pushing Kelln aside. In fact, he felt sick in the pit of his stomach wondering where his friend had gone. Once he found out what the King wanted, he would search out Kelln and apologize to him.

The room was comfortable, consisting of a wooden table, two chairs, a small bookshelf with a few books, a washbasin and a large bed. The books surprised him, but he remembered his father talking about a new printing technique that made it possible to produce more books, rather than having them copied by hand.

The two men reluctantly had to share the same bed. Each took a side and scooted as far away from the other as possible. Darius sank into a deep sleep within moments. His dreams were of Anikari and his mother; every time she looked at him he perceived pain on her face. It disturbed Darius, and he tried to shake himself away from it. A vision of his father and the King appeared to him next. They seemed worried and talked in small whispers. When Darius tried to get closer, they seemed to move even further away. Next, he stood in the Field of Diamonds. Christine was there, but she couldn't see him. The field was brown, and Christine was crying. Again, he seemed to hear another voice urging him forward. Its familiar feeling was stronger now than it was in Belor.

A door crashing open ripped him from his scattered dreams. Before he could move, two large men grabbed him, while a third reached toward Mezar. He watched as Mezar kicked hard, then moved lithely behind the two men and escaped from their clutches. Darius reached for his power, but before he could do anything, a cloth of fowl-smelling liquid pushed against his mouth. It made him dizzy, and he couldn't access his power. He grabbed out with his arms instead and hit one of the attackers while kicking back at the other. One man turned his sword around and smashed the pommel into

Darius's head. Pain flashed through his skull, and he struggled to stay conscious, but soon the darkness engulfed what light there had been in the small room, and blackness filled his vision.

* * *

Mezar, upon seeing Darius struggle against the men putting the rag to his mouth, understood what it was and knew he had to get away before they did the same to him. He had a chance to escape, make his way back to Gildan, and tell his grandfather all that had happened in the Realm. Instead, he decided to follow the men who had overpowered Darius.

He smiled once again at the excitement this land offered and hoped he wouldn't be captured again. That could cause some definite problems. He imagined his father shaking his head at his oldest son's sense of adventure. Mezar's father was more focused on consolidating power than having an adventure. He wondered how his grandfather would react. The old man would probably laugh.

Going down the stairs and into the common room, only a few stragglers were still up this late at night. However, as Mezar neared the bottom of the stairs, he saw a thin figure sneak out a side door. He could have sworn it looked like Leandra, but why would she be in Forest View? She had stayed behind in Belor.

Mezar turned to follow, but the commotion upstairs grew louder, and he had to head out another door to escape notice. Taking a quick look down the street, he moved off into the shadows to await the men from upstairs.

Lanterns burned in the windows of some of the inns down the street, where men stayed up all night gambling. The two attackers came down some back stairs with Darius in tow. Mezar followed discretely, but they rarely looked back. Mezar stuck to the darkest spots and stayed close behind. Even if they looked back, they would notice nothing but darkness. If need be, he could easily take care of the two captors, but he wanted to see where they would take his new friend.

Mezar heard voices up ahead and shrank back farther in the shadows. Through the dark night, he saw a silhouette of a man pulling a cart and horse up, with a girl approaching on the far side. He caught her profile with a splash of the moon and was certain now it was Leandra. She seemed to be arguing with the two men.

The two captors loaded Darius on the cart, and the driver tossed them a bag that Mezar assumed was full of money. Leandra sat up next to the driver as the cart took off. The two men he had been following turned around and headed back into town. They passed within a few feet of him but were too busy talking about the money they had made that night.

"He never knew what happened," one of the men laughed.

"Bet he'll be surprised when he wakes up and finds out he's in the middle of the forest," said the other man. "The other fellow sure high-tailed out of the room. I guess he wasn't much of a friend."

The other man laughed. "Easiest money I've ever made. I would have done it for half."

"I wonder who he is?" said the first man. "Must be important for that much money."

The men continued talking as they moved away from Mezar. Mezar sat in quiet for a moment, then with stealth moved silently back to the inn and went back upstairs to their room.

In their room, Darius had a bag of coins, his sword, and a change of clothes that Mezar grabbed. He left money for the innkeeper and headed back out into the night air. He thought again of returning to Gildan, but something he didn't understand compelled him in the other direction. There was a destiny around Darius that he felt was bigger than any of them currently understood. Mezar was a long way from home, but a few more days might be advantageous to his mission—a secret mission that he was beginning to see was becoming far more exciting and enlightening than his grandfather would have guessed.

The air was cool and dawn still hours away when Mezar entered back into the forest. With swiftness and stealth he ran through the trees, following signs of the wagon in the soft dirt.

* * *

Hours later Darius awoke to find himself being pulled in an old cart. His head spun with pain, and his stomach churned. He tried to remember what had happened, but his mind stayed in a fog. He tried to reach for his power again but found he still couldn't grab hold of it. He began to panic. He closed his eyes and tried to stop the spinning. He suffered the bouncing of the cart and soon fell back asleep.

Darius did not know how long he slept, but the glimmer of morning in the air and the leaves on the trees began to cast long faint westward leaning shadows. By the number and size of trees he saw, Darius figured he was somewhere in the Black Forest. Not deep into it, as most people were still superstitious about it. It gave Darius comfort. The old forest always had. His head had cleared a little, and he began to try to piece together what had happened and why. He had been kidnapped and was being taken somewhere. He didn't think it was the Preacher's men. He wondered if Mezar had been taken also, or if he had escaped during the commotion.

As they reached a small clearing, two men on horseback emerged from the trees opposite them and signaled the driver to stop.

"Who are you, and why have you taken me?" Darius tried to sit up to see his captors but was tied to the floor of the cart. "Do you know I have an army at my command?"

One of the men laughed. "I don't see any great army. Do you, Tam?" he asked the other man.

"No, I don't either. Maybe they are hiding in the trees." The men both laughed, showing Darius a few of their missing teeth.

"They will come looking for me," Darius continued.

The first rider, a large bald fellow, stepped into Darius's view and looked in his eyes. "But they will never find you... at least alive." He gave a hoarse, haunting laugh.

Darius's heart dropped, and he swallowed hard. "What do you want?"

"You will find out soon enough. Our leader will take care of that," said the man named Tam. He had a slight accent that Darius thought was from the Kingdom of Arc, but since he had never been there before, he wasn't sure. Darius reminded himself that either one of these men could kill him in his condition. He wondered what had happened to his sword.

He felt someone step down from the wagon, and low voices followed. A female squealed and Darius wondered who she was.

A voice soon came from behind Darius, telling the two horsemen to blindfold Darius and bring him. Darius tried to resist, but it was useless. His hands and feet were tied. His captors threw him over the horse on his stomach. He heard some other voices up ahead growing louder as they moved. A few minutes later the men pulled him off his horse, untied his feet, and told him to keep walking. One of the men directed him with a large, meaty hand on his shoulder.

He had never realized how much the power had been a part of his life. He guessed now it had always been there. His skill with the sword and bow, his knack for direction and knowing where things were, had all been part of his growing power. Now he sensed the power almost hiding at the edge of his mind, but somehow it stayed blocked. He felt blind and dulled to his usual heightened senses. To him it was like looking through a dirty window or trying to think after too much ale.

The ground underneath his feet changed. It was stone now, and the air was cooler. He had been taken underground into some sort of cave. For some reason he thought about his mother and wondered what she would do if he didn't return? The dream played in his mind again. He had never wanted to hurt her. She had always loved him.

He tried to draw in the power again. There appeared to be a small but subtle shift in his mind—a crack in the barrier that held it at bay.

Somewhere a door scraped open, and the men shoved Darius to the ground. He heard the thudded sound of the door close behind him among a few laughs. Then silence settled in.

Darius, still on the ground, tried to work his knees up to push the cloth off his eyes. The room was dark and still. Finally he was able to shove the blindfold up over his eyes. He could barely see his surroundings, with only a small amount of light entering from the bottom of the crudely made door.

The room seemed to be four walls, but two of the walls rounded together. It was carved from rock. The ceiling hung close to him, barely allowing him to stand without crouching. Off in one corner sat a sunken cot. Besides that, it was empty and lonely. He put his mind to use gathering information for his escape and working to unravel the barrier that had been constructed in his mind.

He wondered what would happen when he did not return to Anikari or back to Belor. If he did not escape quickly, the Preacher would take their men and march on Anikari. Darius grimaced at the thought. It was what he had thought to do himself, but after seeing the type of man the Preacher really was, he knew it wasn't the right answer.

Darius still didn't know who had captured him. Was it because he was the leader of the King's Elite Army or had looked to side with the Preacher or because he was the son of a king's councilor? He wondered if maybe Realm soldiers had captured him. Maybe it was a trick from the King all along, to get him alone. None of it made sense. Most of all, he couldn't figure out how someone had known where he and Mezar were staying ahead of time. Maybe he should have changed out of his armor and gone in with more stealth.

Darius moved from the floor to sit on the cot. His hands, still tied, were swollen and numb. He tried to work the ropes off but soon gave up and lay on his side on the worn cot. Somehow he fell asleep.

Voices outside of Darius's door woke him up. He sat up and tried to listen. He heard sounds on his door as chains and bolts were undone. At last, he would see the leader of his captors and find out what was going on. He sat up to ready himself and tried to stretch as well as he could. His mind had cleared a little, and he was more alert and less groggy than before.

The heavy wooden door swung open, sending in a bright torch light that enveloped the darkened room. Darius tried to see who appeared in the silhouette. Something in his stance seemed familiar.

"Does the light bother your eyes?" whispered the approaching man.

"Who are you?" Darius asked.

"You don't know, Darius? I have been planning this for a long time. I just didn't realize that when the opportunity came it would be so easy and enjoyable."

Darius recognized him now and gasped, "Sean...." The man that had taunted him growing up, teased him for having Christine as a friend from the farmland, and whom he had beaten in his last archery tournament. The last thought gave him small satisfaction now. He had thought when Sean had been in the training camp in the mountains that they had moved past all their juvenile pettiness.

"Surprised to see me, I see." Sean lowered the torch and set it in a hole in the wall. The flickers sent shadows dancing across the room. His hair was still cropped close to his head, but he now sported a goatee that made him look older in the strange light. His pants were pressed, and his lace-bordered shirt hung perfectly on him as if he was ready for a royal gala.

Darius fumed. "What do you think you are doing?"

"I don't think, Darius, I know. I have kidnapped you. And quite easily, I might add. Of course, I did have some help."

"Help... Who?"

Sean turned toward the door and motioned. "Come on in, my dear."

In walked a young woman with her head bent. Darius's heart skipped a beat.

"Darius, you know Leandra." Sean laughed.

Darius opened his mouth but couldn't think of what to say. Anger swelled within and almost overwhelmed him as Leandra approached. Her hair hung down over her face.

With a quick step, Sean moved over to her, grabbed her chin in his large hands and forced her face up. Darius saw the tears in her soft brown eyes. She wouldn't look directly at him.

He couldn't believe she had been the one. She must have followed him from Belor. "How long has this been planned, Leandra?" Darius clenched his fists. "Was our friendship only an act?"

"It has been planned since the beginning, Darius. I planned it," said Sean, puffing out his chest, "and Leandra was kind enough to agree, right Leandra?"

Leandra stood still, not saying anything. Her muscles tensed and soft tears ran down from bloodshot eyes. Darius thought he saw the beginnings of a bruise on her right cheek.

"Right, Leandra?" Sean repeated as he forced Leandra's face up again. He moved over to kiss her. Leandra turned away, and he grabbed her chin again.

Instinct drove Darius forward. Sure he was mad at Leandra, but Sean had no right to do what he was doing to her. Darius might not have loved Leandra, but he had developed a caring friendship toward her. He jumped and brought one leg up, kicking Sean in the stomach. Sean fell to the ground with a roar that brought five guards racing into the room. Leandra stumbled back a few steps.

"I'm all right," Sean said to the guards as he returned to his feet. "It will be his last heroic effort."

Darius stood with hands still tied behind him, glaring at Sean. Once again he had lost control of his temper. It may have cost him a chance to escape. He looked at Leandra and experienced an odd compassion for her. A feeling he hadn't felt in a while. As he did, another crack gave way in the barrier of his power.

"Is that all you've got?" Sean taunted him. "Can't draw forth any of your powers now? I wonder why that is?"

"What powers are you talking about?" Darius's mind reeled at the realization that someone knew about his powers. He was sure Sean was just guessing. "What did you do to me?"

He realized the men that had captured him had put some kind of poison to his lips that stopped his powers from emerging.

Sean shrugged his shoulders, looking back at Leandra. "Just a little something to keep your powers at bay. Anyway, you never treated Leandra right. She was a prize to you, Darius. You don't deserve any prizes."

Darius felt heat on his cheeks as he realized the truth of Sean's words. It grated him to hear the truth from his captor's lips. He hadn't treated Leandra well and had taken her friendship and companionship for granted. But that still gave Sean no right to capture him.

Sean walked back up to Darius. "You took the archery contest away from me. You took away my right to be in the King's army. I should have been a noble's son. I should have had the power you have. You were everything I wanted to be and have everything I want," Sean seethed, his voice getting louder as he spoke. "Well, not anymore, Darius. I will steal it all back from you. I have Leandra now, and for your ransom your father will give me nobility and the rule of a city, or he will never see you again."

"Sean, you are not thinking straight." Darius tried to negotiate. "You can't get away with this."

Sean grabbed Leandra by the arm and pushed her in front of him through the door. "If not, then I will die trying. I am tired of not having what I deserve."

As they walked through the door, Darius heard Leandra whisper, "Darius, it wasn't all an act." Then the door closed.

Darius paced the floor with anger and frustration. His thoughts moved back to Cray, his trainer in the Superstition

Mountains. Cray had been tough on Darius but had trained him well. Darius remembered when Cray had pushed him hard both physically and mentally to see how he would react. It was a test that had made Darius so angry. Cray had answered back that Darius would have to be careful of enemies who appeared as friends and seemed to have warned him all along about Leandra. Why hadn't he listened? Because she was beautiful. Sean was right; Darius had treated her as a prize.

Darius fell to the floor in shame and anger. He delved deep into his own mind, trying to find redemption and help. Sean would not expect Darius to regain his power. In fact, Darius was sure Sean could only guess at how much power Darius really had. He let his anger build. That was what drove his power stronger. But the more he pushed, the further away it seemed to be.

After an hour he tried to reach for the power again and again with his anger, hoping for another small crack. Instead he found nothing. Nothing but anger and fear and hurt. His powers were far, far away.

Darius looked around the room once again. Sean had left the torch on the wall. The room looked smaller in the light.

Reality sunk in. He had no power, no friends, and certainly no destiny here. His wrists burned as his ropes continued to rub his skin raw. He was a prisoner, alone in a dark cave somewhere in the Black Forest. He wasn't even sure his father would pay a ransom for him. He thought of Kelln and Mezar. He had treated them all poorly. He had alienated everyone who could help him. He had made the mistake of not realizing what power was doing to him.

His mind kept hitting a block no matter how angry he became. Anger had always been the best way to bring his power forth. What did they give him that was blocking it?

In frustration he screamed a long, aching wail of desperation.

In a nearby room, he heard Sean laughing.

From a place not too far away, Darius once again felt someone calling him, but with his powers blocked he could do nothing more than lie in anger, frustration, and desperation.

Chapter Fifteen

Richard San Williams, Senior Councilor to King Edward, sank into a high-backed upholstered chair and rubbed his hands over his face, trying to make the massive headache go away. King Edward DarSan Montere sat across from him in an identical chair. It was late in the afternoon, and the ailing king had finally been able to drag himself out of bed. His continuing weakened state concerned Richard more than he could outwardly admit. They had been discussing Darius again and were expecting him to arrive the next day.

Minutes passed in silence, when sounds of struggles and loud voices sounded from the hallway outside of the King's private rooms where they sat. Someone knocked, and Richard looked at the King for direction. He motioned his head towards the door and Richard took a deep breath and stood up.

He opened the door to find a guard trying to hold back a young and dirty man and woman. They pushed into the room. One spoke and Richard recognized him as one of Darius's old friends, Kelln, the son of the swordmaker. The same swordmaker who was rumored to be working with the Preacher in Belor.

"What are you—" Richard began, but Edward interrupted him, demanding to know what was happening. Both Kelln and the young woman started talking at once.

"Stop. Stop. Let's settle down and talk about this slowly." Richard motioned for the guard to leave and close the door.

The three moved back over to where the King sat. Richard stayed standing next to the two visitors. He knew Kelln well, and past moments when Kelln and Darius had to be reprimanded for some trouble flashed through his mind. "Kelln, you mentioned Darius's name. What is this all about?"

Kelln and the woman with him bowed to the king and waited for him to allow them to continue. Kelln then explained to both the King and Richard how Darius had been meeting with the Preacher and seemed to have been swayed by his preaching and scheming. Kelln was concerned for Darius and didn't know what else to do.

The woman, whom Kelln introduced as Alessandra, daughter of the Preacher and a defector from Belor, filled in other information every now and again of the few days that Darius had spent in Belor. After asking a few questions, the King and Richard thought in silence.

"What does he think he is doing, siding with the Belorians in this conflict?" Richard grabbed a book off a table and threw it against the wall. "He is the commander of the King's Elite Army. He can't do this!"

The King gave Richard a warning look. "We will talk to him tomorrow and get his side of the story."

"Darius is coming here?" asked Kelln. "Are you sure?"

"He may be bringing my father and his army," added Alessandra.

"We haven't seen any army. We would know about that. I sent a letter to him requesting his presence." The King coughed hard, and Richard poured him some wine.

"That letter had to arrive after we left," Kelln said softly. "The last time I saw him he wasn't very understanding."

Richard's eyes flared wide. His mouth was tight with anger. "Doesn't he understand who he is? The fool." He walked to the window and looked out across the great city of Anikari. Could the day get any worse?

Richard turned toward the King. "He is a reckless boy who isn't thinking straight. How can he be a ki—"

"Richard!" King Edward bellowed, almost lifting himself out of the chair, then fell back down into it, exhausted from the outburst. "That is enough."

Turning to Kelln and Alessandra, Richard tried to resume some form of outward calm. His frustration had almost driven him to say too much.

The King, with a serious look and in as loud of voice as Richard had heard him use lately, said, "Nothing you have heard here today may be talked about to anyone. If you do, it could cost you your lives. Is this clear?"

Both Kelln and Alessandra nodded their heads in nervous agreement.

"Show them out," the King said to Richard then followed with a whisper for the councilor's ears only, "but make sure they are watched. I am not sure whom to trust anymore."

They reached the door, and Alessandra turned back. "I forgot one thing you should know. His power is growing. If he doesn't learn to control it soon, it will consume and destroy him and maybe others along the way."

"His power?" asked King Edward. "You mean as my commander? It happens to new commanders. The victories go to their heads at first."

Alessandra looked back and forth between Richard and the King. "You mean you don't know?"

"Know what, young lady?" Richard's mouth was tight.

"Darius is a wizard!"

Richard felt lightheaded, his heart tightened, and he began to fall. Kelln rushed to his side and lowered him to a small red couch by the door.

The King lifted up out of his chair. "Get him some help now," he commanded, then collapsed back down.

Alessandra opened the door, leaned out into the hallway, and shouted for the guard to get a doctor. One arrived and came to the couch.

"God help us all," Richard whispered, his face ashen. He felt himself blacking out. He was on the edge. A razor's edge. His heart beat faster, and his chest constricted. A circle of darkness began to close around his eyesight. How could his son be a wizard? There weren't wizards in Anikari anymore.

Richard tried to stay alert for the young doctor, but his heart was racing so fast, and tears filled his eyes. Kelln grabbed some wine from the table, and Richard watched the doctor mix some kaya kava and valerian root into it before pressing it to his lips. The effect came quickly. It began to relax him, and he felt his eyes grow tired. In moments, all went black.

* * *

Kelln and Alessandra were escorted out of the castle and onto the empty streets of Anikari. It seemed surreal, Kelln thought, to be back home again after so long. It had been almost a year, and even though everything looked similar, a new tension filled the air. He took Alessandra by his old home. Two guards shadowed them wherever they went.

Grass and weeds grew up around the home and forge where his father used to make swords and other tools. There was a broken window at the back of the house, and it appeared some vagrants had used the place at some point but had not left it in bad shape. Probably someone down on their luck and with no shelter for the winter.

A nostalgic feeling overcame Kelln as he wandered through the few rooms of his family's home. Thoughts of his life before Belor flashed through in happy memories—working with his father making swords, chasing his sisters, the aroma of fresh-baked bread, and sneaking out at night to visit Darius in some late-night adventure. Breathing in deeply, he let his body and soul relax.

Kelln turned to find Alessandra watching him with a smile on her lips.

"Looks like it was a nice home."

"It was." Kelln sighed again. "It was. But life has changed a lot since then."

"You family is well in Belor, Kelln. I checked on them for you."

"Thank you again," Kelln whispered. He hoped the Preacher wouldn't retaliate against his family for his escaping Belor.

"Let's go to an inn. I am dirty and famished." Kelln headed back toward the door. "There is no food or warm water here. It hardly feels like my home anymore."

Out on the streets of the city again, Kelln began telling Alessandra about Anikari, his family, and exploits with Darius. The longer he spoke, the more his spirits lifted. Up until recently he had had a good life. There were lots of good memories for him in Anikari.

With a short walk they entered the Mighty Stallion, a clean and inexpensive inn not too far from the castle. After bathing and changing into some fresh clothes they had gathered at Kelln's home, they went into the common room to eat.

"What's going on here?" Kelln asked a pretty serving girl. "Why is it so empty?"

"Are you a stranger here? The farmers have cut off all food from us. We have to ration what we have until the King settles things with them."

Kelln knew of the troubles mounting for years between the farmers and the city people. Personally, he had no problem with them. In fact, he and Darius had made friends with quite a few of them after meeting Christine.

He remembered one day hanging out with a few of the farm boys in Karel's barn. They joked around and had fun just like Kelln and Darius did. Most did not have the opportunity for formal education as the city people did, but they were smart and looked no different from those in the city.

"I don't understand." Alessandra turned to Kelln as they waited for their simple food.

"People hold on to hatreds a long time around here. Many assume that the farmers have mixed blood with those kicked out from the wizard rebellion generations ago. It continues to breed mistrust and hatred even this many years later. The farmers are treated as a lower class by many of the nobles."

"But they grow your food and raise your cattle."

Kelln nodded. The serving girl brought them a bowl of thin soup and a few crusts of bread. He paused in the conversation to take a few bites. It was salty and flavored heavily with garlic and other herbs to overcome the fact that there wasn't much substance to it.

Alessandra continued with her line of questions. "So the nobles mistrust magic and wizard powers?"

Kelln looked around nervously, but the inn was empty enough that there was no one close enough to overhear their conversation. "It's not talked about much here in Anikari. It's not necessarily illegal, but exhibiting magical powers is looked at suspiciously."

"Won't they all be surprised!" Alessandra laughed. "If the Preacher and Darius converge on the city, there is bound to be some power displayed here."

Kelln furrowed his brows and frowned at that thought. He had to help his friend. Kelln knew if he could get Darius away from the Preacher, maybe even back with Christine, he could talk some sense into him.

Kelln wondered how Christine had fared over the past year. He wondered if her family was safe or if she had married. He decided he would go see her soon and tell her all about Darius. She would know what to do to help.

"What did the councilor mean about Darius? He was cut off by the King… saying something," said Alessandra.

"I'm sure he meant Darius should be acting more responsibly since he is the son of a noble and the King's commander." Kelln felt uneasy. He suspected what Richard had been going to say, but couldn't understand how it could be.

"The King and the Councilor both seemed nervous. I think something else is going on." Alessandra took a few spoonful's of the weak soup. "Did you see their faces? They are hiding something from us."

"You're exaggerating. I know Darius and his father. They haven't recently gotten along very well. His father worried about Darius's interaction out in the farmlands. They didn't see eye to eye on many things. I do wonder why they asked Darius here, though." Kelln was not as calm on the inside as he showed Alessandra on the outside. The King and Richard were genuinely surprised at Darius's growing power. The shock had almost killed Darius's father.

"Do you think he is bringing my father and the army?" asked Alessandra.

"The King's men hadn't seen an army," answered Kelln. "Maybe he is coming on his own. Let's wait until tomorrow and see. Right now I need some rest."

They rented two rooms in the inn, to the owner's obvious joy, and headed upstairs.

Kelln lay on the too-soft bed and thought about the last year of his life. Things used to be so much simpler when he and Darius were in the academy studying. He smiled at multiple memories of their adventures together. Kelln had to admit it was usually him who got them into precarious situations. Darius had been the level-headed one. At least until he had found the sword and some type of power had awakened in him. Ever since then Darius had been more apt to get angry.

Kelln thought about what Alessandra's grandfather, Alastair, had taught him about God and prayed a silent prayer for Darius. He hoped that Alastair was being cared for by someone. He had hated to leave the old man, but Alastair had said he would be fine. Soon after those thoughts he fell into a much-needed sleep.

The next morning a knocking on his door caught Kelln by surprise, and he sat up in bed with his heart pounding. He shivered in the morning air and threw his cloak on over his clothes before answering the door.

"Oh, it's you," Kelln said to Alessandra as she moved into the room. He sat back down on his bed and started rubbing his eyes. Alessandra let out a soft giggle.

"What?" he asked.

"You look like a little boy just waking up."

"I do not!"

Kelln tried to pat down his unruly hair, but he knew the curls wouldn't do much without a douse of water, and even then they probably needed a trim.

"Your hair is all messy, and you're rubbing your eyes like a child."

Kelln picked up his lumpy pillow and threw it at Alessandra, hitting her in the head. A large smile spread across her lips, and she laughed, her dark, almond-shaped eyes sparkling with amusement.

Alessandra proceeded to throw the pillow back at Kelln. He ducked, and the pillow bounced off his shoulder.

They both dove for the pillow, reaching it at the same time. Kelln, the stronger of the two, tugged the pillow harder and pulled it and Alessandra on top of him. With the pillow partially between their bodies, Kelln reached his head up and stole a kiss from her lips. She frowned slightly but didn't move away so Kelln moved in for another.

This time she did pull away and grabbing a pillow from the side of the bed threw it back at Kelln's face. They both ended up in a fit of laughter. Kelln couldn't remember the last time he had actually laughed. It was a good release for him, and he met the new day full, rested, and optimistic for the first time in many months.

That morning Kelln continued to show Alessandra around the city of Anikari. She had only been there briefly when she had found Kelln, and it had not been for sightseeing. Spring was in full bloom, with late tulips opening and a few dogwoods still dropping their last blossoms. The grasses were greening, and the sun warmed the air. Kelln showed Alessandra the ancient stadium where the festivals were held and the King's field where Darius had won the archery contest.

"You and Darius were good friends, weren't you?" asked Alessandra as they sat on a rock overlooking the field.

"Yes." He paused. "Yes, we were. We did everything together. He would always tease me about getting him in trouble, but I knew he liked it. He always said he wanted adventure, but I don't think any of us thought it would turn out like this."

"Did you know about his power?"

Kelln told her about the library basement at the old academy. They had been trapped in the dark. Darius was thinking hard about what to do when suddenly a light appeared in his palm. It was the first time they realized Darius had some type of power. Later that same afternoon they found a sword in the basement that flared with a bright light at his touch.

"He didn't talk about it much after that, though. He used it a few times around me but seemed quite hesitant. I guess things changed when he left the city."

"What will you do if he comes to Anikari to fight?"

"I will have to stop him."

"But he will kill you."

"I don't think so. Somewhere inside of him his old self is still alive. You don't know the Darius I do: considerate, helpful, humorous, every good quality you could think of... except he did have a short temper. I just have to keep trying."

"Why didn't you stay in Belor and help him, then?" Alessandra put her hand on his arm.

"Because your father was going to kill me!" Kelln raised his arms up in the air as if the answer was obvious. "And when Darius got all caught up with the Preacher, I couldn't reach him. Maybe being in Anikari will help. Maybe if I can find Christine that will help." He told her about Darius's relationship with Christine and a little of the history of the conflicts between the city people and the farmers.

They began walking back through the town. Alessandra reached over and slid her hand inside Kelln's. "You learned a lot from my grandfather, didn't you?"

"Why do you say that?"

"I remember the way he used to talk to me when I was little. He always sees the good in people and wants to help everyone. He is a strong and wise man."

"He is a wizard too."

Alessandra nodded.

"As is your father, the Preacher."

She nodded again.

"And you?"

She stopped so quickly on the street that Kelln almost fell down. "Why do you say that?"

"The power is passed down through bloodlines. So I figured if your grandfather has it, and your father has it, then you must also. That is why you knew about Darius."

"I knew about Darius because I saw him do things. And my father talked to me about him."

"But?" Kelln prodded.

"But?" Alessandra echoed back, then stopped and thought for a moment. Then she laughed. "Kelln, I just don't know. I have never thought about it. I have never felt anything inside. Most of my father's power was learned, so maybe my grandfather's powers didn't pass on to him or to me."

After looking around the town they circled back to the inn. All of a sudden a man stepped up in front of them, and the two guards that had shadowed them came forward.

"You two need to come with me," the man said in a commanding voice. Kelln recognized him as one of the King's guards.

"Where?" Kelln asked.

"The castle," was the only answer they received from one of the guards. "Just be quiet and follow Roald here."

Kelln and Alessandra were led quietly to a side entrance through the outside castle walls and then into the castle's lower levels.

"Who wants us?" asked Alessandra.

"Councilor Richard San Williams."

"Richard?" repeated Kelln.

"You shouldn't be so informal with his name," Roald stated.

The group walked into a small room. After entering, the two men closed the door and then moved a large bookcase in front of it. They continued walking down a long hall filled with pictures of past kings and queens, until they came to Richard's office. They knocked and then entered. Richard sat at his large mahogany desk. He motioned for Roald and the two soldiers to leave.

Richard stood and paced a few short steps, stopping in front of a book case. He looked recovered from the night before. His color had returned, and he seemed back in control. "Darius has been kidnapped."

Kelln's mouth hung open as if to respond, but he didn't say anything.

Richard continued. "We know he was in Forest View last night and was taken from his room. Another man was with him, a Gildanian, if things are to be believed, but we don't know where he is. We received a ransom notice in the past hour, with additional instructions to come later after the ransom is paid. It was eluded that the kidnapper would like to be set up as a ruler of one of our cities."

Kelln opened his mouth to speak but couldn't think of what to say again. Who would kidnap Darius?

Richard looked back and forth at Kelln and Alessandra, then continued. "We will obviously not meet these demands but must rescue him instead. We cannot send an army of our own men, because we are not sure where loyalties lie right now and don't want to cause any undue alarm. Darius must be brought back as soon as possible without anyone knowing he was taken. So he must be found and brought back without incident. There is an undercurrent of unrest in Anikari right now, and we can't afford anyone to have a reason to start fighting."

"Mezar was with him, it seems," stated Kelln.

"Mezar?"

"The Gildanian commander Darius captured… though Darius treats him more like a friend than a prisoner, from what I have seen."

Richard's jaw tightened. He invited the two young people to sit down.

"Kelln, I know you are a bright young man, but we also know that your father is in Belor. Can I trust you?" The councilor looked Kelln directly in the eyes.

"I'm not siding with that crazy man in Belor. He wants to kill me." He looked at Alessandra apologetically. He knew the Preacher was her father, but it was hard to remember at times. The two seemed so different from each other.

Richard smiled. "Good. Good."

"I will find Darius," Kelln said sternly.

A knock sounded at the door. Richard glared at the door and spoke quickly. "You will be provided an escort. He knows the forest well and has already been briefed on the mission."

"Come in!" Richard said in a loud voice.

Richard stood to meet the young man who entered. The man flashed the three a brilliant smile but lingered longer over Alessandra. She blushed.

"Kelln and Alessandra, I want you to meet your escort on this mission... Sean San Ghant." Richard scowled at Sean.

"I know Sean," mentioned Kelln. "I'm not sure I agree he is the best to help us, though."

The councilor raised his eyebrows at the statement.

Kelln continued. "Sean and Darius haven't always seen eye to eye on things." Sean had goaded Darius most of their time in school. The young man, two years older than Kelln and Darius, was the quick-witted, handsome son of a minor noble who wanted power and attention. Darius, who was the son of the first councilor, could have all the political power and attention he wanted, but he despised it. Sean had never understood that and was always trying to put Darius down.

Sean laughed and didn't take his eyes from Alessandra. "Just normal friendly competition between two noble sons. Nothing to worry about, Kelln. Now who is this striking young woman?" Sean strode forward, his red jacket tightenedaround him with gold buttons up the front.

Alessandra introduced herself, and Sean took her hand, bowed, and left a soft kiss on it. When she didn't respond,

Kelln nudged her, and she remembered to smile and thank Sean.

"All right, everyone knows what needs to be done," Richard said. "We must find my son soon. Three horses and supplies are waiting for you outside of the north gate behind some trees. Be careful when going out of the city. Send word as soon as you find out anything. And we need to keep this quiet."

The three headed toward the door, with Sean leading. Kelln was the last to go. Before leaving the room, Richard called Kelln back in.

"Go on ahead," Richard told the other two. "I need to talk to Kelln for a moment."

Alessandra looked at Kelln, but he nodded to her that he would be fine. She turned a corner with Sean, and Kelln turned back toward the Senior Councilor.

In whispered tones, Richard said, "Kelln, I trust you to find my son. I know you have been his best friend for years and know him probably even better than I. You must find him, Kelln." Richard paused and lowered his voice. "You do understand why, don't you?"

Kelln smiled nervously, remembering back to what he thought Richard had been about to say. *Was Darius really to be a king?* "I think so."

"What you think is true, Kelln. You don't need to know why or how right now. I barely understand it all myself. Only the King and I—and now you—know the secret. Trust and tell no one. Not Alessandra or Sean… and certainly not Darius."

Kelln felt dizzy and put his arm against the wall to steady himself. All he could do was to nod his head in the affirmative. Why would the councilor tell him all this?

"You are the only one able to save him, if he can be saved. You had to know. You have to succeed."

Kelln still didn't know what to say. "Darius as K—"

"Don't say anything out loud," warned Richard, "even to yourself. This has far-reaching political implications."

Kelln laughed uncomfortably. "Councilor, Darius has always hated politics."

Richard allowed himself a small, grim smile. "Don't I know."

"This will kill him," Kelln paused, "or he will kill us all."

"Our destroyer or our savior," whispered Richard as he opened the door for Kelln.

Kelln strode down the hall and around the corner, catching up to Sean and Alessandra, but his mind was miles away. He thought back to when he had been imprisoned in the dungeon prison in Belor. He had felt lost and full of despair. Now, only weeks later, he had talked to the King and had been given a command by his Senior Councilor to find Darius, his best friend. The next king! He said a silent prayer that he would be guided to find his best friend and that Darius would accept whatever came to him.

Chapter Sixteen

Later that evening, the three-person search party set up camp next to the east bank of the Black River, just south of Anikari. It had been a long, unproductive day. Sean seemed to be winding them around the long way. At one time Kelln thought they had found some wagon tracks, but Sean dismissed them as being old and of no concern.

On the first evening the group talked around the campfire, planning their next day's activities. Sean mentioned he had seen Darius a few months earlier in the Superstition Mountains and they had become friends and had a good time talking about the city. Kelln tried to appear interested, but he didn't believe for one minute that Darius and Sean had become friends. Sean was hiding something.

"Did Richard tell you anything about the ransom?" Sean asked Kelln.

"Only that they hinted at causing more trouble if they didn't get it. I don't think he knows who they are. I can't imagine why anyone would kidnap him."

"Me either," said Sean. "He is a fine young man, with a fine future..."

"What do you know of his future?" asked Kelln. He worried that Sean knew more than he was saying.

"Only that he is a noble and his father is second in power to the King. He has a life many of us wish for."

"From what I saw of him, I don't think he wanted that life," added Alessandra.

"Then he is a fool!" Sean almost shouted. "Maybe he is better off where he is."

Kelln was becoming more suspicious of Sean. "And where might that be, Sean?"

Sean coughed. "That's why we are here, right? To find out."

Kelln watched Sean stare into the fire and smile to himself. He brushed his goatee with his fingers and a small chuckle escaped his lips.

"What do you find so amusing, Sean?"

"Oh, I was just thinking how no one is ever happy with what they have. Take Darius, for example. He is the son of the King's closest councilor, with the ability to follow in his footsteps and to become a great councilor with power. Then, over and above that, he has some kind of magical powers giving him even more advantage. But he doesn't even care about these things. Then there is this Preacher in Belor, who wants change and power but can't seem to get all he wants."

Alessandra looked over at Kelln. Neither of them had told Sean who Alessandra's father was, but Alessandra shifted uncomfortably.

Sean continued. "Then, there is you, Kelln. I don't understand your motivation in all this."

"My motivation is to help out my friend. And what do you want, Sean?"

"Oh, that is easy. I want power and influence."

Kelln looked at Sean with distrust. He was hiding something. In fact, as Kelln thought back on the day, it seemed like every time they found a clue, Sean had dismissed it. At first they had trusted in his abilities. Richard had sent him along with them, so Sean must be useful to their task. But the more Kelln thought about it, the more he didn't like having Sean around.

Kelln felt heaviness within him when he realized the burden he carried in the awesome secret. *Why did the councilor trust me?* he asked himself repeatedly. Looking over at Alessandra, he longed to tell her the secret. But she had betrayed him twice already, and even though he really wanted to trust her, deep inside he couldn't. Not yet.

Kelln shook his head at such thoughts. Beautiful, lovely Alessandra. She had been caught in her father's unrighteous quest for power. He felt bad for her and gave her a smile.

She smiled back at him and moved to lie down inside her blankets. The night was cool, but not uncomfortably so. Soon the small camp fell asleep.

By lunch the next day no new clues had been found. The small group had moved farther east on Sean's instructions. He said maybe it would be best to backtrack to Forest View and start from there.

"We don't have the time," Kelln explained, becoming angry over Sean's self-proclaimed role as leader.

"What is another day, as long as we find him?" said Sean.

Kelln knew the other two did not feel the urgency he did. "I think we should look closer to the river and farther south. Alessandra has seen some signs."

Sean laughed. "The councilor sent me along to be your guide, didn't he? What does Alessandra know about tracking?"

Kelln had had it. "Look, Sean. You have been leading us around in circles and seem to be ignoring signs we have found. Alessandra grew up outside of the Everlasting Meadows and the south side of the Black Forest. I'm sure she has spent more time out here than you have. I think we should listen to her. You are obviously not getting us anywhere."

"Oh, Kelln," Sean became condescending. "You comprehend so little about politics and power. I have had enough of you two getting in my way and disrupting my plans."

Alessandra looked over at Kelln with a look of warning.

Sean grabbed his sword and began moving toward Alessandra. She had taken off her knife when they sat down to eat, and she eyed it on the ground, too far away from her to do any good.

Kelln pulled his sword out. "Get away from her."

Sean jumped without warning, reaching for Alessandra with his outstretched sword arm. Kelln stared in horror. He was still too far away. Fortunately, Alessandra was quicker than Sean. She jumped to the side and tried to move behind a tree, but on the second swipe from Sean, the sword caught her just below the elbow, drawing a deep gash. She yelled for Kelln and fell behind the tree. Kelln maneuvered up behind Sean and moved forward.

The young noble spun around and with wild eyes drove his body into Kelln. The ferocity of the move caught Kelln off balance, and he tripped on a root of one of the old cedar trees.

Sean brought the sword down hard, but Kelln rolled away to his right, jumped up and regained his footing. Growing up the son of the kingdom's best swordmaker, Kelln made up in control for what he lacked in size and power. The drills he had gone through in his early days of Belor also came back to him.

Kelln moved from defensive to offensive. He went after Sean with determination and small, controlled strokes. He pushed him back toward a tree, trying to wear him out so he'd make a mistake.

Sean fought back hard. Unexpectedly, he dropped and rolled away from Kelln, forcing Kelln to react in an awkward move and almost lose his balance.

"They didn't teach you that in swordsmanship class, did they?" laughed Sean.

It was hard to fight a man that didn't think right or play by the same rules.

Alessandra picked up a large rock with her unhurt arm and tried to throw it at Sean. The problem was, by the time the rock arrived, Sean and Kelln had changed places in their duel. The rock hit at Kelln's feet. On reflex, he glanced at the stone.

The quick diversion was all Sean needed. He drove into Kelln with his sword and sliced him across the thigh. The blood ran down Kelln's leg, distracting him. Sean was stronger than he had thought and continued advancing forward, forcing Kelln backward into a tree. He was trapped.

Sean stopped for a moment as he brought the sword closer to Kelln's throat. "I guess it ends here."

"What does?" asked Kelln, trying to buy some time. Alessandra began to move. Sean ordered her back or he would slice Kelln's throat.

"I will get what I deserve now. I should have power and riches, like Richard. Darius does not deserve what he doesn't want."

"What do you know about Darius?" breathed Kelln.

Sean just laughed. But his laughing was cut short as the point of another sword touched the back of his neck. He straightened, stiff as a board, with surprise plastered on his face. Kelln limped to the side.

"Who... Who are you?" asked Sean to the brown-skinned man who had a sword at his neck.

"Not your friend."

"Mezar!" Kelln exclaimed, "What are you doing here?"

"It's a long story. First, what do you want me to do with him?"

Kelln glared at Sean. "I could think of a lot of things I would like to do."

Sean paled.

"Just tie him up for now against a tree," Kelln said.

Alessandra brought some rope over from her pack, and they tied him to the tree. Sean shouted obscenities at them and yelled until his voice was raw. Finally Mezar put a gag in his mouth so the rest of them could talk. As they did so, they bandaged Alessandra's arm and Kelln's leg. Alessandra's wound was deep, and she had a hard time moving her arm. Mezar wrapped the bandage over Alessandra's wound, and then held his hand there a few minutes longer. Alessandra gasped and declared how good it felt.

When Alessandra turned away, Kelln gave Mezar a questioning look. The young Gildanian just smiled and put his finger to his lips. Kelln had a hard time believing what he saw. His head exploded with the secrets he held. Darius a wizard. Darius possibly the next king. In addition, now obviously Mezar was some type of wizard also. It was getting too much to bear. He put his hand on his head to steady his headache.

Alessandra mistook his emotional strain for physical pain. She moved over to him and helped bandage up his leg. The cut was not as deep as they had originally feared.

Mezar told them what had happened in Forest View and how he had followed the kidnappers and found a cave where they were hiding Darius. He explained to Kelln and Alessandra that he had seen Sean there also, that he seemed to be the leader.

The hiding place was not far away. It was down the river, where Alessandra had wanted to go all along. They discussed what they would do with Sean. The three decided they would have to bring him along for their plan to work.

Mezar walked over to Sean and knocked him out with the hilt of Darius's sword that he still carried. They draped him over the back of his own horse. They looked overhead and saw the sky growing darker with clouds of an approaching storm. They hoped to rescue Darius before it hit. Kelln gave his horse to Mezar and he jumped up with Alessandra on hers. Then urging the horses forward, Mezar led them out in quick succession.

After a short time of riding due south, along the banks of the river, Mezar slowed and warned them they were near. He closed his eyes for a moment, as if resting. When he opened them again he pointed down a small hill around the bend of the roaring river. The constant sound would help mask their approach. It was colder close to the river, and a late spring breeze blew past them and caused Kelln to shiver.

They slowed their approach. Through the dense trees they spied two bored guards in casual conversation. Their words drifted on the wind toward them. The men were hoping for a warm meal soon. Obviously, they did not expect visitors.

Kelln, Mezar, and Alessandra put the plan into action. Alessandra dismounted and hid behind some larger scrub bushes. She was to stay hidden in case something happened. She knew her way around the forest and would be able get back to Anikari in a few hours, quicker than the others could. She would ride to Anikari and inform Richard they had found Darius. If they did not return the next day, then Richard would have to decide what to do. Kelln wondered what she would do if the storm was too fierce, but that was the chance they were all taking.

He smiled at Alessandra, and she returned it with a wave of her hand. His heart fluttered a moment at her bravery, and he felt emboldened. He and Mezar moved out on their horses, with Sean still draped across the back of his.

"Sean's been hurt!" yelled Kelln to the guards, hoping Sean had used his real name with them. He figured that with Sean's ego he would have. It appeared he was correct.

Worried looks crossed the guards faces as Kelln continued. "Some thieves beat him and left him in the forest. He needs to get inside." Kelln did all of the talking, as Mezar's slight accent would alert the guards.

Without hesitation, the guards opened a crude door to what appeared to be a cave inside a rock formation. Kelln and Mezar dismounted from their horses, commanding the guards to tie the animals to a nearby tree. Moving swiftly to gain as much time as possible, the two carried Sean inside. Once inside, they realized it was a rather large cave, divided into different rooms. Others directed them toward an area that Sean used privately. Kelln told them Mezar was a healer and a friend to the cause. During all of the confusion they did not question his lack of speaking. Once Sean was in the secluded area, Kelln informed them the healer needed privacy. They were left alone.

A short time later, Kelln left Mezar alone with Sean. He had to find out if Darius was really there, but he knew how careful he must be. While wandering the corridor in the small multi-room cave, he saw he saw a room with a thick wooden door. It had a guard posted outside of it. That must be it.

"What do you want?" asked the guard. Suspicion lined his young face. The man was much larger than Kelln, with a short black beard and small beady eyes.

"Sean woke up a little while ago and wanted to know if the prisoner was still here."

"Why shouldn't he be? He can't just disappear now can he? When I took him his last meal, he was just lying on the floor moaning." The guard laughed. Two large swords hung at his side. Kelln knew he couldn't fight the man alone. He excused himself and went a little farther to the outside door. Upon his leaving the cave, the same two guards from earlier approached him.

"No one is supposed to leave here without Sean's permission," they stated.

"I just need to check on our horses. We had to run quickly through the forest to get him here."

"All right, but hurry," said the second guard with a strained voice for the protocol they were violating. Kelln walked over to where the horses were tied. He bent over, pretending to inspect their shoes. He heard a faint rustle through the bushes in front of him.

Without looking, he whispered to Alessandra. "He's here. But it will be morning before we can get out again." The sun was quickly leaving the sky ahead of the incoming clouds. "Are you sure you are fine out here alone?"

"Yes. I should beat the storm back to Anikari. I will steal one of the other horses here. They are tied up loosely on the other side of the cave."

Then just as quickly, Alessandra was gone. Kelln hated sending Alessandra alone, but he had to admit to her highly trained skill in the forest. He remembered the first journey they had made together. From Anikari to Belor. It had been Kelln's first time in the Black Forest, and he had been so paranoid. He smiled at the thought as he walked back to the cave.

Back inside he returned to Sean's quarters. People were asking questions about him, and Kelln had to keep them away with the guise that Mezar was still seeing to him. Once inside Sean's room, Kelln pulled some leaves out of his pocket that

Alessandra had found earlier. Given to Sean, they would ensure he slept at least through the night. Mezar ground the leaves up, mixed them with water, and poured the liquid down Sean's throat.

Looking at Sean lying on the ground, Kelln thought again, for a brief second, of just killing him and doing away with the trouble. He knew, however, that no matter what Sean had done, he couldn't kill like that in cold blood. Also, they would need to use him in order to get Darius freed. Mezar and Kelln sat down on the ground next to Sean and waited until all was quiet.

Chapter Seventeen

A few rooms away from Kelln, Darius picked himself off the cold ground and sat on the worn-out cot. He'd lost all sense of time in the dark stone cell, but figured since he was fed a few hours before, it must be late in the evening. He thought about escape until his head hurt, but he found no way out until they brought him out of this room, or until the drug that limited his power wore off. They had untied his hands and feet. Sean told him he had to go help Richard but would be back soon. Darius hoped his father could see through Sean's antics and send help.

He continued trying to reach for his power. He knew it was close, but they must be putting something in his food. He thought about not eating but decided he needed his physical strength more than his magical strength. He trusted it more, anyway.

His time thinking had brought him to the conclusion that Sean was correct in the fact that Darius couldn't trust anyone anymore. Anger flooded through him, thinking about Leandra for the first few hours, but then subsided into mere frustration. Darius thought about Belor and the Preacher. He thought about his father. He thought about Kelln. Could he trust anyone? The Preacher wanted him just for his power. Kelln wanted things to be like when they were younger. He just didn't understand that Darius was different now. His powers would always make him different. The King and his father wanted him to be a political leader. None of them understood and cared about what *he* wanted.

Darius himself was not sure what he wanted either. At first it was simple. While at the academy he learned about the Realm and wanted to be a leader that protected it. He wanted things to be fair among all the people that lived there. Then he found out about his powers and everything changed. He was different now. Anger seemed to fuel him, he became frustrated more often, and he saw more clearly injustices that were done throughout the Realm.

He had to trust someone, but whom? Who could guide him and help him be what he wanted to be and do what he wanted to do in life? He felt a tugging inside that said he could trust someone.

Kelln's few discussions on God as they crossed through the Black Forest on their way to Belor came to Darius now as he lay on the broken cot. Kelln always seemed to be jumping into something. Thinking of Kelln and growing up together brought Darius's mind once again to Christine.

The memories of the last year with her before he had left Anikari made him smile inside. He had felt so happy and alive then. He remembered the Field of Diamonds and felt a calmness come over him. Picturing the dew on the grass, the tall trees surrounding the small lake, and the Superstition Mountains off in the distance, his breathing slowed. His mind began to relax.

Christine was so charming and understanding. He remembered some of their talks. Christine seemed to believe in

God even though her people from the farmlands were persecuted. Her simple faith and joy in life had always attracted him to her. He thought about these things and felt a small stirring of joy inside him. With this joy, his power began to rise once more. He felt an excitement as he reached for it, but it was still locked behind a barrier.

He continued thinking of the past, and his thoughts took him to the King and his father. They had, with no explanation, sent him away at sixteen as the youngest person among the new recruits to train in the Superstition Mountains. Anger built again, and he felt the power subside. He groaned out loud and became discouraged once more. *What is happening to me?*

Then a stark realization brought him to his knees. *Am I any better than they?* He had done nothing to become the person he truly wanted to become either. He had entertained thoughts of marching against Anikari and the King. Why? Because of his relationship with his father? It had never been *that* bad.

All of a sudden, nothing made sense. He and his father had not seen eye to eye in the last year before he left home, but he had fond memories of him when they were younger. It was his father who had instilled in him a sense of duty and love of the Realm, had taught him the bow and the sword. Their disagreement over his relationship with Christine had caused a large rift. That was the one thing Darius saw that was hurting the Realm. The councilors couldn't see how divisive things were becoming.

However, the King and his father had sent him away, and in the end, he ended up being a leader in the King's army. Wasn't that what he had always dreamed of his entire life?

Didn't he want to protect the Realm and keep it strong? He'd marched to Denir and conquered the Gildanians. Then he'd marched to Belor, finding Kelln on his way.

Poor Kelln. Darius had treated him like the enemy. He thought of their childhood antics—the library, the trip to White Island where they had brought back Christine's Cremelino for her, the games they played. *He must hate me now!*

Darius stood and began to pace the room. Maybe he was better off here, he thought, where he would do no more harm to anyone he cared for. He had become something he hated. He had not handled the power of his magic or leadership very well. What would Christine think of him?

"Ahhh!" he yelled out loud as he pounded a fist on the cold hard wall. He tried to figure out where his loyalties were. He knew now that the Preacher had manipulated his feelings, but on second look, it probably wasn't too hard for him to do so. Darius had just been looking for a justification for his own thoughts and pending actions. *Who is right? Whom can I trust?*

Darius thought Sean horrible for using everyone, yet hadn't he done the same? He had used Leandra, Mezar, Kelln, the Preacher, and anyone else who got in his way. The thought scared him more than anything else had. How had he let his own power and insecurities rule him? Had he gone too far to be saved?

Trust me, a small voice seemed to whisper to him at the back of his mind. It echoed through his mind and heart. Where was the voice coming from? It sounded familiar, but he couldn't quite place it.

Darius lay back down on the cot and tried to sleep. Maybe he should be looking at what he could give to others, not what they should have given him. He whispered back in his mind to whoever it was that was reaching out to him. *Free me, and I will do better,* Darius promised whoever was calling to him. *Free me and I will trust again.*

He knew it was an unfair bargain. But it was all he could do for now. Thoughts of his mother and Christine came to him—their smiling faces and their love for him. He breathed in deeply and let the love wash over him for the first time in months. Peace overtook him on the dirty cot. His body relaxed as his mind drifted further away. Peace, warmth, and love burned through to his soul, a purifying fire that washed away the anger and evil thoughts.

As sleep engulfed him he felt his power once again flow through his veins, as pure and strong as ever before. It felt like light had infused his soul and chased the fear and darkness away. A contented smile turned his lips. The rapture made him feel as if he would burst out of his body. But he couldn't help but fall asleep, taking his power with him into his dreams.

* * *

The next morning, loud noises outside of his dark cell invaded Darius's slumber and brought him awake. Sitting up, he tried to remember what he was thinking before he fell asleep. He realized that the power was his once again. Smiling, he took a deep breath and let it out slowly. He felt at peace for the first time in the last year.

The door opened, and Sean fell into the room unconscious. Kelln and Mezar stood behind him. Darius jumped from his cot to his feet, trying to put together everything he was seeing.

A feminine voice in the hallway followed behind them. "Who are you? What's going on?"

The men turned toward the sound.

"Leandra!" Mezar exclaimed. He quickly grabbed her up and hugged her as he pulled her into the cell with them.

With a weak reflection of a torch from the hallway they each looked through the shadows at each other in the cell.

"Is he...?" Leandra looked at Sean.

"Dead?" finished Kelln, "No. Just a little confused."

"Take me with you, please," Leandra begged, looking at Mezar. Darius looked away, pain filling his eyes.

"Kelln... how...?" Darius stammered. "And Mezar—"

"We will explain later. We have to go before the other guards wake up. Do you want her along?" Kelln asked Darius.

Mezar realized what must have happened. "You turned him in?" he said to Leandra.

"I didn't want to... Sean made me." She began to sob. "It was his plan all along. He threatened my family with harm. Please take me away. You can drop me off anywhere. I just don't want to be here when he wakes up."

The men looked at each other. Leandra's fears were well founded.

"Fine," said Darius. "But let's go."

They left Sean in the room on the floor, closed the cell door and moved around a guard lying on the floor. They wrapped Sean's cloak around Darius to hide his face and moved to the outside door. As soon as they opened it, two guards approached them, demanding to know what was going on.

Kelln glimpsed the faintest signs of morning brightening the eastern sky, sending small silhouettes of the large cedars into the front of the cave. The ground was wet, but the storm had seemed to blow away during the night.

"Sean needs to go to Anikari. He is very sick," said Kelln, pointing to the bent-over Darius. The guards saw Leandra and questioned her. She assured them it was all right. As the group turned to go, one of the guards saluted them with a shout. Darius, without thinking, turned around too quickly, and his hood came off his head. The guards now shouted for reinforcements from the cave and began to run after them with swords drawn.

With a calm look on his face, Darius lifted his right palm toward them, and a barrier of air blew into them. They stumbled to stay upright, fear covering their faces.

"That's fantastic," Kelln exclaimed.

The escaping party followed Kelln through the trees to where their horses were tethered. Kelln and Darius hopped on Kelln's horse, while Mezar and Leandra jumped on the other.

One of the guards stood back up and shot an arrow at them. It hit Leandra in her shoulder, and she yelped with pain. They couldn't stop riding but pounded north through the forest at a breakneck speed. Soon others would be after them.

Darius breathed in the morning air. Never had it felt so good to him. His head seemed clear. His power was back, but with more purity than before. He almost felt giddy with excitement. He would have to set things right, but his life had been spared.

Chapter Eighteen

Jain was eating ham and bread in the kitchen when Christine walked in. It had been two days since the councilor approached her. She hadn't said a word to Jain since returning home that day.

"What did the councilor want from you, Christine?" Jain broke the silence.

Christine didn't want to talk to him. "A truce."

"A truce? Really? And you agreed?"

"Yes. For a few days." Christine sliced a piece of bread for herself. She had spent the last day talking to others in the farmlands and deciding on how she could stop the fighting. She didn't have control over everyone anymore. Some of the younger farmers were hotheaded, still rearing for a fight.

"Can you do that?"

"I don't know, Jain." A deep sigh escaped her tight lips. "But I guess I owe the councilor a chance. He did come to me."

"Christine…" Jain opened his mouth to say more, but Christine stopped him.

"Jain. We don't have time to get into this now. Later." Her eyes flashed at him. She knew he felt bad at what he'd done, and they would work through it eventually, but not now.

"I'm going to the gates to see what's going on," Jain said.

"I will be there soon," Christine informed him. "But don't let them start fighting."

Her mother walked into the room as Jain left. "Christine, will it stop?"

"I don't know," Christine said softly. "Maybe earlier something could have been done. But it might be too late. The councilor was adamant that some news may be coming that would stop the fighting. I can't dream of what that would be, but for the sake of Darius, I will honor his father's request."

Christine left the house, closing the door softly, and went to the barn to get Lightning. On her Cremelino it would be a short trip to the city gates. The road was still muddy from the rainstorm the previous day. Brown mud kicked up behind the white horse as they approached the crossroads in front of the north gate to the city.

Jain stood in the middle of the road. A group of farmers were marching in from the farmlands. Suddenly a loud crash turned Christine's attention towards the gate. A group of soldiers emerged. At least a hundred of them. Armed and ready to fight. Her heart pounded. Had she brought them to this point? The city soldiers would slaughter the farmers.

Down the road toward Forest View a group of farmers pulled down a man from his horse-drawn cart. He had most likely been trying to get food to the city. A few other city dwellers were running toward the gate, trying to get in before the other group of farmers caught up to them.

Jain seemed to be caught in the middle of everything. He yelled for the farmers to stop their approach, but of course, they wouldn't listen to him; he was just a boy in their eyes. These were Christine's followers. They were ready to fight.

Then Christine saw a large horse ride up behind the soldiers at the gate. *Richard!*

She galloped out to join Jain.

"You promised to stop this!" Richard's voice floated to her over the din of gathering men.

"Call your men back!" she demanded of Richard.

The councilor looked shocked at the command but turned toward his men and repeated the command to return into the city gates.

With dragging steps, the city guard and the few other townspeople in attendance obeyed their Senior Councilor. Down the road, small skirmishes still arose between soldiers and farmers. Christine galloped down to stop them. One of the farmers left ranks and ran to help his friends. That brought a yell from the group of soldiers.

"Get back!" yelled Christine at the lone man. "You'll get yourself killed!"

Another farmer ran to help, and others followed him. The soldiers stood looking at Richard for direction.

An arrow shot out from the midst of the soldiers. It hit Christine's horse in the thigh. The horse reared in pain, and Christine slid off into the dirt and mud.

I'm sorry, Christine.

Christine jumped up and ran back to her horse. *Don't be sorry. Are you hurt badly?*

I will recover, but we must stop this. You must do as the councilor wants. It's the only way. The prophecy is at a crossroads. Decisions are being made.

What is it? What do you know that you're not telling me? Christine could feel the pain from Lightning as she stroked her. She could tell the horse was trying to hold it back.

Something that will shake the Realm. Something that will change you forever.

What do you mean?

Soon, Christine, soon. He is coming!

Seeing Christine fall off the horse was all it took to move the other farmers to action. The main band of farmers ran forward toward the soldiers at the gate. Christine tried to call them back. She really did. In her mind she saw them running to their death against the highly trained city men. Tears streamed from her eyes. She couldn't let it end like this. Even with her horse's injury, she mounted Lightning and mustered all the strength she had.

"No!" she yelled as loud as she could. Drawing on the power from Lightning, she yelled again, and her voice carried across the field of men and filled the air louder than any normal voice would carry. The sound stopped the men in their tracks.

Richard turned toward Christine with silent thanks in his eyes. He ordered his men into the city again.

Once the soldiers started to retreat, the farmers become bolder and, despite Christine's yelling, pursued the soldiers toward the city gates. Christine knew it would be a slaughter. Was this what she had led her people to? How had she been so blind?

Jain stood next to her in silence. She knew he hurt also. Their friends were going to die.

The soldiers scrambled inside the gate, but it was too late. The farmers attacked the back row, and the soldiers turned to defend themselves. Richard stood up in his stirrups as high as he could and yelled for the gates to close. He rode in behind his men, the last to enter the gates before they were closed and locked.

As they closed, Christine heard horses coming down the road from Forest View. She could tell by the sound that they were traveling fast, but she couldn't see who it was over the other farmers and remaining skirmishes. One of the men in the new party drew his sword and tried to break up a few fights on his way towards the gate. Another man sat at his back. As the horses came closer she could see two others on the second horse, but one, a girl, leaned against the man as if she was hurt.

The horses were heading straight toward Christine, Jain, and Lightning when the man in back on the first horse shouted to the other. "The west gate. Go around the city. That should be safer." Then only a moment later he yelled, "Kelln, stop!"

"What? We'll be killed. We have to—"

"Just stop! It's Christine."

The second horse skidded around the first and kept going along the road, but the first horse stopped in front of Christine.

Christine and Jain looked up in response to hearing her name yelled. Her dagger dropped to the mud in surprise. Jain stood with eyes wide.

She recognized Kelln and his red mop of hair, but it was the man behind him who caught all of her attention. The man

Christine looked at wore a tattered blue uniform and his hair was longer than it used to be. He looked older and hardened. But seeing him almost made her fall back to the ground. He had returned.

"Darius?" Christine said in disbelief. "What—Where—" Tears came unbidden to her eyes.

"I don't have time now, Christine. What are you doing here?" he asked, pointing to the group of fighting men still trying to get into the city gate.

"Darius..." urged Kelln with a small smile at Christine. He had changed also. There were dark circles around his eyes, but his red hair still sat unruly on his head.

"Christine, we've got to go. I...."

She watched him not knowing what to say. Tears came to his eyes, but he brushed them away with a dirty hand.

He looked over at Lightning for a brief second. After a short pause, Darius laughed out loud.

"What?" Christine didn't understand what was so funny.

"I'm sorry, Christine. Lightning has a puzzling sense of humor sometimes."

"You can hear her too?"

Darius smiled a real smile of joy now. Lightning limped forward. Darius leaned over and placed his hand over the horse's wound. He closed his eyes, and a smile came over his face.

Christine's eyes widened as she saw the arrow fall out and the wound close up and heal.

"Darius, we have to go." Kelln urged the horse forward. "Mezar won't be able to get in the gate without us."

"Meet at the field at sunset," Christine yelled after him. She barely saw him through her tears. She couldn't believe it was actually him. *Oh, Darius!* Her heart pounded, and her legs shook.

I told you something important was coming. Christine could feel Lightning's joy. *I told you he was coming!*

"Our field!" Darius shouted over the noise of the other farmers.

That was all he had to say. Memories flooded back, forcing tears to run unashamedly down Christine's face. She thought about the fighting she had started. She stood watching the back of Darius until he rounded the corner and the dust disappeared.

Oh, Darius. Will you still love me?

* * *

Darius turned around only once as they rode away toward the west city gate. Christine was still standing there next to Jain and Lightning. His heartbeat raced and wouldn't slow down. He breathed deeply to stop himself from being too emotional. He didn't know what to think. Upon seeing Christine again, his transformation from the prison cave now seemed complete. Joy ruled his mind rather than despair. Love controlled his powers rather than anger.

However, he had changed, and Christine didn't know who he was anymore. *He* hardly knew who he was. Would she even care for him anymore?

"Kelln, why did you come for me?" he asked from behind as they rode toward the west gates. The large horse was slowing down, tired of carrying the two men.

"Your father asked me to."

Darius frowned.

"And because I wanted to."

"Why? I was willing to have you killed in Belor."

"That wasn't the real you." Darius could hear Kelln smile. "I know you too well."

"Who am I? I don't even know. How can you? Someone or something deceived me into thinking I could take over Denir, Belor, and then Anikari. For a while I wanted to rule the Realm, to show the King and my father they couldn't push me around. Isn't that crazy?" Darius laughed heartily and slapped Kelln on the back.

He felt Kelln stiffen in front of him, but the normal jovial friend said nothing back in response.

Mezar and Leandra sat waiting for them on the other horse as they approached the west gate. The guard stopped them. "Sorry, orders are no one from outside is to enter."

"Whose orders?" demanded Darius.

"Councilor Williams."

"Well I am the Councilor's son, Darius San Williams, and commander of the King's Elite Army." He showed the guard his personal signet ring.

The old guard opened his eyes wide, bowed awkwardly, and stuttered before letting them through. Darius watched the old guard eye Mezar with suspicion as they raced past.

The streets were full of chaos. People ran everywhere. The children looked thin and hungry, and the adults were arguing and fighting. Darius wondered what had been going on by the north gate.

They slowed to a trot as they approached the castle district. They passed Darius's house, and memories of his mother flooded through him. He felt embarrassed for what he had done and had been about to do. As they neared the castle, soldiers approached from a northern road, led by Richard.

"Father!" was all Darius said as they approached. What could he say? He had left in anger and had spent the entire time he was gone vowing revenge. He was still worried about being manipulated again.

"Let's go inside," Richard motioned, as he called over some of the soldiers to help Leandra. He, like the guard, eyed Mezar. "A Gildanian?"

"Yes, Father. My prisoner from Denir." He saw Mezar stiffen at that. "But also my friend and savior, along with Kelln."

Richard raised his eyebrows but just motioned all of them inside, away from prying eyes.

The soldiers took Leandra off to the palace healers, and Richard took Darius, Kelln, and Mezar into the palace offices. They walked down the long echoing hallways toward Richard's private office. Darius knew the way well. One part of him felt happy to be back home, but another part felt anxious, wondering why he was called back so abruptly.

Upon reaching Richard's office, they all sat down. There was silence. Everyone looked at everyone else. Darius had never been great at communicating with his father.

"How is Mother?" Darius finally said. "I received her letter."

"She has been a little unwell lately." The councilor glanced out the window in the direction of their home. "But doing better."

"I need to go and see her."

His father nodded but seemed distracted. "In a while."

Darius tried to gather his thoughts together. He was still trying to come to grips with everything that was happening. *What was Christine doing out in the middle of the fighting?*

"Councilor, did Alessandra reach you?" Kelln asked. "Sean is the traitor. He was the one who kidnapped Darius."

Richard let out a deep sigh. "Yes. She did reach me. I am not sure what to think. I knew Sean was ambitious, but I didn't think he would go this far. Rest assured he will be taken care of. A group of guards headed out as soon as the girl reported back."

His father would not look him in the eye. Something else was going on.

"Darius." He sighed deeply once again. "You need to talk to the King before you see your mother."

Darius looked at him skeptically. His father looked very tired.

"The King... why?"

"Aren't you the leader of his Elite Army?" his father said gruffly.

"Well... yes... but..." Darius didn't know what to say. Had the King found out what he was planning? *Is he going to imprison me or strip me of my title?* Did his father know? He knew something, that was sure. Too much tension filled the air. Maybe Richard was even enjoying the discomfort and secrets.

Darius stood up. *Might as well get this over with.*

Leaving Mezar and Kelln with a guard, Richard led Darius down the hall toward the King's quarters, their footsteps echoing in the silence. A guard let them into the King's suites. Pausing at the bedroom, Richard knocked and slowly entered. King Edward stirred in his bed and mumbled.

"Edward, Darius is here."

"Oh... Darius!" The King rolled over to face the father and his son. He sat himself up with great effort, his face pale and gaunt. The powerful King of the Realm, Edward DarSan Montere, was physically drained and barely able to hold himself up.

Darius didn't understand what had happened. The man looked so pathetic and sad that Darius could hardly feel anything other than pity for the man who had pressed him into leaving Anikari, his friends, and his family.

"Richard, please leave us." Edward tried to wave his hand but instead started into a coughing fit.

Richard bowed and began to walk out. Before leaving the room, he turned and looked seriously at his only son. He did look him in the eye this time. Piercing, stern, and serious.

"Listen well, my son." His voice was deep and gruff and full of emotion. Closing the door behind him, he left Darius alone with the King of the Realm.

Chapter Nineteen

The Field of Diamonds didn't look as Christine remembered it. Dew sparkling on a soft green carpet of grass lying next to the Lake of Reflection—that was how things used to be, but now... maybe it had been the winter harshness and late spring. Maybe she wasn't seeing it through the same innocent, youthful eyes from before. The field was greening with the spring rains, but it just didn't look as special as it once did.

Christine stood for a moment leaning against a tree on the edge of the field. She took a deep breath to try and ease the apprehension before meeting again with Darius. Fresh leaves covered the tree, seeming even greener in the overcast and gray light of evening. Lightning stood nearby. The Cremelino grazed on tufts of new grass. Christine had pulled her long blonde hair back so the wind wouldn't carry her locks around. She watched the back of Darius up ahead of her. He must have arrived early.

At seventeen now, Darius seemed to be taller than before he left, and his shoulders were definitely broader. She had heard stories about him—or were they merely rumors? He had become severe and demanding, they said. He had saved Denir by order of the King but had defied his command and marched to Belor on his own. It didn't sound like Darius to her, but then she had done things in the past year that were also hard to believe. She had met with the King and his Councilor, led raiders against the city, and stopped listening to her friends.

The moment Christine had seen Darius on the road leading into the city, her life changed once again. She had heard people talk before about how one event or one moment in time changed them. She now believed it. The instant in which she saw Darius again had re-ordered all her thoughts and feelings. It had changed her. Feelings broke through barriers in her heart that she had set up for far too long.

Go, child. It will be all right. Lightning nudged her on with calming thoughts.

Christine looked back at Lightning and thought about the miraculous healing Darius had performed earlier in the day. How had he done it? He'd merely placed his hand over the horse's wounds and healed her. What had he become while he had been away? She walked with some fear and trepidation as she approached him.

Darius stood now at the edge of the lake. He was picking up small rocks and throwing them in, breaking up the smooth gray waters. There was a tautness to his broad shoulders. His almost-shoulder-length hair hung loose, blowing in the breeze. He threw the rocks farther and farther, harder and harder. Finally, he heaved a large rock and yelled toward the sky.

Christine ran the remaining way across the field toward him. Something was wrong. "Darius, what is it?"

He stood still, continuing to face the cloud-covered Superstition Mountains. When he finally turned around she saw a new heaviness in his eyes. Almost pain. "Oh, Christine, how are you?" he stammered and tried to smile, but she noted the exhaustion in his voice.

Christine smiled warily but didn't quite know what to say.

"You've become the talk of the town." Darius smiled more and let loose a short laugh.

Christine shared in his laugh. The release felt good. "I guess you've heard what's been going on with the farmers?"

"My father and the King filled me in. I am surprised my father approached you like he did."

"My father died, did you know?"

Darius frowned. "I'm sorry, Christine. I really liked him."

Sadness hung in the air. Both just looked out across the lake. She didn't know where their relationship stood at the moment.

"Did you get my note?" asked Darius suddenly, referring to the day he had been forced to leave Anikari so quickly. Because of the suddenness of the King's command, he had not been able to say goodbye, as Christine had been off in Forest View with her father.

Christine choked back a sob at that memory, took a step toward him, and instinctively wrapped her arms around him in a fierce hug. Darius held her in a tight embrace while she sobbed. It had been so long since she had cried. Only once since Darius had left, when her father had died. Since then she had become numb to everything but violence. The lost feelings of love had needed something in their stead.

With a deep sigh she let all the pent up feelings out now— all of the fear and frustration she had gone through, and all the relief she had found since seeing Darius return. Her mind seemed clean for the first time since he had left.

Tears ran down Darius's face, warming Christine's own cheeks. His shaking arms held her tightly. She could see she was not the only one who had suffered in the past year. Finally they pulled apart.

"Will you tell me about your travels?" asked Christine after she had run out of tears.

Darius brushed some dirt off a couple of large rocks, and they sat down at the edge of the lake. The sun peeked out briefly over the Superstition Mountains as if to say good-bye before it went down for the evening. It sent a momentary glow across the lake. They wrapped their cloaks around them against the growing coolness of evening.

Darius told her about his ordeals, his successes and failures. He seemed embarrassed by some of the telling, but she could see a sense of pride in him also at what he had accomplished. He told her about Denir and Belor. He ended by explaining the feelings he had experienced while being held captive by Sean, thinking at first that he had lost all friends and all hope.

"Something called out to me in the cave," Darius said. "I think it was your Cremelino."

Ah, he heard me, came the reply in Christine's mind.

Both Christine and Darius looked at each other and laughed.

"Once I felt joy and love again and realized there was hope, Kelln and Mezar arrived," Darius continued.

Christine listened attentively to Darius while holding his hand, rough with calluses. He finished up where they had seen each other that morning. There was still a look of pain in his eyes. He held something back from her. She thought about all she had gone through that year and realized she couldn't tell

Darius of everything that had happened to her in just a few minutes either.

"Darius, what did you do for Lightning?"

Darius sat silent for a moment as if struggling with what to say. Finally he stood up and, pointing his hand toward a small pile of large stones on the shore of the lake, moved his right hand upward. The stones began to rise up off the ground. He then threw the stones high into the evening air and into the lake. The splash reached their feet.

Darius looked at Christine, waiting for a response. Christine, wide-eyed, opened her mouth but then closed it again.

"You think I'm a freak, don't you?" Darius held his head down.

Christine found her voice. "Oh no, Darius. I just don't know what to say. I've never seen anyone do that before. You did heal Lightning, didn't you?"

"Yes, I did. That was the first time I have done something like that… something good with my power. It felt so nice. As I told you, when I was held captive by Sean, I hit the bottom, and it was only when I let love and hope enter my heart that I broke through the barriers holding my powers away from me. Before that I thought it was anger that drove it. That was a hard lesson to learn, but it is so clear now. Love is so much more powerful than hate. I couldn't bear to see Lightning hurt." He looked intently into her eyes. "Or you hurt."

Christine's eyes glistened with tears. She tried to blink them away but had to use the side of her hand.

Lightning nudged up between them and looked at Darius. He nodded after a moment.

"Christine, you have a pushy horse."

Christine laughed. "You gave her to me."

"So I did. From the beginning she whispered to me that I needed to bring her from White Island. She obviously knows more about what goes on around us than she shares."

"Don't I know." Christine smiled and ran her hand down her horse's mane.

"She wants me to tell you what I am now."

"What you are? I don't understand." Christine furrowed her brows.

"Christine, I am a wizard. One of a few in the Realm. I am a wizard with wonderful natural growing powers… many of which I still don't even understand."

It's about time.

They both looked at Lightning at the same time and laughed.

"She speaks to you as well as me. I wonder why?" asked Christine.

Of course I do. Lightning spoke to both of them. *It is the right of a wizard. It is why we were bred. It is they whom the herd of Cremelinos serve. It has been a long time waiting for a worthy wizard to walk the Realm again.*

"It was also you I heard calling in my mind while I was in Belor, wasn't it?" Darius asked the horse out loud.

Yes. It was hard to reach you that far. But that is one of our gifts.

"And talking to me?" Christine asked.

That was a little more surprising. You must have some old wizard blood in your ancestry.

Darius looked like he wanted to ask more but instead he grew solemn again.

"Darius, what is it?"

"There is more."

"More?" she stood up and stroked Lightning on the nose. "What more could there be after telling me you are a wizard? The first in many generations in the Realm. I admit it is all quite strange and unreal, but exciting also."

"And dangerous. Remember, there has not been much tolerance for wizards since the wizard uprising."

Christine nodded. "You said there was something else?"

"I... uh... You won't believe it, Christine." Darius stumbled on his words. "I don't know how to tell you."

"What?" Christine asked anxiously. "Your father told me his mother was a farmer. I always knew you had some good in you. Did you know my father's father was from the city too?"

Darius smiled. "It's not that. Oh, that's part of it, but there is still more to the story that you don't know. No one knew."

"More?"

"The King is sick—"

"I know. The whole city is on edge. Declaring a new king might mean open warfare. A few factions among the nobles have already approached us about our support. Your father asked me to stop the fighting until an announcement was made. He seemed to think that maybe things would work out. I sure wouldn't want to be the next king."

"Neither would I, but..."

"But what?" her eyes opened wide. Her heart fluttered and jumped.

"But I am. I am going to be the next king." Darius didn't look to be joking. "There, I said it. Maybe it will help me believe it. I am going to be the next king, Christine. The next king of the Realm."

Christine sat down hard on the ground. She was stunned. Darius leaned down and then knelt beside her. His hair was longer and his jaw more firm. She wondered if she looked much different from when they last saw each other.

"Go ahead and laugh if you want. I did at first." A crooked smile emerged from Darius's lips. "I have a lot to atone for and a lot to learn."

"How can it be?"

"A little confused? So am I. It seems my father's father, Alric, and King Edward were brothers. My grandfather was the oldest brother. He married a girl from the farmlands. His father, King Charles, disowned him for it and sent him away with a story to the people that he had been killed in battle. It was then that the old king had another son in his older years. That was Edward. So my grandfather should have been the next king, and then my father, and then..."

"You!" exclaimed Christine. "I can't believe it. And no one ever told you?"

"No. My father said he didn't even know until last summer. I guess that was why the King sent me away. I had to learn to lead, to be a king." Darius laughed. "I almost fought against the King and my father because I hated politics. I blamed all of my problems on them. Now I am going to be king. Now others will blame their problems on me. How can I do this?"

"Can't you deny it? Not take it? What about your father?"

"That's the same question I asked of King Edward. When Alric was banished, my father Richard was already born, so he was included in the banishment also."

"There are no other options?" Christine asked.

"Not any good options. Naming someone outside of the royal line could cause civil war. The King told me about all of the fighting between farmers and the city. He said I was destined to be a king. Since he has no children alive, I am the only one who would be able to keep others from contesting the throne, as I am of the direct line. I alone could reunite the Realm, and since I am part farmer and a friend to those outside the city…"

That brought a smile to Christine's lips.

Darius continued, "I could help heal the rift between the two groups. Of course I argued every point I could think of… but it was of no use. I have been walking around for the past hour thinking and trying to talk myself out of this. I don't have any idea how or what I am going to do as king, but I feel good inside after thinking through it all. I'm not confused anymore. The timing of it all is too coincidental not to be right. A few months ago I would not be ready for this. But I have come to peace with myself, and if this is my destiny, if that is what has been given to me, then I will do my best."

"You will be wonderful." She leaned over and kissed him on the cheek.

"I don't know who knows about my growing powers though. That might still ruin everything."

"Will you tell them?"

"How? I think they suspect something, but people don't ask me directly, so I haven't said anything."

"You'll find a way, Darius. I believe in you."

A huge smile spread across Darius's face. "Thank you, Christine. I have missed you so much! I have done some things I am not so proud of, but when I am with you, I feel that everything will be all right."

Christine felt she would burst with happiness at seeing him smile again. Her heart lifted, and she, too, felt better being next to him. "Both of us have learned a lot this year."

Darius nodded.

"When will they tell the people?" Christine asked.

"Tomorrow, at a meeting in the coliseum. All the dignitaries of the Realm will attend..." Darius paused as if thinking. "Oh no! I have to go!"

Christine watched Darius jump up. "What's wrong?"

"The Preacher I told you about, he is bringing his troops here to meet me... tomorrow. I have to stop him."

"Will he listen? We have heard about the unrest in Belor."

"I don't know."

Darius ran to his horse and Christine to Lightning, and both headed back through the forest and then down the road through the farmlands. They stopped briefly at Christine's house, and Darius told Christine good-bye. They lingered a moment, not quite knowing what to do. Darius reached over and gave her a hug before leaving.

* * *

Darius rode at a quick pace, skirting around the merchant section of town, and went directly to the castle. He looked up at its lofty stone towers and ancient, high walls. The pit of his stomach churned. This would someday be his home. Not just his home, but his castle. He shook his head, trying to clear away what seemed like a dream. But this was no dream, and the fear didn't go away.

After talking to Christine, his spirits were higher. It had gone better than he had supposed. Actually saying out loud that he was a wizard and the heir to the throne had been good for him. It made it seem more real. Of course the throne could be years off still, as he was sure the King would recover from his illness. But his powers as a wizard would have to be dealt with much sooner.

Roald, one of the guards saluted him as he walked toward his father's office. Rumors were still flying around of who he had become and what he had done in Denir and Belor. He imagined there were some of the Elite Army soldiers who were not too fond of him by now. He truly felt sorry for anyone he had treated badly. It had been wrong for him to act the way he did, and he would have to find a remedy for that also.

There were so many things to take care of at once. And now, having to work with his father seemed to be another inevitable chore he would have to get through.

Darius entered his father's sitting room and found Richard writing at a table. Darius quickly revealed the Preacher's plan.

"I'll send a battalion of men out to stop him." His father moved to call a messenger.

"That will only start a war, Father."

"Already thinking of the Realm like a king, I see."

Darius didn't smile. "I hope not for a long time." The next day's ceremony was not to anoint him king, only to declare King Edward's intention of succession and Darius's lineage. "I will go myself to him."

That did not sit well with Richard. "Darius, you must stay safe."

"I have thought this through. The Preacher knows me as a leader of the King's Elite Army. He will assume I have returned to finish our plan together. I will take Mezar with me."

"The Gildanian?"

"Yes. The Preacher knows I left Belor with him, so it won't be surprising. Do you have a problem with that?"

Richard sighed. "No, Darius. It's just I am not used to you being a commander. You have grown up this past year."

Darius realized his father was trying hard to make things work and nodded to him at the compliment.

"I don't know if you should trust Mezar," Richard added.

"Do you trust me?"

Darius saw Richard blink at the question. This is what everything came down to, didn't it? Could they trust each other? Could Darius trust himself? He didn't blame his father for mistrusting him. Just a few days prior he had been planning on bringing his army to Anikari to fight. Now, with newfound feelings and new information, it seemed ludicrous. Of course, his father didn't know the extent of his powers either, so maybe his father shouldn't trust him.

His father looked up at him. "Since you have arrived you have not given me any reason not to trust you, Darius." He smiled genuinely. "Not yet, at least."

Darius saluted, realizing how hard it must be for his father to let go. They both had to learn to trust one another.

Before riding off to intercept the Preacher's men in Forest View with Mezar, Darius asked Kelln and Alessandra to ride back to Belor and tell his army there what was happening. He rode off within the hour with Mezar at his side. He felt stronger now. With his new basis of power growing within him he could fight off the Preacher's spells. He realized the man had just enhanced through magical means what Darius's frustration and thoughts of revenge had already been.

Now his thinking was different. He also felt more comfortable with Mezar at his side.

The two rode the horses hard and arrived in Forest View that evening. The Preacher's army would be staying in the smaller town that night. Belorian soldiers filled the taverns and inns. The local citizens looked nervous, but they had long gotten used to foreigners stopping in the night before they arrived at Anikari from Belor, Mar, and other foreign kingdoms to the south.

Darius was not sure how to find the Preacher. They decided the best way was to pretend the old plans were still on. Once Darius met him, he wasn't sure what would happen next. The two of them went into the nearest inn and found someone from Belor. Darius asked where the Preacher was staying, and the man, recognizing Darius, directed him to The White Sands Inn on the other side of Forest View.

Darius led while Mezar followed. The buildings in this part of town were larger and sturdier on their foundations. The inns and shops were clean and straight. The White Sands Inn was no exception. Two large double doors out front greeted them, with a man guarding both. Sounds of a late-night meal floated past Darius. The smells made his stomach growl. It had been a while since he had eaten.

The inn's common room was filled to capacity. These were men ready for battle. They drank up to bolster their bravado in preparation for the fight that was to come.

Dark, polished wood from the edge of the Black Forest paneled the walls, and the hall was filled with white tables of marble from White Island. Definitely the nicest place in town. Nobles sat in small groups around the three stone fireplaces.

"Almost like home," Mezar whispered.

Darius turned to him with a questioning look.

Mezar continued. "As a young boy, one of my friend's father owned an inn in the nicer part of Gildan. We would try to sneak down and listen to the stories of the travelers who would board at the inn. Many times we were caught by his mother, and I was sent home. My parents didn't think an inn's common room was a place for someone like me."

"Now they are not here to stop you." Darius smiled. He still didn't know what he would do with Mezar, but for now at least, Mezar seemed just as comfortable staying around Darius. They were almost more alike than Kelln and Darius were.

After waiting for what seemed like too long, Darius watched the Preacher approach. Sliding gracefully but purposefully across the wooden floor, the man seemed larger than life. Darius steeled himself against any possible manipulation.

"Where can we talk?" Darius asked.

"We can talk here. On the eve of battle I have nothing to hide from my men."

Darius had to be cautious. He realized more than ever how dangerous an alliance with this man would have been. He thought about arresting the man and dragging him to Anikari, but looking around the room, he knew he would have a hard time getting through the Preacher's men, in addition to having to face the man's magical powers.

"Let's sit." The Preacher motioned to a table.

The Preacher and Darius sat at a table in a corner by the fire. A serving girl brought them a cool drink. The Preacher used his power to glide the glass down the table toward Darius. The server's eyes went wide and she ran off across the room. Darius figured it was the Preacher's way to remind Darius of who he was. The simple use of power also reminded Darius that he wasn't the only wizard in the Realm either.

Darius tried to clear his head. It had been the longest day of his life. He had entered Anikari that morning amongst fighting, had found out he would be king, reunited with Christine, and now had ridden to see this dangerous man. His heart and mind had been in a constant battle all day. As he sat down he realized that this day would be longer yet. He felt the weight of the kingdom on him already. And in a way, he supposed it was. The Preacher was here because of him. It was now his duty to make things right. "Have you received an invitation to the coliseum tomorrow?" asked Darius.

"No." The question surprised the Preacher.

"The King has invited the leaders from all of the cities in the Realm to a special announcement tomorrow." *Some announcement.* "But, then, Anikari doesn't recognize you as the leader of Belor."

"I am the only leader in Belor!" The man slammed his fist on the table.

Why hadn't Darius seen how volatile this man was? Kelln had tried to warn him. *Good ol' Kel. He's always been there.* The Preacher's men surrounded the table as if preparing for battle. Their hands rested mere inches from their swords.

"I realize you are the leader." Darius had to humor him. "That's why I am here. We can't fight until the announcement is made." On his way here Darius had tried to make a plan, but he realized he would have to wing it to some degree depending on the Preacher's reactions.

"What do you mean?" the Preacher asked with suspicion in his look.

"There are rumors they will be naming a new king. Since King Edward has no children it will have to be someone outside of the royal family. Fighting may start after the announcement. It would be much easier for us to go in then."

Darius watched the Preacher's body relax.

The Preacher laughed heartily. "My, you are good, Darius. I didn't know if I should trust you, but you have this set up very nicely, haven't you? How did you find out all of this?"

"I am the commander of the King's Elite Army and son to the Senior Councilor, aren't I?"

They both laughed.

The Preacher ordered another round of drinks.

"Where are my men?" Darius asked. "My unit that I left in Belor?"

"They were left in Belor. They wouldn't follow me, and I wasn't sure about your intentions. You don't blame me for being careful, do you?"

"No, no. That's fine." *Or was it?* "Will you come back to Anikari with me tonight? I will get you into the meeting, and then we will know what to do."

"Fine. I can leave the men here for a day. The townspeople shouldn't mind so much. They are getting rich off all of us." He took a long drink and smiled. "By the way, have you seen your old friend Kelln or my daughter Alessandra?"

Darius kept a straight face and hoped the Preacher wouldn't see through his lie. "I have been meeting with the King and my father all day." He skirted around the question.

"My daughter can be impetuous at times, and Kelln is still my prisoner. You will tell me if you see them, won't you?"

The Preacher talked to his men for a moment and gathered up a few belongings before the two leaders headed back toward Anikari. The steadiness of the horse's gallop seemed to lull Darius into a state between full sleep and consciousness. He was so exhausted he barely stayed on his horse. *Some king.* He wondered why the Preacher didn't look so tired. Maybe something in the power he had. He would have to learn about that.

Darius left Mezar in Forest View with some of the Preacher's men as a gesture of goodwill. He knew his father wouldn't approve of letting the Gildanian out of their sights, but Mezar didn't seem to mind. It was almost a game to him. He still couldn't figure the man out.

The two travelers barely spoke during the trip back to Anikari. It was easy to see that neither Darius nor the Preacher trusted the other more than a few feet. Somewhere in his sleep-ride Darius figured out what he would do with the Preacher and his army.

As they neared Anikari the sky was still dark, and the city sat in a quiet that is only reached a few hours before dawn. The crickets from the farmlands filled the night air as the two approached the gate. The air was cool but promised a warmer day. A few early-morning birds flew out of the giant oaks. The gate still stood closed for the night. Darius explained to the Preacher the problems between the farmers and the soldiers.

Darius could have talked his way in, but he didn't want to cause a scene right then. He wanted the Preacher inside Anikari as little as possible. They took some blankets they had brought and laid down under some newly budding trees to rest until the gates were open for the day. Darius didn't trust the Preacher and tried so hard to stay awake, but his body was just too exhausted, and after fighting it for an hour, he gave in.

The next thing Darius knew he heard loud voices waking him up. There were men on the road in the early hour. With a quick look around he noticed the two horses and the Preacher were gone. If it would have helped, Darius felt like shouting and screaming, but it would only give him a sore throat. He berated himself for falling asleep and not staying on guard. Jumping up off the ground, he raced toward the city gates.

Chapter Twenty

Darius sprinted through the now-opened gate as fast as he could. The puffs of smoke rose from the early-morning vendors selling food to the growing crowds. The beautiful mid-spring morning was already warm, and many people were out and about. Excitement filled the air as rumors abounded.

He began to look for the Preacher. He thought of telling his father, but that would make him look incompetent. Darius realized there was no way he could find the Preacher without help. Before getting too far into the city, he turned back around and headed out to the farmlands. He would need Christine and her family to help.

With his horse gone, he had to walk to Christine's house. It was good to stretch his muscles. He began to run. He took longer and longer strides as the power built up in him. Not realizing how fast he had been going, he soon found himself at the Anderssn's property. He steadied himself against a tree to catch his breath and balance.

Darius described the Preacher to Christine and Jain and explained he needed them to gather some friends to help him look for the man while he went back to his father and prepared for the large gathering.

Jain asked what the large meeting was about, but Darius couldn't tell him. He assured Jain, however, that it would be good news for the farmers. Jain gave him a skeptical look but didn't prod any further.

Darius returned to the city and proceeded to his father's office. He was surprised to see Sean sitting on a chair talking to his father. This time, though, he wasn't wearing the smug face he usually displayed. His clothes were ruffled and his hands tied. Sean turned around to look at him. He sneered and turned his head away from Darius.

"Sean has been telling me who hired him to kidnap you. I think we will wait until after the assembly today to determine what to do." His father let off a grim smile.

Richard called in two men. One took Sean to the prisons, and one he introduced to Darius as Roald, a fit but middle-aged man who gave a flourishing bow to Darius upon entering.

"Darius, I think you should stay in the castle until this afternoon," Richard directed.

Roald proceeded to inform Darius that he would escort him anywhere in the castle that he would like to go.

"It's only for your protection," Richard said firmly.

Darius wanted to tell his father he didn't need protection. His power emerged stronger every day; he could always feel the sensation at the edge of his consciousness. He wasn't ready to tell everything yet, though, so he walked out feeling like a prisoner. It was a fine line he toed. He could slip away unnoticed, he was sure, but he was trying to uphold his father's faith in him. He wanted to run out and find the Preacher, but he knew that wasn't the actions of a king. He needed to be calm and calculating. He trusted Christine and her friends to be discreet.

As he was only allowed to wander the castle grounds, the afternoon dragged on slowly for Darius. He went to the library and looked at maps of Anikari and Forest View. He ate a boring lunch of cold chicken on fresh-baked barley bread he had talked the cook into giving him early. The assembly was approaching, and Roald informed Darius of the clothes he would have to wear.

While dressing in the royal colors for the announcement ceremony, he struggled with Roald wanting to dress him. He had been taking care of himself quite well out in the mountains and forest for almost the past year. "I can dress myself, sir."

"I am sure you can, Commander," Roald said as he continued to straighten Darius's clothes, shine his leather boots, and clasp on his cloak.

Darius nearly choked as he observed himself in a full-length mirror. *I am going to be announced as the next king!* The thought seemed almost blasphemous. It had never even entered his mind. What would ruling entail? Whom would he choose as his councilors? Surely some of the existing councilors had masterminded his kidnapping to gain some political advantage from Richard.

But that would be in the future. Darius continued to assure himself he had plenty of time to learn. King Edward was still young. In fact, he was two years younger than Richard, even if he was ill.

My father should have been king. It was still somewhat confusing, but King Edward had explained it to him twice now. Since Richard was alive when King Charles had officially disowned Alric, his father was under the same decree.

Later in his life, King Charles' heart had softened, and he had allowed Richard to become a noble and even add a San to his name. He had informed Edward on his deathbed of the situation. *Why couldn't Edward have had more children? Then we wouldn't have to mess with all of this.*

"Darius?"

Darius turned around, the familiar voice snapping him out of his thoughts. "Cray! What are you doing here?"

Cray had been Darius's teacher and trainer at the Elite camp in the Superstition Mountains. Still a master swordsman in his sixties, the dark-skinned man had been legendary throughout the Realm army for years. He had been one of the first to notice and comment on Darius's power.

"Coming to hear the big announcement, same as you, I suppose." Cray nodded to Roald, and the guard walked a discreet distance away from the two men, although he stayed in the suite of rooms.

Darius thought it unexpected that the guard had followed Cray's unspoken directive. He didn't know that the old time general still had any pull in the castle.

"But why?" Darius asked.

"I am the King's uncle. I have uh… you might say… an interest in the outcome today." Cray's eyes flickered around the room nervously.

"I didn't know King Charles had brothers." Maybe this was a way to get out of taking the crown.

"No. I'm not related to Charles," Cray almost spat. "To his wife. I am his wife's younger brother."

"Does King Edward know you are here?" asked Darius.

Cray shook his head. "We don't get along well." He glanced around behind him.

"Why?" asked Darius.

"Because he should have never been king!" Cray's voice lifted in anger, echoing off the high stone ceilings. Roald glanced over but then continued to be busy doing something else.

Darius stood still, not knowing for sure what to say. This was not like his trainer. He looked tired, nervous, and strained. Darius guessed everyone was worried about the succession of the King, and everyone had their own ideas and candidates.

"There was another son, you know. Charles's first born, Alric," Cray continued, lowering his voice to a more controlled level.

"So I have been told."

Cray looked at Darius but Darius gave nothing else away. He could not betray his true identity yet, though he was sure Cray surmised the connection.

Cray continued. "Then you were taught that Charles sent him away to war, eventually getting him killed. He was the rightful heir. He was a kind and strong friend and would have made a great king." His voice lowered almost to a whisper for the last sentence. "He had powers like you Darius."

And Darius now knew why. He wanted badly to say something. He could tell that his trainer was pained still at the thought of losing his friend so many years before. But he stayed silent until Cray understood that he would receive no new information from him. "You must excuse me, I need to go."

Cray turned around and bumped into Richard, who had just entered the room.

"Cray! I haven't seen you in years. Seems retirement has been treating you well."

Cray grunted, "I'm busier in retirement than I was leading the army."

"Have you two met?" asked Darius.

"Cray was my sword teacher years ago." Richard smiled.

"Darius, remember when you knocked me off the wall and I said there had only been one other time?" Cray asked.

"You mean..." Darius stared at his father.

Richard smiled. "I used to be quite a swordsman. That is, until I got into this councilor position and spent much too much time in meetings and formal banquets." He patted his stomach.

Cray slapped Richard on the back as he once again tried to exit. "You'd better watch your son, Richard, he may be better than you."

As he reached the doorway, Cray stopped and turned as if to say something.

"Cray?" prompted Richard.

Cray hesitated a minute, then turned around and left as quickly as he had entered.

Richard dismissed Roald and side by side, father and son left the castle. Their strides were similar now. Darius glanced out of the corner of his eye at his father and wondered if he had been too harsh on him the last few years.

"Did you know Cray is King Edwards's uncle, on his mother's side?" Darius asked.

Richard nodded. "He usually tries to hide from it."

"He became angry talking about Alric. I don't think he realizes he was your father."

"That is unlike Cray. Usually he has complete control over his feelings. Everyone is on edge today it seems."

A coach pulled up to take them to the meeting in the coliseum. The footman opened the door, and they entered. It was just the two of them. The curtains were open, allowing air to breathe through the carriage.

"Will they accept me?" Darius whispered.

"They will have to." Richard's voice was gruff. "There will be civil war otherwise."

"But won't some of them think we are making the relationship up? I'm so young, barely seventeen."

"Remember, you aren't king yet."

Darius nodded.

His father continued. "Others in our past have been young kings. Charles was close to your age when his mother, the Queen, died and he became king after her. Anikari has always protected and defended her leader. The farmers... and the other cities, especially Belor and Mar... who knows?" Richard shrugged to let Darius know he wasn't so sure about them. "Though I hear you have some inside influence with the farmers." Richard smiled.

Darius's cheeks reddened, but he didn't say a word. It wasn't only what his father said, it was the way he had said the words. With a smile. *How I have longed for that smile!*

In front of the carriage they heard shouting and commotion. The guards leading out in front of Darius and

Richard halted their horses. Some townsman had fallen off his horse in the road and yelled in pain. The guards went to go look. As they did so, someone rushed to Darius's side of the carriage, leaned in, and whispered, "Red and purple," then disappeared.

Darius tried to see who brought him the information, but they left faster than they had come. All he knew was that it was a young man. The man who had fallen off of his horse seemed to be suddenly feeling better.

"What was that?" Richard asked.

"Just some information," Darius smiled.

"About what?" Richard was annoyed.

"Doesn't a future king need to be informed?" Darius was having fun. His father was not amused.

They continued their ride into the coliseum itself. Darius began to feel overwhelmed by the size of the gathered crowd. He had been to the coliseum many times before but never for the naming of an heir to the throne. *Red and purple!* That's what the messenger had said. The colors of Belor and Anikari.

Darius looked around, trying to see if there was any sign of the Preacher, but among so large a crowd it was impossible to tell. Colors swirled everywhere, signifying a city where each person had come from… colors tied to hats or as sashes around waists or as cloaks. Denir in blue, Mar in yellow, accented by a multitude of other colors, Sur in gray, Forest View with green and black and Tean with earthy brown, and red from Belor if anyone actually showed up from there besides the Preacher. In all the swirls of color how would he ever find one man?

His mother already sat on a raised stand above the level of the crowd. The wives of the other councilors sat next to her. The Queen, had she still been alive, would have sat at the head of the group. Darius and his father made their way through the crowds toward an even higher stand. Here the King's chair sat tallest, with his three closest councilors on his right and the other councilors on the left. An extra chair sat on the right for Darius. *They will never believe it. Me, a king?*

Chapter Twenty One

Darius took his seat and looked out at the crowd. They all seemed to be looking at him. Well, why shouldn't they? They would wonder what he was doing up with the councilors. His cloak moved about him in the slight breeze. As one of the King's commanders, his sword was at his side. By now everyone had heard of his victory in Denir. He hoped no one knew about Belor, at least his professed siding with the Preacher. But he had to keep the ruse up with the man to get him to come with him to Anikari. His hope had been to turn him in and get him in prison. However, since he had escaped and was now probably in the coliseum, Darius would have to be careful. He continued scanning the large assembly. He had to be prepared for something to happen.

Looking out across the gathering, he glanced over the other dignitaries, nobles, and city leaders in the front few rows. Higher up in the stands he saw a few of his friends from school. *I hope Kelln is all right with this.* He hadn't shared the secret yet with his best friend. Thinking of Kelln had him wondering if he and Alessandra had reached Belor in time to bring back the rest of his Elite army with them.

Darius's mind swam and he found it hard to focus. He was juggling so many secrets and plans at the moment. He breathed deeply and drew some power into him. Not enough for others to see, just enough to calm himself.

The only one missing was King Edward. Soon, heads in the crowd turned away from the stand and toward the entrance of the coliseum. He watched the carriage with the King's flag waving in the slight breeze. Four proud Cremelino horses led the way. He wondered if anyone else knew the secret of the Cremelinos and their ability to speak to the minds of wizards.

This had been the first time the King had been out in public in many weeks. Darius heard the whispers in the crowd. They all expected him to name his new successor. *Won't they all be surprised?*

The King was brought to the stand on a chair held by four men dressed in royal purple. He stepped from the chair and onto the podium, his walk slow and deliberate as he moved to his throne. The crowd fell silent. Darius heard a few sounds from outside of the coliseum, vendors selling their wares and children playing. He gave a quick glance at his father. King Edward looked so much older than his father did now, though only two years separated them.

King Edward DarSan Montere stood up in front of a portable throne and rested one hand on its polished gold inlaid armrest. The other hand he raised to the crowd.

The crowd erupted as if on cue. The citizens of the Realm stood and cheered. Anikari had always rallied around its kings. The people loved Edward. Until the recent events, he had kept peace in the Realm for almost fifteen years. Neither the Gildanians nor Arcs had even tried an attack in over ten years.

The King seated himself. An expectant hush fell over the crowd as the King began to speak from a sitting position, his voice raspy and weak. The crowd had to strain to hear the words. Each person leaned forward so as not to miss anything. The King began by telling about his father, Charles, the previous king. The speech was well rehearsed to only say what was necessary. Darius looked around and saw soldiers throughout the crowd. They were prepared if trouble began. He thought he saw Jain moving through the crowd once, but he quickly became lost. Still no sign of the Preacher.

At the back of the crowd, Darius saw movement. Cray silently sending men around to the sides of the coliseum. Was he expecting trouble or… causing it? Darius wondered what authority Cray had anymore and began to worry that Cray was acting outside of the King's direction.

The crowd's tension mounted as Edward told of the old king banishing his son Alric, the rightful heir. This would be news to those who knew recent history. They all assumed King Charles's son had died in battle. Some of the nobles leaned forward even more, realizing all of a sudden that there still might be a royal line. Darius wondered exactly how the King would announce the succession.

"My older brother did not die in battle at sea as our history has been told. He lived in disguise the rest of his life raising his son. This boy, who was two years old when I was born, was included in his father's banishment of the throne, but the next generation was not." The King slowly gazed over the crowd. He wanted his words to sink in. He led them along magnificently. The tension was at a crescendo.

Cray halted, signaling to his men something that Darius couldn't tell. They looked ready to attack, not defend.

Darius felt as if he was going to be sick. He began to panic. *I can't be king! No! No!*

King Edward stood, this time with no support. "I announce today there is still one of the direct royal line. My Senior Councilor Richard San Williams is actually my nephew, the son of my banished older brother and..."

The sentence seemed to take forever. The beginnings of murmurings and whisperings spread throughout the crowd. Darius's heart nearly burst. The sun beat down on his face, making him sweat.

"...his son, Darius San Williams, first Captain of the King's Elite Army, I proclaim as my rightful heir to the throne of power. He will be your next rightful king of the Realm."

King Edward stopped speaking. Darius's heart missed a beat. The crowd took a deep, simultaneous breath. But when the breath came out, so did chaos. Through the crowd, Darius caught Cray's eyes in a brief flicker. His old trainer's eyes were open in surprise. He gave Darius a slight nod of respect and a large smile, then signaled for his men to stand down.

The people cheered... or was it yelling? Darius couldn't tell. Maybe both. The King motioned for Darius to join him. The crowd quieted down somewhat as Darius walked forward, hard black boots clicking on the wooden stage.

He stood beside the King clothed in his royal garb, his dark purple cloak swirling around him in a growing breeze. Power rose within him and amplified his persona. He put his hand on the hilt of his sword. It wanted to be drawn and to feed on his power, but Darius kept it in check.

The King motioned for Darius to kneel before him. Drawing his own gold sword, Edward tapped Darius on the right shoulder. "Darius San Williams, Commander of the King's Elite Army, great grandson of my father, King Charles, through the direct royal line. I, King Edward DarSan Montere, of the great Realm of this people, anoint you to be the servant of all and the King of all after I have departed this mortal life. You are now named Darius DarSan Williams, heir to the Throne of Power and next king of the Realm, with all rights, privileges, and power associated with that high and noble title."

The power built inside Darius. He strained to keep it under control. *This must be a dream!* He almost laughed with giddiness but kept it under control.

The King continued. "Be it known that anyone who contests this anointing is an enemy of the Realm and shall, with his family, be known as traitors in our kingdom."

Darius wondered how long this would go on. The official part was over. Now it was a sick king trying to prevent civil war. Darius saw a movement out of the corner of his eye and turned his head slightly. *Red and purple.* It must be him. And...

Darius jumped up with a shout. With a speed that many would talk about later, he pushed the King out of the way as a red arrow flew past him. The crowd jumped as one and chaos ensured. Soldiers ran through the crowd as another arrow shot through the air. Darius ducked, trying to get a look at the shooter at the same time, but the King had moved to the side, and the arrow struck him in the arm.

Richard lunged to the King's side as Darius leaped off the stand. Red arrows. The color of Belor.

As he ran through the mass of people, the crowd's eyes followed him. *Is this the way a king acts?*

"Well this is the way I act," he mumbled under his breath. Among all of Anikari, only he, along with maybe Kelln and Alessandra, realized how dangerous the Preacher really was.

Darius saw a group of soldiers running toward a small door in the back of the coliseum. The room should be locked. It led into a giant kitchen rarely used. As Darius caught up to them, the Preacher was nowhere to be seen. Darius stood on top of a bench and scanned the area. Only a short distance away he saw the back of someone. *Red hat. This is what the messenger had alluded to.* The Preacher had a purple cloak and red hat. Darius jumped down and muscled through the crowd, stooping low so the man wouldn't notice him.

Right before he got there, a dark blur ran in front of him and tackled the Preacher to the ground, holding him by force.

"Is this who you were looking for, Sire?" Cray seemed to emphasize the last word.

"Yes. Thanks, Cray."

Cray turned the man around, facing the Preacher toward Darius.

The Preacher's face was red with anger. "Traitor!" He spat. "No one will follow you."

The crowd had gathered to watch what their newly anointed king-to-be would do. A boiling rage surfaced inside of Darius. His eyes sharpened as the power built. He lifted up his hand to strike the Preacher, but as he did so he remembered Sean's words about Darius learning to control his temper if he was ever going to be great. Darius cringed again at the thought that Sean, of all people, would say something that would be of benefit to him. With his hand still in the air, he waved for some of the guards to take his prisoner away to the dungeons.

Darius wiped the spit from his face and glared at the Preacher. "You will never see Belor again."

Darius turned to go but, out of the corner of his eye, saw power gather around the Preacher. The Preacher pulled his hands away from the guards and held them forward. Sparks began to jump forth from his hands. Darius moved to intercept but was afraid to show his powers yet. Suddenly, Cray came up from behind the Preacher and with muscled arms held a cloth over his mouth. The Preacher struggled for a brief moment and then sank to his knees. Darius gaped at Cray. It was the same reaction Darius himself had in Forest View when he was captured. The mixture in the cloth seemed to dull the power in an instant.

Darius looked sternly at Cray, wondering why he had the concoction ready to go.

Cray whispered, "I didn't know about your ancestry—that you were of the direct royal line, but I knew about your other power and your previous anger. I had to be prepared to protect the kingdom if need be."

Darius nodded his understanding and realized that Cray had been prepared to take him down if he would have shown aggression to the Realm. Cray was loyal to the Realm.

Darius motioned for the guards to put the Preacher in a dungeon cell until he could talk with his father and the King.

The King!

Darius raced back through the crowd toward the stand. His soldier training had taken over when the King had been shot with the arrow. Now his lungs filled with flames as he raced with all of his might. He prayed mightily for King Edward to still be alive. He was not ready to be king yet.

Richard and some other men had put the wounded Edward in his carriage during the commotion. A palace healer sat in the carriage with him, extracting the arrow. As Darius reached the carriage, he saw Jain standing next to it. Darius smiled his thanks to him. Jain bowed and turned to leave.

Darius leaned over to him. "Tell Christine to meet me in the field."

As soon as Darius made sure the King was being taken care of, he left the coliseum with some of the King's guards following behind. Cray noiselessly approached him from around a corner. Darius stopped and saw a small crowd of men a ways off, watching their interchange. His guards hung back.

"Darius," his voice had softened from earlier in the castle. "I didn't know about your lineage. If I did, I wouldn't have... You must understand I would have never hurt you. I was only prepared to avert a civil war if that was your intent."

"You don't need to say anything, Cray." Darius put together what Cray must have been planning. Not knowing that Darius would be named as the next king, Cray was afraid of Darius's power and his reaction to the King's announcement. "You remember my motivation from before? How angry I was with everyone and the revenge I wanted?"

Cray just nodded.

"Then you can appreciate why no apology is needed. What you planned was done without all the information, and in support of your King."

"When did you find out about your heritage?" Cray asked.

"Just yesterday."

"Now I see what I recognized in you… a grandson of my best friend."

"A grandfather I never knew, who should have been king."

"And what kind of king will you be, Darius?"

He looked hard at Cray. "I assure you, Cray, that I will rule when my time comes in fairness and with honor." Darius softened his retort. "I have found peace within myself, and I understand my duty to my people."

"I just don't know if everyone will accept all of your abilities." Cray looked back at some of his men.

"Cray, do you remember when you planned that mock attack against me and you told me to be careful of who my friends and enemies were?" Darius's hand moved toward his sword. The handle began to glow.

Cray only nodded again.

"Tell me now, who are you really? Friend or foe?" He smiled to show Cray he wasn't angry, but he needed to know right now if Cray would remain loyal to the crown or not.

Cray didn't hesitate to kneel in front of Darius. "I pledge my service to you, Darius DarSan Williams, the rightful heir to the throne of power, grandson of Alric, my friend." He stopped for a few seconds to compose himself. "I swear my loyalty to you and to your family to the end of my days."

Cray stood, and Darius gaped at him speechless. The pledge was far more forceful than needed and maybe not altogether appropriate since he wasn't the king yet. However, he smiled and only said, "Thank you, Cray."

"Sire. You will be a good king. I am sure of it."

"And your men?" Darius motioned towards the others.

"They will follow me." Cray sent a hand signal, and they dispersed.

Darius relaxed. "So you knew my grandfather?"

Cray smiled and began telling him of boyhood adventures with Alric. Darius enjoyed hearing about his grandfather.

Darius then excused himself, telling Cray he wanted to continue the talk later. They parted, and Darius ran back to the castle to get something, then had to sneak away to avoid the eyes of his father and his men. As the next heir, he would be guarded day and night now. He used his powers to silence his steps and to ditch his guards. For one last time he wanted to be alone. *Well, not all the way alone.*

* * *

Late afternoon found Christine walking into the Field of Diamonds once again. The sky and air had turned bright and warm. She basked in the feel of the spring sun on her face. The grass in the field continued to green, even more so from the day before. She looked more closely. Flowers. *How could that be? Flowers this early in spring. They weren't here yesterday.*

As Christine reached the flowers, she bent down to pick one. There were about a dozen flowers, not planted, just stuck in the ground. She brought one up and breathed in, thoughts and feelings of springtime abounded in its soft scent. Large hands encircled her from behind. She turned around.

"Like them?" Darius had a grin from ear to ear.

"They are beautiful. But how?"

"Nobility does have some benefits. The King has a private indoor garden. I took a little early prerogative."

"They smell like spring. Like this field does later in the spring." Christine looked around, as if remembering.

"Remember when we used to come here when we were younger?" Darius spoke.

Christine laughed. "It wasn't that long ago, Darius."

"Seems like it was." Darius blew out a deep breath. "A lot has happened this past year."

Christine's eyes glazed over, remembering back to the first time they had found the field. They had been running through the forest after a rainstorm. As they had reached the field, the sun had broken through. The reflection of the droplets of rain on the ground had given off the glimmer of diamonds. Things were so simple then. "We've both grown up since then. Back then it seemed so innocent and fresh and… so..." she struggled for the right words.

"Romantic?" Darius finished for her.

"Well, I guess. Except we didn't know what romance was back when we first met. Anyway…" Christine looked down at the ground.

"What?" Darius prodded.

"Nothing."

"Come on, Christine. What were you going to say?"

"It doesn't matter now."

"What doesn't?"

"Us." A few tears leaked out of her downturned eyes.

"What?!" Darius exclaimed. "What do you mean?"

"You are going to be king. How does it feel?"

"It feels... uh... I don't know. I'm not any different. King Edward will recover soon; I am sure I still have a while."

"But one day you will be king."

"Yes, but what are you saying, Christine?"

"It may sound silly now, but when you first left I always dreamed you would come back for me and we would be... married." She turned away in embarrassment. *A silly girl's dream.*

Darius reached over and turned her head softly back to him. "We still can!"

"What?" Christine was taken by surprise. But the words made her heart skip a beat, and she took in a sudden breath.

Darius bent down on one knee. "Christine Anderssn, will you marry me?" Darius almost seemed to be begging. "It's perfect. If we marry, then the farmers and city people have to be united. Our son will be the first true king of *all* of the people."

"Aren't you the first, Darius?"

Darius thought briefly. "I guess I am. I keep forgetting that my father's mother was a farmer. Still, it will be perfect, you and me."

Christine considered the excitement in Darius's voice. She remembered all of the times they had together. He was her best friend. She loved him very much, but...

"I can't, Darius."

Christine's heart ached watching the pain surface on her best friend's face as he stood back up from the grass. She could hardly stand it.

"Why? Christine, what are you talking about? I know I've made some mistakes this past year. If it's about Leandra, don't worry. She is only a friend to me, nothing more. When I saw you in the road the other day, I knew in that instant that I needed you in my life forever. Please don't do this to me. I love you." He choked on his last words. Tears filled his eyes. "I can't do all of this without you by my side."

"It would seem like you are just marrying me for political reasons."

"Political reasons!" Darius was shocked. "This isn't only about the kingdom, it is about us. I want to marry you because I love you. Even if I weren't going to be king, I would want to."

"I know that, Darius. But you will be a king, so that changes things."

"How?" His gray eyes flashed in anger and confusion.

"I don't know," Christine stammered. Tears filled her eyes. "It just does. I'm a farmer, an outsider. The city people still treat us poorly. Look at the mess that happened with your grandfather marrying a farmer. King Charles disowned and banished him. What if King Edward or your father banishes us?"

"They won't, Christine. King Edward wouldn't do that to me after naming me the heir to the throne. And my father... well, my father has been hard on the farmers, but I think he is coming around. We will make it work."

Christine just shook her head. It was so hard to say no to him. It was the moment she had dreamed about for years, but not now and not this way. "I just need more time. I need to know this is real and not us just caught up in the political maneuverings of the Realm."

Darius stepped up to her. "I don't want to hurt you, Christine. I guess it's just too much to ask right now." Tears filled his gray eyes.

Christine's heart broke. She couldn't bear to see Darius in so much pain. Pain she was causing. Things weren't fair. Why did this all have to happen? Why couldn't they have a normal life? She could see he thought it was possible. A lot of things seemed impossible before Darius. But he had a way of making things work. Maybe it could.

"Darius, I'll think about it." Christine touched him lightly on the arm. It was all she could promise at the moment.

Darius looked up, and over his tear-stained face a broad smile spread. His eyes sparkled with hope once again.

With tenderness, he grasped Christine and held her tightly. He was so strong. She could feel the muscles that had developed while he was away. Her heartbeat fluttered and slowed down to match his. His power washed over them both, giving them strength and hope.

Chapter Twenty Two

Loud voices outside the castle walls woke Darius out of a dreamy sleep in his warm bed. As heir to the throne he had been given a suite of rooms in the castle. He still couldn't believe how soft the bed was compared to where he had slept for the past year. He lay still for a moment, listening to what had awakened him. He heard the sound of horses and yelling. Then, he thought he heard his name. Darius tried to wipe the sleep from his eyes as he dragged himself out of bed. Yesterday had been an exhausting day he hoped he would not have to match anytime soon.

"Darius, you will never be king over Belor!" shouted a fading voice. Darius jumped to the window opening and shaded his eyes from the rising sun. He watched men on horseback riding out of the castle gates. He recognized the voice now: the Preacher.

Darius grabbed his clothes, still half-dressing himself as he ran down the empty hallway to the front of the castle. They would be long gone by the time he got outside, but he had to try. As he ran, he wondered who the other men were. Someone from inside the nobility of Anikari, most likely. Someone who had the means to get into the cells and unlock them without being caught. There wasn't any other way the Preacher could have escaped. Not with the dose of drug they had given him to stop him from using his power.

By the time Darius reached the large main doors of the castle, others joined him. He realized he was not the only person in the castle to be awakened by the noise. Leandra stood next to them in her nightshirt, blinking her eyes. He had forgiven Leandra's deception while he had been held prisoner in the cave. Now he just felt sorry for her. She had been through a lot and had been injured when they arrived in Anikari. Her ashen face had begun to show signs of color again.

"It was Sean," she whispered half to herself. "I am sure of it. He was working with someone from inside the castle."

"What?" Darius shouted, and then ran toward the dungeons. One of the guards stopped him and told him he needed to check for danger first. The cells were no place for a future king to be. Darius reluctantly agreed with the strong soldier.

A few minutes later Darius, Leandra, Richard, and a few of the guards gathered in one of the many castle meeting rooms. Darius was glad a fire already burned in the fireplace. The clear night had brought in uncommonly low temperatures for this time of spring.

Richard surmised the Preacher, as well as Sean, had been helped by some noble, perhaps even some of the other councilors who wanted to stir up the people against the announcement of their new, young king. Darius insisted on going after them. If they reached Forest View and had time to organize the Preacher's men, they could attack Anikari that very day. The city was not ready for an all-out war, especially not after the recent fighting with the farmers and lack of food. The people would be confused as to whom they should follow. The

King seemed to be failing rapidly. Would they now listen to Richard or to his son? Or to someone else? He hoped Alessandra and Kelln were making their way north from Belor with the rest of the Elite Army. He hadn't heard from them yet.

"Darius, you can't just go running off every time there are problems. You must stay here and be protected." Richard's lips were tight in frustration.

"If I am going to be a king, the only way both the city and the farmers will accept me is if I show them I am on their side… that I can protect them. All of them. I have to prove myself to them, and I have to prove myself to me, Father. I am the one who brought the Preacher here. I thought he would be safe in our cells." He said this last remark while looking at some of the councilors who had joined the group. Some of them did not return his gaze. "But I guess I was wrong."

"What do you propose, son?" Richard sighed.

Darius could tell his father would have a hard time letting him form his own plans, but he had been out in the field preparing and fighting for the past year. If there was one thing he did know, it was field tactics. "You organize the Elite soldiers here. Take them out on the road to Forest View. Not all of the way... only about half way. A buffer zone to protect fighting from coming to the city."

"But..."

"We can't afford an all-out battle in Forest View, if it comes to that. We have to protect the people. But hopefully I can stop the fighting from reaching that level."

Richard nodded.

"I will bring a small group into Forest View with me to try to stop anything from happening. You will be informed if it gets out of control and I need your help." Darius was scared to death. What if he was wrong? What if he failed? He would not be popular and unpopular kings or kings-to-be didn't live a long time.

"But the Preacher and Sean will get there first." Leandra said her first words since the informal meeting had begun.

The men in the room looked at her, wondering why she was there.

Darius answered her question to the others. "Not if I hurry." Darius gave a few more instructions, ran to get a few things, and bolted to the castle stables to get his new horse, a quick black Andalusian that had been kept at the King's stables for him.

He jumped on his horse and rode at a frantic pace to Christine's house, catching Jain as he was about to leave. He gave Jain a key and told him to go to a room under the library in the school, take Karel and Thomas with him, and grab as many swords as he could. He gave Jain some papers signifying that he had permission to be in the school. Darius hoped there wouldn't be any problems there. Jain was to pass the swords out to as many farmers as he could, then meet Darius in Forest View.

Darius pulled out a map and spread it on the ground. He had drawn on it a different road into Forest View, one that bypassed the main road. The smaller trail stayed north of the Black Forest but was used only on rare occasions. He instructed Jain to take that road. That would keep them away from his father and the city soldiers.

Jain looked a little bewildered as he bowed awkwardly to Darius. "You can count on us, uh… Sir or Prince or…"

Darius smiled at Jain's red face. "Just call me Darius for now, Jain. I hope to have a long time until I am king, and prince just doesn't sound right." He saluted back, and Jain rode off.

"We need to ride Lightning to Forest View." Darius turned to Christine.

"I thought you said she would only take one rider at a time."

"I think she will take me." Darius smiled.

Speaking to Christine's mind, the Cremelino spoke boldly. *Don't worry, child. I can carry you and the wizard.* The beautiful white horse trotted up next to them, looking anxious to run.

"But I thought they would bond to one rider and one owner?" Christine asked.

It almost seemed as if the horse smiled as it spoke in both their minds. *Darius is a wizard, and they may ride us anytime if their heart is true. But don't worry; my bond is still with you, Christine.*

Darius leaped up and then reached his hand for Christine to join him. His strong arms drew her up behind him in one long pull.

"Let's go!" Darius yelled. "The peace of the kingdom depends on you, Lightning."

Oh, no, wizard, it all depends on you.

They rode with the speed of a stormy wind over brush and grass. The thin trail had grown over in spots, but Darius kept his hand out in front of them and, drawing on his power, burned the brush and small trees away as they rode through. The horse was fast, but Darius still worried about whether or not they would beat the Preacher and his party to Forest View. His plan depended on him being there first and the element of surprise disarming the Preacher.

The ride seemed to take forever, but Darius knew it was only his mind playing tricks on him. Christine didn't say a word. He wondered what she was thinking. Had she made up her mind yet about marrying him? It felt good having her arms around him. The side of her head rested on his back. He breathed in and smiled at her lavender scent. With Lightning's increased speed, the enjoyment lasted less than an hour before they reached the edge of Forest View.

"The city is too quiet." He panned the area with a slow turn of the horse, making sure he didn't miss anything. They slowed and trotted from the north around to the east side of the city before entering. They saw his own soldiers up ahead, and Darius stiffened. He looked around for someplace that would be safe for Christine. Someone shouted his name.

A few of the Elite soldiers came running toward him. Darius smiled and jumped down off the Cremelino.

"Commander," said one, "we have heard the news. Congratulations." They nodded their heads to him in acknowledgement of his new position as heir.

Darius smiled and shook hands with a few of his Elite soldiers. Some still seemed reluctant and untrusting. Darius couldn't blame them.

"You got my message in time, I see."

"Yes. Alessandra and Kelln must have ridden through the night. All the way from Anikari to Belor in one night is an astonishing feat. We could hardly believe it," said one of the Elite Army captains. "We came to Forest View as fast as we could, as you instructed."

Just then a young woman stepped out from the crowd. "It wasn't too bad. I guess a lady had to show these men what could be done." Alessandra smiled.

Christine moved closer to Darius. Was that jealousy on her face?

Darius introduced Christine to Alessandra.

Kelln walked up, and Darius and he clasped arms. "Thank you, my friend." Darius spoke in low tones.

Alessandra moved over next to Kelln. Darius felt Christine relax somewhat when it became apparent Alessandra was more interested in Kelln than Darius.

"And my... father?" asked Alessandra. "Where is he?"

"He is on his way and should be here any minute," Darius informed her.

"Your father," Christine gasped, "is the Preacher?"

Alessandra looked ashamed but nodded.

Darius asked for a horse other than Lightning, motioned orders to a few soldiers, and rode out to the entrance of the city. The Preacher's men from Belor stood uncomfortably around the city gates as they eyed Darius's small group of Elite soldiers. He positioned himself inside the tall, elaborate city gate and watched as the Preacher arrived. Darius smiled inside at the shock that spread across the face of the self-proclaimed leader of Belor.

"You are a devil!" the Preacher yelled. A small group of men arrived behind the man, led by none other than Sean San Ghant. It seemed it hadn't taken them long to forge an alliance in prison and find some men to let them out and follow them into battle.

"What do you want here?" Darius directed his question at the Preacher, trying to stall for some time.

"I want you."

"I thought you wanted peace and freedom for Belor. Isn't that what your soldiers are fighting for? They don't want me. I am nothing to them."

The Preacher glanced around at his men. They were obviously considering what Darius had said. "Your death is a means to that peace," he said to Darius.

"My life is the only way to that peace!" Darius let some of his power seep through him, and his voice bounced off of the nearby buildings. The power filled him with righteous anger and determination. He turned to the Preacher's soldiers. "I have been proclaimed today to be the next king of the Realm by King Edward himself. I promise you that I will listen to your grievances. I will even sign a proclamation to make Belor a safer and better place."

Many of the soldiers nodded in agreement. They had wives and children. If they could get what they wanted without fighting, so much the better. The Preacher's fanaticism had moved beyond what many of them had originally signed on for. Darius knew they served him now only through fear.

"You are a liar," shouted the Preacher. "You deceived us before. And now you lie again."

"I didn't deceive you. I had deceived myself." Darius continued prancing his large brown horse in a circle. He wanted to make sure the entire crowd heard him. "Hasn't there been a time in each of your lives when you didn't know what you were searching for? Haven't there been times when you made mistakes? I have been proclaimed to be a king, not a god. I am not perfect, but neither is your leader, the one we call the Preacher. I promise you I will do all I can as the next king to help your city, and to help the entire Realm have more equality among all of her wonderful and diverse people. But if you don't listen to me, I also promise you will receive the utmost punishment for continued rebellion against the Realm. Put down your arms. I am still commander of the King's Elite Army, sworn to defend the Realm and have the King's authority to maintain the law."

The men began to talk and argue among themselves. Some pulled out weapons. The Preacher tried to regroup them, but they were out of his control now. Many of them, convinced of what Darius had said, were tired of fighting. They wanted to go home. The portion of the Elite Army that had come up from Belor started to form a semi-circle around the outside of where the Preacher's men stood. Somebody from within the rebels shot an arrow and hit a Realm soldier. Some of the soldiers retaliated and drew their arrows and swords.

Darius cringed as the fighting began. He hoped he had changed enough minds. He looked around for the Preacher. The man had somehow disappeared from the crowd. Darius heard a shriek from Christine. He turned around, and an arrow hit him in the thigh. He roared with pain as he searched out the shooter. "Sean!"

"Now we will see who the best aim is." Sean lifted another arrow up to shoot. The last time they had faced each other with bows and arrows was in an archery contest at the end of Darius's last year at the academy. Sean had taunted him then, and Darius had lost his temper. In the end, however, Darius had won the tournament. Sean had been bitter about that loss ever since.

Unexpectedly, someone jumped on Sean's back. It was Kelln. Darius sighed in disbelief. Impetuous, adventuresome, loyal Kelln.

Sean dropped to the ground and rolled, with Kelln still holding on. Finally Sean jumped free, and Kelln got back up off the ground. Sean grabbed a sword from a neighboring soldier and began to approach again.

"You!" The Preacher yelled at Kelln, as he came running hard from behind a nearby blacksmith's shop. "I will have you once and for all."

Sean moved closer to the Preacher and stared at Kelln and Darius with a smug look on his face. The Preacher's power must have not been fully functional yet, or he would have blasted Darius earlier. Now, though, Darius saw fire run down the length of the Preacher's sword.

The Preacher slowed to a deliberate stride and continued moving toward Kelln. "I am tired of you escaping me. Now you will die. You can't escape from death."

"No, Father!"

The Preacher froze and looked toward the voice. Alessandra stood in the muddied street. A look of shock ran across his face; then rage contorted his lips. "You're as bad as he is. You will die next."

The Preacher's eyes were afire, and his veins popped out of his neck. Power began to crackle around him as he broke free of the drug that had contained him. The wizard took two giant strides, bringing his sword up high in the air above Kelln.

Darius took a step forward, but before he had gone any distance a shout came from close by.

"No!" shouted a new voice as Kelln's father jumped between the Preacher and Kelln. The power-filled blow of the Preacher's sword hit him on top of the shoulder, almost severing his arm.

Blood splattered over those who were close. Darius rushed to Kelln's aid, who had fallen down to the ground. His father cried out in pain.

Careful of showing too much of his power, Darius, with a quick motion of his hand, pushed the Preacher back with a thrust of air. Another of Darius's soldiers grabbed the sword away from the man. The fire had vanished from the Preacher's sword, his still-limited power spent for the time being. Others quickly bound him and Sean up with heavy ropes.

Darius stood up, and Kelln knelt down beside his father. "Father..." came a choked sob.

Alessandra stood next to Darius.

"They talked last night," she whispered to Darius. "His father came with us and apologized for what he had done. It seemed that many of the people left in Belor were freed from the Preacher's powers once the Preacher had been gone a few days. Kelln and his father laughed and talked about old times. Kelln sure has a way of not giving up on people." Alessandra left Darius to kneel down next to Kelln and his father.

Darius nodded and smiled, understanding completely what she meant. He thought about his own father. What if he died now? The things Darius had said to him over his life needed to be rectified. He looked around at the fighting that still continued on the outskirts and caught Mezar fighting a group of the Preacher's men all by himself. A serene smile spread across the Gildanian's face. Darius marveled at the smooth and effortless sword strokes, different from the Realm's way of fighting. It was more fluid and graceful—almost an art in the way that Mezar danced around his opponents. Once again Darius wondered about the man he had captured and what else the Gildanian was hiding.

Darius turned to find Christine standing next to him. She smiled at him, and among the sadness of the fighting, joy once again filled him just by her being there by his side.

Darius winced as he remembered the wound in his thigh. He sat down slowly, and Christine wrapped his upper leg in a torn up piece of cloth. It throbbed but wasn't severe. Kelln and Alessandra bound Kelln's father's wound as well, but he had lost a lot of blood and was unconscious.

Darius moved over to Kelln and was about to bring his hands over his father's bleeding wound, but Kelln must have felt his intentions and caught Darius's eyes. Kelln shook his head to say that it was all right.

"You need to conserve your strength. I will take care of him."

Thoughts about his own father continued swirling around Darius. What would happen to his father by the time he became king? How would the leadership really work? Would Richard be jealous of his son?

A group of the Preacher's men appeared, marching at a brisk pace toward Darius. Elite soldiers moved in to block them. They demanded the release of their leader. When Darius declined, one of them drew his sword and lunged forward. Darius rolled over on the ground and bounded upright as he pushed Christine behind him.

Sword struck against sword. Back and forth the two men dueled. One would retreat and then the other. Everyone marveled at Darius's use of the sword against the skilled swordsman opposite him. Another rebel joined in against Darius. Suddenly Mezar was at Darius's side.

Soon the battle rose to a new fury. The Elite solders were in an exhausted state at marching so quickly from Belor. It was wearing on them and slowing them down. The Preacher's men had two days in Forest View and had plenty of rest and strength. Some of the Preacher's men had decided not to join in the fight on either side, and stood on the outskirts and watched what the outcome would be.

Darius wished to use his power and end it once and for all. But the people weren't ready for it yet. An acknowledged wizard had not been seen around Anikari for at least two generations, if not more. He didn't want to be like the Preacher. He wanted to earn the right to be king on his own.

But he was torn. He felt so exhausted. If he didn't use his power soon, he was afraid they would lose the battle, and possibly the kingdom.

Two men jumped toward him at once. Darius howled and retreated, but stumbled on his way.

Off in the distance new yelling was heard. Down the street came Jain and a large group of armed farmers fighting through the group toward Darius. The Preacher's men, not knowing who the others were, but expecting it was the King's army from Anikari, began to retreat. From where he was tied up, the Preacher ordered them to continue fighting, but many began to lay down their weapons and surrender. The Elite Army gained new hope and energy and forged forward until the Preacher's dwindling group of fighters became surrounded on all sides by the new mixed army of farmers and Darius's Elite Army. The battle was finished.

Darius was still sitting on the ground, where he had stumbled. Someone had kicked him in the back of the leg, causing his previous injury to rip further. Blood soaked through his pants. The Preacher yelled out again, and one of Darius's men clubbed him over the head with the hilt of a sword. The Preacher slumped unconscious to the ground.

Christine ran over to Darius and helped him stand. She held him close to her side, looked into his strong, gray eyes, then leaned in and whispered, "I will marry you, Darius DarSan Williams. I don't want to ever lose you."

Darius grinned, then laughed out loud with joy.

Limping over to the group of soldiers, Darius felt the peace of Christine at his side. The Preacher's followers, still in defiance of Darius, stood in a group together but now were unarmed. Darius directed the band of farmers to begin marching the prisoners toward Anikari. The rest of the Preacher's men—those who agreed to leave in peace, he let go back to Belor and instructed them that representatives from the Realm would join them soon to re-establish an appropriate government.

He motioned for some of his army to help Kelln load his father's injured body into a wagon, but noticed tears streaming down Kelln's face. Darius ran over to his friend.

"He's gone, Darius."

"So quickly? I thought… I could have..." Darius stumbled with what to say to his best friend. The last he had seen of Kelln's father, it looked to him as though he would recover from his injuries.

Kelln half smiled. "It's not your fault, Darius. The injury was too much for him. We made peace in the end, and he will rest well with God. I will never forget his sacrifice for me. He saved me in the end. He gave his life for *me*." A sob escaped his lips.

Darius put his arm around him. "He was a wonderful man. I will honor him with full honors as a hero in defending the Realm," Darius said.

"Why? Why did he go to Belor?" Kelln whispered, barely able to talk.

"Kel, I have learned this past year about many things we don't understand. Only a few years ago we were children with hardly a care. Today we are men who are shaping the future of the Realm. Who knows why it is us at this point in time? The reasons may not be evident for years, but I have learned there are reasons for everything."

"So wise now, huh?" Kelln smiled, his eyes still full of tears.

"No, not wise, my friend, just finally figuring out some things."

Kelln reached around Darius with both arms and gave him a quick hug and strong slap on the back. Christine, Alessandra, and Mezar stood close by. There was no shame in the sadness of that moment. Their lives had crossed, friendships bonded, and though they would never be the same again, they would remain friends no matter where their intermediate travels would take them.

Darius's head picked up as he turned toward a sound off in the distance. It was a yell for him. A rider appeared around the side of an old house. His purple cape flew in the air behind him. He was one of the King's messengers, only a few years older than Darius himself.

"Your... men... said you... were still here." The messenger barely seemed to notice the somber mood. "You must... must return to Anikari... immediately," he said in between quick breaths.

"What is it?" asked Alessandra.

The messenger eyed her suspiciously. Darius nodded his approval of the question.

"Senior Councilor Richard San Williams sent me. He told me a strange message. He said you must ride the white horse if possible... I don't know what that means."

Christine smiled. "It's my Cremelino. He must want you to return quickly, Darius."

"The King?" asked Darius anxiously.

The messenger didn't know, but Darius did. Whether it was the newfound kinship they shared or the imminent passing of the mantle of king to his heir, Darius knew King Edward DarSan Montere was passing on.

Darius swayed on his feet, paled, and fell to his knees. A rush of power filled him. Tears and fear clouded his vision momentarily. Kelln rushed to his side and leaned down to him.

"It's time. I must be strong," Darius whispered almost to himself.

"Time for what?" asked Kelln.

He looked up to his old friend, tears streaming down his dirtied face. "My time in history, Kel. The time we never thought possible. The time I never wanted."

"You don't think..."

Darius stood up again slow and deliberate, his power bringing him strength. "I know. I can sense things happening. It is time for my destiny to take an unexpected turn, my friend. And once again I must ask 'why me?'"

"I will get Lightning." Christine began to run off, but Lightning was already approaching.

"Please join me as soon as possible," Darius said to Kelln, Alessandra, and Mezar. Mezar's eyes held his own for a brief moment. Darius felt something there. A power he hadn't felt before. Mezar smiled and bowed his head in slight obeisance. He would have to trust Mezar to return on his own without taking him along with him. Somehow he did trust the man.

Turning to Kelln, Darius spoke to him alone. "Take whatever time you need with your father. I will send a rider to Belor to bring back your family to Anikari."

Darius motioned for Christine to join him on her horse and rode off down the road to Anikari. Darius silently prayed with all the fervor he had. If he ever needed guidance and extra strength, it was now.

They soon came up on the men marching from Forest View to Anikari that had previously left with the prisoners. He spoke a few words to Jain, and they continued on their way. He gave some of the herbs to Jain to make sure the Preacher's power would not return anytime soon.

Darius sat lost in his own thoughts as they galloped, and he realized they were halfway to Anikari when two units of the King's Elite Army approached them on the main road. Darius informed the unit commander that an army from the farmlands was bringing in the captured rebels from Forest View and they were not needed for the battle, but they should accompany the men back to Anikari.

Christine laughed behind him on the horse. "Darius, you set that all up, didn't you? Did you see the look on that captain's face when you mentioned that the farmers were bringing in the rebels? You are amazing. You tied together the Elite Army and the farmers with such skill that no one knew what was happening until it was over. Then you made sure that the King's army here knew the farmers had captured the rebels." She leaned in and kissed his cheek.

They reached the gate and rode through in a blur without stopping. The two arrived at the castle, handed their reins to a stable boy, and ran inside. The royal chamberlain met them in the hallway and directed them to the King's room. The long halls seemed to take forever. Darius limped painfully and trembled from the exhaustion of battle. The weight he felt sat more heavily on his shoulders with every step he took.

Being led into the King's chambers, Darius saw his father, a doctor, a religious leader, and a guard encircling the King's bed. King Edward didn't look like he had passed on yet. Darius breathed a sigh of relief. In a somber mood, Richard motioned him over to a corner. He looked tired and ready to fall over himself.

"The doctor says he only has a short time. Are you ready?" He looked Darius directly in the eyes. His father had never looked so intent in his life.

Darius wondered if he should try and heal King Edward. He didn't know if he had the strength to even try. He was exhausted to his core.

"I am." Darius's knees shook. *I must be strong!*

"The battle?" asked his father.

"*We* won." He emphasized the *we*. "The farmers and the Elite Army fought together."

His father smiled and relaxed a bit. "It seems I have underestimated your abilities."

"And I yours." Darius thought back to Kelln and his father. There was still a chance for Darius and his father to become friends once again.

The King coughed, and they moved back to his bedside. His tired and heavy eyes fluttered open and searched out

Darius. Speaking to the others he said, "Leave me alone with Darius for a few moments."

The doctor looked uncertain, but Richard led the others to a far corner of the room.

King Edward whispered, his voice deep and husky, "I am sorry to put such a burden on you at such an early age, Darius. Times will be difficult."

"Sire." Darius reached his hand over to the King's forehead and pulled upon his power. It was hard to do. There was so little left in his exhausted state. He concentrated and felt deep into the King's body. There was poison there, spread deep throughout his body. It would be difficult to remove, but he had to try.

The King reached up with a weakened hand and pulled Darius's hand away. "No. It is my time. I have nothing left here. I go to be with my family and I leave the Realm in your hands."

Darius nodded but kept silent, moving his hands back to his side.

"There will be many who disagree with you and want to see you dethroned. Some, who, I am sure, have been planning my succession for years. There is only one way for an Anikarian King to be dethroned..."

Darius nodded again, realizing what the King was saying. *Death!*

"I see you have special abilities, Darius. The rumors are true. A wizard King will walk the Realm once again. Be careful with what you do, but be proud of who you are. The kings of the past were wizards and ruled us well. Show the people that power can be used for good." The King stopped and coughed a few times. He closed his eyes.

Darius turned to look at his father and motioned him over.

"Richard," the King turned his head slightly to his trusted councilor, "take care of your son and guide him. He is strong and full of enthusiasm, but he still has much to learn. If he will, I request that you continue as his councilor. He will need your knowledge and wisdom."

Darius thought he would get tired of nodding, but it didn't seem right to speak just yet.

The King closed his eyes once more and the doctor stepped forward to feel his pulse. He still lived, but only barely hung on to life.

King Edward opened his eyes once again. "You must be strong, Darius. Others may see you as unfair, hardened, and uncaring at times. That is the lot of a king. But if you follow what you know is right, you will be all right. You will feel the peace... the peace inside. Like I do now. Knowing finally that wrongs are being righted."

The King took a deep, ragged breath and continued. "Others will want your power and riches. Remember, though, you must serve the entire Realm. Sometimes this may make you unpopular with certain groups. Your times are different than mine..."

He faded off again. Darius looked at his father.

A few moments later he opened his eyes once more. Looking at the back of the room he pointed a weak finger toward Christine and asked Darius, "The girl?"

"What about her?" Darius asked.

The King laughed himself into a coughing fit, smiled, then turned back to Darius. "She would make a beautiful queen."

Darius saw his father's eyes widen in disbelief.

"Times change, my old friend," the King said to Richard. "From the first time I saw her come into the castle with that petition from the farmers last year, I sensed she was destined for greatness and now I see how. Royalty will suit her well."

"We will be wed soon," Darius said. The joy he had felt when Christine had told him yes! He didn't know what had changed her mind. They would talk about it later. But for now he knew with her by his side he could handle what would come.

The King looked pleased, and then turned to Richard one last time. "Goodbye, my faithful councilor, my nephew, and my friend…" A smile spread across his lips, and his light gray eyes took one last blink before closing.

It was the first time Darius ever remembered seeing his father cry. Tears spilled without shame down his face. The doctor checked the King's pulse for the last time and nodded solemnly to the gathering.

Christine was escorted out, and Darius left her and the others to be by himself. Taking a few steps down the hallway, he entered his own rooms. Placing his palms on the stone windowsill, he gazed out the window over the entire city. The great city of Anikari! It was beautiful from this vantage point. Oil lamps began to flicker on throughout the city, giving it a sparkling glow before darkness settled in. The power of the Realm and even the whole western world was seated here. He could see the fields where farmers toiled for a mere subsistence.

Darius looked toward the Superstition Mountains. They stood dark and shadowy with the setting sun just behind their jagged peaks. He thought of his training up in those mountains.

Darius remembered standing on top of some of those foreboding mountains, feeling like he would conquer the world. His decisions this past year had led him to his destiny. The King of the Realm! How unprepared he felt for that role.

Slowly he sank to his knees. With the last echoes of the sunset reflecting a burnt orange off of the stone walls in the room, Darius pleaded for a chance to redeem his previous evil thoughts and desires. He asked for divine help as he began his stewardship as king.

Darius sensed his father walk by his room and stop. An impression of satisfaction rose from Richard as he softly closed the door, leaving Darius to himself.

Though his eyes remained closed, Darius could distinguish the room darken as the sun fell fully behind the mountains. The room was dark, but his soul seemed to remain bright. Power and magic infused his being, and he recognized it as the power of kings—the power all kings used to hold. The power of a wizard *and* the power of the throne. He had a great responsibility now.

If this was what his destiny held, he knew there would also be a way for him to accomplish the almost unbearable tasks that lay ahead of him. He finished his pleadings and, without getting up, laid his head down against the soft comforter hanging from the bed and fell asleep.

Chapter Twenty Three

The few people assembled in the large dining room sat in a somber mood. One by one, they had entered and taken a seat at the formal table. Not a word was spoken. The oil lamps on the walls lightened the room in a dramatic, yet artificial way. The large mosaic window on the north wall and the many crystal goblets along the long mahogany table reflected droplets of this light, making the room as bright as daytime.

A simple fare of light refreshments of breads, cheeses, and pastries had been set on the table, but no one made the move to be the first one to eat. A servant stood at each end of the room, awaiting instructions.

Darius sat at the head of the table in a simple, but pressed, pair of black pants, a white linen shirt, and a buttoned-up black jacket with the purple emblem of Anikari embroidered on the front right breast. He looked up at the wooden carvings along the edge of the ceiling, then down to the paintings on the walls. Some were portraits of prior kings; others were scenes from different places around the Realm. He realized how much he didn't comprehend about the business of the Realm. He had read all of the books in school but, until the last few days, had not thought he would need the knowledge much. Now he would need to learn fast.

His eyes moved to the person at his right. Christine! She smiled at him, and excitement overwhelmed his fears for a moment. He reached over and squeezed her hand. *So beautiful and calm!*

Next to her sat Alessandra and Kelln. Darius wondered what they were thinking. Alessandra's father, the Preacher, now taken prisoner, and Kelln's father killed by him. He worried for his friend and hoped that Alessandra would not break his heart again.

Across from them sat Mezar and Jain. Along with the rest of the group, they had proved invaluable to Darius's plans over the past day. He waited a few moments.

The door opened, and Darius stood and motioned for Leandra to sit next to Mezar, on the other side from Jain. She gave Darius a brief smile, but her eyes lingered on Mezar far longer. Darius detected a slight blush to her cheeks as she sat next to him. Darius wasn't sure if he trusted her yet, but she had been through a lot, and he would give her the benefit of the doubt for the time being.

Darius dismissed the servants. This needed to be private.

This would be the hardest thing Darius would have to do over the next few days. He had to reconcile his past with his friends.

"Thank you for coming tonight. I have something I need to ask from each of you." *What if they wouldn't?* "Most of you know to one degree or another what I have done this past year. I have treated many of you badly." He glanced at Kelln and didn't finish the sentence.

He cleared his throat and continued. "I became deceived by revenge, power, and glory. I was confused and didn't grasp what I was doing. I wanted revenge, at some point, on something I didn't have all of the information about. Each one of you has helped me overcome my weaknesses in one way or another. A few hours ago King Edward passed on." He paused for a moment to let his words sink in.

Each of them followed Darius with even more interest as he stood and paced behind his red velvet high-backed chair.

"I am now officially the Protectorate of Anikari, King of the Realm." Darius smiled, but there was sadness in his eyes. "But I need the support of every one of you. I need your forgiveness. Will you forgive me for the way I treated all of you?" He braced his hands against the back of the chair, waiting their response.

Christine reached over and took his hand back into hers. He knew she forgave him. They had already reconciled their past earlier in the day. It was the others he worried about.

Mezar cleared his throat, and everyone looked his way. "I forgive you, Darius," he said with his slight Gildanian accent. "Even though you captured me and held me as your prisoner, you treated me fairly. We developed a sort of friendship, a closeness that I don't think you totally understand."

Darius nodded in the affirmative.

"I am not sure where to start," Mezar continued. "You all know I was in Denir. But you never really knew why. I was sent with my men to test your defenses with no intention of going any farther into the Realm. However, during the confusion, I, along with a few other men, were supposed to leave the city in disguise and travel the Realm for a time. It was never our purpose to cause any trouble. I was instructed to report on your living conditions, army strength, medical advances, trade, nobility structure, and general observations of your kingdom—a spy, if you will." Mezar's tilted eyes smiled in amusement.

Darius's eyes went wide. He had harbored a spy from Gildan. What would his father say to that? As King, it would be his duty now to decide what to do.

"The problem was, we didn't expect an army to meet us in such a quick and efficient manner in Denir." The Gildanian smiled at Darius, who gave a small laugh in return. "Some of my older lieutenants had grown careless and had stayed up drinking too late. I tried to warn them, but they didn't listen. They thought I was too young to know better. Well, anyway, I have seen more of the Realm and in a different way than I had planned. I even grew to like many of the people."

Leandra smiled at Mezar.

"Did the king of Gildan send you?" asked Jain, becoming excited by all of the travels and stories being told around the large table. Darius knew the boy had never been farther than Forest View, and now he sat in the castle with the new king.

"Yes, my grandfather… the Emperor of Gildan, sent me." Mezar paused.

Darius stiffened at the unexpected news.

Mezar continued. "My older brother died last year due to an outbreak of a plague, so I became second in line. I will be Emperor of Gildan, your equivalent to king, when my grandfather, the Emperor, and my father, the general, pass on. That is why Darius and I had some sort of special comradery. There is more that I need to discuss in private with King Darius, but that will have to wait until later."

Darius paused to think about what Mezar meant, and a sudden realization washed over him. He remembered crossing the Black River and feeling someone else with power. He was also surprised at how quickly Leandra had healed. He smiled knowingly at Mezar.

"Wow!" Jain said, echoing the thoughts of all.

Darius began to laugh, and they all joined in. The whole story was what made books and fairy tales, yet they were in the middle of it all.

"Seems like only yesterday when we were all children, playing carefree games. Now we are shaping the future of not only the Realm but the Empire also." Darius laughed again. It felt good. One by one the rest of the group expressed their forgiveness to Darius. A heavy burden lifted from his heart. Running a kingdom was going to be hard enough without having to worry about if his own friends accepted and trusted him.

Darius called for the servants to come back in and pour drinks for everyone. It had been a long day, and they all laughed, talked, and ate heartily. Darius, though, was already thinking about his next meeting.

"Darius?" Jain asked, "Where did those swords come from that you had us take to Forest View? They had some unfamiliar writing on them that I couldn't understand."

"I've been told that the writing on my sword came from the old Kingdom of Mar. A language spoken before the Realm was formed. It was created by a great wizard. Those other swords were not magic, but hadn't been used for a long time.

The Preacher seemed to understand the words that were inscribed on them."

Alessandra almost choked. "What?"

"He translated the writing for me. It was some type of instructions for finding knowledge when you entered the old Kingdom of Mar. The Preacher seemed to know quite a bit about Mar and its historic underground," continued Darius.

Alessandra dropped her fork and covered her face with her hands. "He told me he had never been to Mar," she whispered.

"Alessandra, I am sure he told you many things that were untrue," added Kelln.

"You don't understand. When I was young," Alessandra continued, "my mother disappeared. My father always told me that she died. However, my grandfather said she hadn't died, but had left my father and returned to Mar and that my father had gone in search for her. When my father returned years later all he said was he had traveled the Realm and then over the sea to the Eastern Kingdoms. I never told him that I knew my mother hadn't died and he would never admit going to Mar. Soon afterwards my father became obsessed with his power, had an argument with my grandfather, and sent him away." Alessandra took in a deep breath, trying to sort things out as she spoke.

"One thing I gathered from him was that nothing in Mar was worth anything anymore. Those were his words," added Darius. "He seemed quite bitter about the place."

"She may really be dead, Alessandra," said Christine. "Do you think she is still alive, and in Mar?"

"I'm not positive, but I think it's time for me to find out. She is my mother and if she is still alive…" Alessandra sniffed back her tears. "Maybe my father will tell me finally what he knows."

"I will help you," offered Kelln. "You can't see him alone."

"Your father will be tried for treason," Darius said solemnly. "Not just for the uprising in Belor. I might have been able to be lenient there. But for multiple murders and the assassination attempt on King Edward. That is not forgivable."

Alessandra just nodded.

A messenger came in and told Darius that fighting was going on in the lower section of the city. The news of the King's death had already begun to spread, it seemed. Darius dismissed himself with a sigh. Time for his next meeting. He wished everyone well, kissed Christine, and left the room.

Richard met him in the long corridor heading to the other end of the castle. "Are you ready?"

Darius nodded. It was all he could do. He knees felt like buckling again. *I must be strong. I am the King!* They walked into the assembly area of the castle. Sheets of silk hung around the outside to enclose the area from the night air. Lanterns dotted the outdoor sitting area. Darius looked at his father and remembered the last time they had been there together. It was the day he had left for the Superstition Mountains. His father had slapped him in front of the others and embarrassed him. The anger welled up inside of him once again, but now he knew how to push the negative feelings away.

Most of the councilors and other high nobility were already assembled and seated. He smiled at a few of the guards who had come in from the Elite Army. They nodded back. He hoped they trusted and accepted him. He hadn't always been the nicest of leaders, but they had been taught to obey, and he hoped obedience would suffice until they found their own acceptance of him.

Richard led Darius up to the stand. They sat and waited until everyone arrived. Darius observed the hard faces of seasoned men looking straight at him, trying to figure out what their role in this new leadership would be. Many weren't looking incredibly happy; they were most likely the ones that would have put their own names forth if a true heir hadn't been announced. *And many more will be even more unhappy after this.* Most of them were still in town from the ceremony at the coliseum.

Richard stood and walked to the podium. "Councilors, Ambassadors, Mayors, and Nobles, this day is a sorrowful one for the Realm. Our beloved King Edward DarSan Montere has passed away." They all had been informed already, but it was the official role of the First Councilor to direct the meeting. "He has left us saddened at his passing but has named a new Protectorate and King for our Realm, continuing a long line of kings. We are here to crown our new King, Darius DarSan Williams, friend of the people, protector of the people, and one of the people."

Darius saw a young man come out from behind a small door holding the crown and the royal staff that had been used by many kings in Anikari over the ages. Darius walked toward his father and knelt. His father placed the crown on his head and handed him a staff. Darius thought of how difficult this must be for his father. He should have been the King.

The ceremony was simple. A more formal larger one would be held in the arena the next day for all the people to attend. But as of now Darius was officially the King of the Realm.

As he held the staff, he sensed a great power, similar to that of his sword. He wondered how many other objects of power survived, scattered throughout the Realm, and if Edward had known about any of them. He concluded that King Edward, not being a wizard himself, probably had not known. There had been no sign of wizardry or power in him that Darius knew about.

Darius stood and replaced his father at the pulpit. Many of the crowd squirmed in their seats. He began his acceptance speech.

"I am Darius DarSan Williams, newly crowned Protectorate of Anikari, King of the Realm, and still named as commander of the King's Elite Army. I am the defender and the servant of this great people. I ask now for your pledge of loyalty and support, which you, along with me, will serve according to the laws of this great kingdom." Darius paused, scanning the crowd before starting his next sentence. "Are there any who protest this motion?" This was the official wording to be recorded. He hoped everyone didn't get up and run out.

An elderly man in front stood up… Jonathan, one of King Edward's councilors. The man's hair was gray and receding, but his large frame stood in defiance. Before he could say anything, Darius spoke out first.

"Jonathan San Alver, is it only I whom you protest as king—or anyone else other than yourself?" Some of the crowd looked puzzled, others worried. "Do you deny that even before the announcement naming me as King; you were scheming in secret against King Edward, to position yourself as the next heir to the throne?"

The long-standing councilor cleared his voice and began to protest. "There was no heir before."

Darius cut him off before he said more. He had something more incriminating. "And do you deny it was you, along with your supporters, who let the Preacher and Sean San Ghant out of prison?"

Many in the crowd gasped.

"I do not have to take this harassment," Jonathan stated as he turned to leave.

"Guards!" Darius called them forward. "This man may leave the castle with an escort in peace, stripped of his rank, never to return, or you have my permission to take him to the dungeon. He is no longer welcomed in Anikari."

Darius could see his father out of the corner of his eyes. They had discussed this earlier. His father did not agree with Darius's approach. Darius knew he had to show firmness to the other leaders at first. His father thought a more softened approach would best support his new reign; but he in turn supported the new king.

"Are there any others among you?" asked Darius, hoping for one more.

"You are too young. You do not understand any of the politics of the Realm," shouted another of the councilors.

"Aaron San Silva, I am surprised. I am surprised at all of you. You sit here in your cozy rooms in Anikari, thinking you know her people. How many of you have slept for a week in the Superstition Mountains alone? How many of you have led an army to Denir in the middle of the winter and conquered without losing a soul?"

Darius let some of the power come through his voice and magnified it louder. "How many of you have marched across the Black Forest? Or through dark and ancient tunnels into Belor?" He could see heads dropping. *Good! It was working.* "When was the last time any of you walked out in the fields surrounding our great city to consider how much work goes on out there in order for you and your families to have food on your tables?"

Darius moved away from the podium and paced the length of the stand as he spoke. "I may be young. And I do admit I have things to learn. Many things. But so do each and every one of you. We will council together to meet the needs of our great land, but I am the King." Darius hoped he wasn't shaking as badly on the outside as he was on the inside.

The group sat stunned. They didn't know whether to call his bluff or not.

"Aaron, would you like to resign from the assembly of councilors?" Darius was giving the man a way to leave on his own terms. Aaron was not a bad person and had not worked behind the King's back as Jonathon had done, from what Richard's research showed. Darius wanted to encourage opinions spoken by his councilors, but he couldn't have one of the councilors voice concerns about his leadership at this point and time.

Aaron nodded once, but kept his chin up.

Darius softened his words. "You may retain your home here in Anikari, your riches, and any estates accumulated during your term as councilor. Thank you for your service to the Realm."

Aaron looked mildly surprised at the concessions and left without any further problems.

There were only a few young men and women in the crowd. That would need to be remedied. Age brought experience and wisdom, but youth brought enthusiasm and new ideas. Once again he asked, "Any more objections?" No more objections were raised. Darius's plan had worked. The councilors would follow him. Darius realized they would test him at every turn. But he would be ready. His power would guide him, and his power was centered in his heart. He would temper firmness with compassion for all citizens of the Realm.

Darius continued his speech and announced the Preacher would be sentenced to death for his crime of attempting to assassinate King Edward, for murdering and torturing, and inciting rebellion in the Realm. Sean would be sent to the Twin Cities to work in the mines there. The prisoners brought in by Jain and the farmers would be led around the Realm for two years, performing manual labor for the King in rebuilding roads and homes, and then returned home to Belor.

Richard returned to the pulpit and announced that the next day an official declaration and ceremony would be made to the entire Realm in the coliseum. It was there Darius would announce his new councilors. *And one other surprise!* Darius thought.

Afterward, some came up to Darius, congratulating him and trying to get into his good graces before the announcements. Weakened and tired inside, he smiled and continued to visit and talk to people. He would have to get used to the new hectic life of a king. He reminisced inside on the easy days at the academy with Kelln.

* * *

Just outside of the city walls two men came riding out of the gates. Christine and Jain had just left Anikari and were walking back home to see their mother. Lightning had been left behind this time and had not accompanied Christine to the city. One of the men kicked his foot out and hit Jain in the head, knocking him to the ground. "Stay out of our city, outsiders!"

Christine screamed and moved out of the way, barely missing the kick of the other man. The two riders started to move in closer but stopped at the sound of riders coming fast down the road from the direction of the farmlands.

"Go back to your mud," said one of the young men as they turned the other way and rode out toward Forest View.

Christine leaned down to see how Jain was doing. His arm had hit a sharp rock, and a small amount of blood dripped to the ground. She helped him sit up. Four horses came into view from the farmlands. Christine flagged them down for help. It was Karel, Thomas, Anya, and Stephanie. In quick succession, the friends ran to Jain. Scrapes and bruises already showed up on his dirtied face.

Christine explained what had happened. She expected sympathy but only got cold looks from her friends.

"Well, what did you think would happen?" asked Anya. Her lips were pursed, and a scowl covered her face. "One minute you are fighting against them, and now you are cozying back up with them in their big castle. They will never accept us, Christine."

"I will always be from the farmlands. I might have gone about things the wrong way, but it was all I knew to do at the time. I still want peace for us."

Karel nodded his head, but no one else said anything.

"All I want is peace. Real peace. For both peoples. There shouldn't be any differences in how we are treated."

"Some of them might like us now." Jain added his support to his sister. "We did help to stop the Preacher's army in Forest View."

"I'm sure they will find a way to explain the battle to make them look better than us," Karel said. "Christine, you think peace can be found. I just don't know if it can."

"A way will be found, Karel. Darius…I mean the King, is fair-minded. When I live in the city I will find help for us."

"You are going to live in the city now?" interrupted Anya. Her eyes flashed in anger, and she paced back and forth. "That's just great."

Christine tried to calm her friend down. "I'm not supposed to say anything yet until the official announcement, but the King and I are engaged to be married. I thought my friends should know."

"Congratulations, my Queen!" said Thomas as he made a mock bow.

Karel stood in shock. "You know, Christine, I may have been wrong. You've always wanted to marry him. I told you it was impossible, him being a city boy and the son of a councilor. But now, who knows, maybe there will be peace after all. If the two of you can marry, maybe there is hope for peace."

Stephanie and Anya began asking Christine about the wedding plans, what dress she would wear, where it would be held, and the three young men stood off to the side and talked about how it would be to be friends with the King and Queen.

The more they talked the more they felt better about things. Christine and Jain joined two of them on their mounts and soon were riding back into the farmlands. Christine couldn't wait to tell her mother and sister the news.

Chapter Twenty Four

That evening while Mezar and Kelln met with Darius and his father to further discuss recent events, a lone visitor made her way through the dungeon tunnels. It smelled of mildew and mice, and the young lady, dressed in black, tried not to touch the cold, hard walls. Up ahead she heard voices. It sounded like two men. They would be no problem to her.

A lone torch flickered against the walls up and down the corridor, sending larger-than-life shadows across her vision. She shielded her eyes and stayed close to the walls. The two men noticed her as soon as she rounded the corner. One of them ran up and grabbed her, forcing her over to where the other was so they could see her better in the torchlight.

"Who are you? What are you doing here?"

"I just came to visit you two lonely men." She batted her dark eyes at them.

"No one is supposed to be here," said one of the guards. "Orders."

"Well, I don't think I can find my way back. So I guess I'll have to stay for a while." She moved up close to one of their faces and smiled.

The guard smiled back, but his smile soon turned to horror as a cold knife swiftly appeared up against his throat.

"What... do you want?" his voice was hoarse.

"The keys to the door."

The other guard tried to back around her. She kicked her foot out and knocked him to the floor. He stared up at her in fear.

"This knife can cut two necks as well as it can cut one," she said with a gleam in her eyes.

"But we can't... He'll kill us."

"Who will?" she demanded.

"The new King. We are ordered to guard the prisoners."

"He won't kill anyone. He's too soft. But I can." She pushed the knife a little sharper into the guard's neck, drawing a small droplet of blood. Her heart beat with wild betrayal at what she had to do. She hated herself for it, but it was the only way she could think of to get the information she needed to find her mother.

"Give her the keys," the other guard said.

The guard with the keys gave them to her. She unlocked a door to an unused cell, then at knife point pushed the two guards into it, locking the bars behind her. She then stepped over to the cell holding her father, the Preacher.

"Alessandra." The Preacher looked surprised. "What are you doing? How did you…" His voice dropped to a whisper. "Are you here to kill me?"

"That depends on the answers to a few questions. You've lied to me. I heard from Darius that you spent some time in Mar. Why? What did you want in Mar so badly?"

The Preacher laughed out loud, and he grabbed two of the bars that made up the cell door. "Alessandra, let me out of here, and I will make you a queen."

"I don't want to be a queen. Why did you go to Mar and lie to me?" Her voice grew louder, and her body shook with anger.

"It wasn't any of your business, Daughter. Why all of the interest in Mar? It is a dirty city run by criminals, with nothing of worth there anymore. Now Belor..."

"Is my mother there?"

"Your mother is dead. I have told you that before." The Preacher's eyes hardened.

"She didn't die. She left you because you were out of control. You used to preach peace and love, and you would motivate people. Now you teach fighting and death. All you want is power. Now, where is she?" Alessandra yelled, not caring if her voice carried out of the cell. Tears poured from her eyes and streamed down her face.

The Preacher dove for her through the bars, trying to grab the keys, but she jumped out of the way and kicked his hand back.

"Who told you this? Have you been talking to your crazy grandfather again?"

"Do you want out of here or not?"

The Preacher's eyes brightened. "You would let me out? I am sentenced to die."

Alessandra knew what she was doing could bring her own death, but her heart ached to see her mother again. "Only if you lead me to my mother."

"But I said—"

"I heard what you said," Alessandra interrupted. "Do you want out?"

"Yes." The Preacher's lips stretched thin. He never liked relying on others for help.

"Is she in Mar?"

"I don't know anymore." The Preacher sighed and his shoulders slumped down. "She once was. I can take you to people who knew her before. Perhaps they know. Maybe she will see you. She wouldn't talk to me ever again."

A look of regret flashed across on his face, but was gone quickly.

Her father continued. "Don't think she is so wonderfully perfect compared to me. She has her own dark secrets too, Alessandra. All of Mar does. As I said, it is a place ran by criminals."

"Do you promise to help me find her? I don't want any tricks. I don't want you to use your power on me as soon as we are out of here. Grandfather told me how to protect myself from your power."

"Oh, he did." This perked the Preacher up. "And I thought I had learned all of his tricks."

Alessandra ignored his curiosity. She had to get this done quickly. "Remember, I have a new friend who happens to be the King now. I walk away from here or turn you in later and you are dead. You lead me to her and maybe you will stay alive."

The Preacher looked surprised at her vehemence, but Alessandra was beyond caring. "But if they find out you let me go, they will have your head as well as mine," he said.

"That is a chance I have to take for my mother."

"I will take you."

"What about him?" she pointed toward another cell where a lone man lay on the filthy ground. He glanced their way but said nothing. She gave the Preacher the keys and a map of the tunnels under the castle.

"Sean may be useful to us," said the Preacher. "I will see what motivates him."

"The map should show you a tunnel that leads out the back of the castle under a small hill," Alessandra directed. "I stole this from the archives. You should leave as soon as you can. You will not be noticed until the guard change in a few hours, and everyone else will be at the ceremony. That's all the lead you will have out of the city."

"And where will you be?" asked the Preacher.

"At the ceremony. I can't give them anything to be suspicious about." Alessandra tried to keep her voice steady. "I will be by Kelln's side as I've been for the last day." Deceiving Kelln once again was going to be the hardest thing she had ever done.

Alessandra unlocked her father's and Sean's cell doors and began to walk away, needing to get back before anyone noticed. She brushed tears from her eyes. Guilt almost buried her at what she was doing. She had committed treason against those who had actually helped her and cared for her. But desperation to find her mother after all these years overcame all of Alessandra's rational thoughts.

The Preacher went over to Sean's cell as Alessandra turned the corner. Before she was out of earshot, the Preacher called to her, "Be careful my daughter. I will meet you in Mar in three weeks. I will leave a message at the Boar's Head Inn."

The plan was foolhardy, she knew, but she couldn't pass up the smallest glimmer of hope. Her heart ached, and tears burned her eyes for her betrayal, but hope rose inside her as she remembered her mother's face. It had been so long she could barely make out the features in her blurry mind. *She had dark red hair like me.*

Chapter Twenty Five

Darius sat in a carriage on the way to the coliseum. The morning was warm but threatened rain. The leaves on the trees were fuller every day and flowers adorned the entry way of shops along the way. The city held a nervousness that seemed to be barely under control. City guards were abundant in the streets, and so far the general citizenry were behaving themselves.

News had reached Darius that there had been sightings of soldiers from the Kingdom of Arc gathering in the northwest across the border from Sur in the city of Herro. Nothing serious had happened yet, but it was a problem Darius would need to face in the coming weeks. Soldiers from Denir had also reported a Gildanian buildup of men across the border, but Darius had talked to Mezar. As soon as the ceremony was over, his new friend would be going back home, meeting with the Emperor and his father, the general, and taking care of any confusion at their southern border. Darius sighed. He had not inherited a peaceful Realm.

Belor also still sat in upheaval, as no one firmly ruled the city. A few men, who had sided with the Preacher but now had removed themselves from him, tried to regain some control, but the people were not very supportive. Darius would have to help find and appoint a governor there quickly.

The hours between his meeting with the councilors and the official announcement had been filled with meetings and planning sessions. He had met with councilors, ambassadors, farmers, mayors, and religious leaders, as well as his father many times. They disagreed on many things and agreed on a few, but progress was made. By the time the ceremony in the coliseum approached, Darius felt confident.

His mother, Elizabeth, had been a great comfort to Darius in the last few days. Just knowing she was there to talk to helped Darius feel more confident. They had spoken a few times the previous day about Darius's wedding plans. She was so excited to be able to help plan a wedding. She had not met Christine's mother yet, but Darius knew they would get along well. His mother got along with everyone.

Six white Cremelino horses pulled the large carriage. They were all from White Island and it was hard to stop them all from trying to communicate to Darius at the same time. They had not been able to speak with the previous king and so were anxious to voice their thoughts and support. The Cremelinos were also able to keep in contact with one another across great distances. They were almost giddy with excitement to have a wizard on the throne again and someone to communicate with. It was what they were born to do, but been deprived of for a long time.

Darius opened the curtains. He smiled and waved at onlookers as they drove their carriages and walked to the assembly. Slight butterflies grew inside of him. His mother affirmed it was natural. She looked better since moving into the castle yesterday. Richard had been spending more time with her also.

"I won't have much time to see you," Darius said to his mother. "I'll miss our home."

She smiled and patted him on the head. It was kind of silly, but Darius knew the gesture meant she loved him.

He entered the coliseum between two large white stone pillars. A rumble sounded across the large expanse as everyone rose to their feet. He was startled. "I wasn't prepared for this," he told his mother and father, who sat opposite him in the carriage.

The ancient structure of stone seemed to be larger than before and held an over-capacity crowd. He remembered back to times when he was younger and had seen King Edward enter. Now he would be the one the crowd cheered for. Tears threatened the corner of his eyes. He keenly felt the loyalty and love of the people as he began his entrance. As he waved to the crowd, he recognized familiar faces. He realized they would treat him differently now.

Ahead of him, he spotted the colors of Anikari and the four major cities of the Realm: Mar, Denir, Sur, and even Belor. He wondered who had come from Belor and hoped for no trouble on this day. Colorful flags had been posted and waved over their respective leaders.

The King's procession was almost to the stand when he saw Kelln sitting next to Alessandra in the front of the crowd. He waved at them, and Kelln waved back. He was dressed in his finest clothes, which looked too formal on him. Kelln's hair was still unruly and hard to keep in place, especially in the growing wind. Alessandra had dark circles under her eyes and looked tired and nervous. When Darius looked at her, she did not meet his eyes but looked down instead. Once again he got a nagging feeling that he would have to watch her more closely.

Darius ascended the stand, and the crowd sat. He hoped it wouldn't rain. The skies were threatening, with bulging black and gray clouds gathering over the city. The breeze rippled the flags that stood around the border of the stand.

Richard San Williams, councilor to a king but never to be one himself, stood up and approached the pulpit. He rested his hands on the unique carving of olive wood laced with gold.

"My fellow citizens of the Realm, I welcome you to this assembly. Today we join in a joyous occasion of welcoming our new King and Protectorate, King Darius DarSan Williams." His voice broke ever so slightly, but the applauding crowd covered it up.

Darius stood and walked to the pulpit, standing beside his father. He looked over the crowd. He touched his sword at his side and gained comfort through its power. Christine smiled up at him from a side chair. He hoped they would accept her. *Should I tell them first or last?*

Darius stood in his full kingly attire, dressed in the black and red of Anikari, his purple cape of royalty blowing behind him in the increasing wind. Richard lifted up the crown, and Darius knelt in front of the crowd.

"Upon the death of King Edward," Richard continued, "Darius lawfully became the King. Today we formally acknowledge that bestowal and set upon him the crown of the Realm, and welcome him as our King and Protector to inherit the Throne of Power that is now his by right." Richard placed the golden circlet on his son's head. His piercing gray eyes looked down at his only son and a small smile escaped his lips. "You may now arise."

The crowd erupted in applause and enthusiasm. Richard went back to his chair and Darius approached the podium. "Welcome, my friends and fellow citizens. I regret the passing of our former king, King Edward DarSan Montere, a great man that led us in a period of unequaled peace. As we all know, new problems have arisen of late throughout the Realm. I pledge that the problems will be corrected, that wrongs will be made right, and the Realm will continue to be looked upon by our neighbors as the peaceful, successful, and great kingdom it is."

This brought applause again from the crowd. Many seemed pleased to hear their new king speak so openly and candidly of troubles.

"With the passing of any great king, changes need to be made. So it is today." *Here it goes.* "My father will be Senior Councilor to me, the same position he held previously under King Edward. His word and command will be as mine own, except in things a king cannot delegate. As a member of the royal family, the title Dar will now be added to his name." He glanced at his father and smiled. His father looked genuinely surprised at the additional words and title Darius had added.

"My second and third councilors will be Jarad San Newlyn and Michael San Lazier, if they will accept." He motioned for them to join the other councilors on the stand. Jarad was known as one of the older religious leaders throughout Anikari. It was the first time people could remember a religious man being put into the nobility as a councilor. Michael was in his mid-thirties but had as a junior councilor proven his loyalty to King Edward many times.

Darius next announced that Cray Dreydon would also be a councilor. Cray had been surprised and flattered when Darius had approached him about the appointment earlier that day. He would be the King's military councilor.

The other new councilor was Martin Halverssn, a man from the farmlands who had gone with Christine to deliver the farmers' petition the previous year.

Martin approached the stand, and whispers grew throughout the crowd. Dressed as well as he could, his homespun wool pants and worn boots still marked him as a farmer. Some yelling came from the back of the crowd, and Darius called for his soldiers to remove the troublemakers. There were even hushed whispers among the other councilors.

Many did not like this decision of putting a farmer formally on to the council, but Darius had decided any future problems of discrimination between the two groups could not be blamed on him. He was doing his part.

He named Kelln El'Han as his ambassador at large, to travel the Realm and report back to Darius on conditions. Kelln smiled from ear to ear.

Finally, Darius brought Mezar forward and announced him in his official capacity as second heir to the Gildanian Empire. The crowd cheered and seemed impressed their new king had already established such contacts.

Now it's time, while they are cheering, he thought to himself.

A misty rain began to fall around them, and the crowd tried to cover their heads. Darius paused and took a breath. He called Christine to come forward. She looked radiant in the new light blue silk dress she had designed herself. Seamstresses had worked nonstop to get the dress completed on time. Her soft blonde hair cascaded down over the burgundy cape she wore. Her curls bounced softly as she stepped forward. A servant walked beside her, covering her head with a large parasol to keep off the rain.

The crowd strained to see who she was. They surmised that it must be the daughter of some high noble. Her green eyes had a new edge to them but still held their dramatic sparkle. Darius took her hand as she approached.

"Along with naming my new councilors, I would also like to announce my engagement and impending wedding to Christine Anderssn." The crowd cheered for a moment for their young and handsome king, but as the last name sunk in, the applause thinned. "She is from the farm lands surrounding Anikari."

Darius thought the entire crowd stopped speaking at the exact moment he finished his sentence. Thunder roared overhead, and the rain picked up.

His announcement had taken a moment to sink in, but now the crowd was in confusion. Some of the farmers cheered from the back and were quieted by neighboring city people. Others began to shout up at Darius. Even some of the councilors had looks of disgust on their faces. Darius felt anger grow. He was the King! Why shouldn't he marry whom he wanted? The division between the different factions of people had gone on too long and had affected too many lives.

"Stop!" The power-filled shout echoed throughout the coliseum, the words seemingly coming from the heavens, even louder than the thunder itself. Even Christine, next to him, shivered at the sound. Power seemed to emanate from Darius's body. "Look at this woman, whom I love." The crowd looked, and Christine blushed. "Nothing is wrong with her or with any of you. Whether we are farmers or born in the city, whether we come from Mar, Belor, Sur, Denir, Anikari, or any of the smaller towns in our Realm, we are all the same. We have a shared heritage as members of the Realm. Even the reign of the kings has been affected by the great inequality among us, as my grandfather was denied his place as heir when he married someone from outside the city. Fighting has erupted in Belor because someone thought they were better than others and deserved power. All of us, whether from Mar or Denir, from outside or inside a city wall, are all created equal. We all have our own intelligences, talents, powers, and perspectives. Let us celebrate our differences and let old hatreds disappear."

Darius drew his sword with a ringing sound and held the powerful relic up high above his head with one hand, the other still holding onto Christine's hand. His muscles bulged with strength and control. His sword glowed a golden color, and with a release of his power he sent a bolt of lightning high up into the cloudy sky. The power spread out over the people in cascading colors to form a dome of power stopping the rain from touching those within the coliseum. Some of the dignitaries in the front began to shrink back in fear. Such use of power had not been seen openly in Anikari for as long as any man could remember. Darius prayed inside that his power would be accepted and that he hadn't just made a cause for a full-scale revolt.

"I challenge any person who disagrees with my choice for peace to come forward." He looked back at the councilors and nobles. "And, that includes any of you."

The crowd fell silent. The look on their faces mirrored the questions in their minds. Who was this fierce young man who had become their king? Could he defy the entire assembly at such a young age? What power did he hold?

Darius stood silently, tall and proud next to his fiancée, holding his golden sword high in the air. Kelln walked forward next to him and held his sword high next to Darius's. As his sword touched Darius's, the white light engulfed him also. He looked at Darius nervously.

"As his Ambassador I accept his pledge of peace," he proclaimed to the crowd with a smile to Darius, "and will publish that peace in all reaches of our Realm."

Mezar came forward next. "I, Mezar Alrishitar, named second heir by my grandfather the Emperor of Gildan, hail your King and support him until the end of my days."

The people realized this was not an oath to be taken lightly by their southern neighbor. The Gildanian Empire had always been a powerful neighboring kingdom.

Mezar pushed his hands up into the air. The sleeves from his golden cloak fell down his brown arms. His eyes turned a lighter color of brown, and golden fire erupted from his fingertips to join with the lightning from Darius's sword. The entire Coliseum was bathed in a brilliant mixture of yellow, gold, and white. The crowd stayed transfixed.

Out of the corner of his eye, Darius saw someone else stand up and walk toward him. He walked deliberately, but proud. A look of respect and awe covered his face.

"My son is your king, so named by King Edward. His word is law, and his law is just and righteous. I, Richard DarSan Williams, accept his proposal of peace, bow to him, and pledge my sole support." He smiled over at Darius.

Cray walked forward, holding his fist in the air. "As the general commander of his armies, I, Cray Dreydon, pledge the support of the entire army of this great Realm in defense of Darius DarSan Williams and his laws of peace."

The other two Senior Councilors also joined Darius on the stand.

As if on cue, a single clap echoed through the crowd. Then another. The applause continued until the entire coliseum rocked with support and acceptance of their new king. The sound was deafening, but sweet to Darius's ears. He knew he had caused quite a spectacle, but that is what the people needed. They needed to be shocked from their complacent ways and join him in finding peace. In quick bursts he had thoughts about the last year of his life. There were many paths filled with decisions. He was glad he had chosen the way he did. He felt right about where he stood.

Darius lowered his sword, and the normal color returned. Mezar turned his arms in a circle, and the golden light rapidly expanded with swirling circles around the tops of the walls of the coliseum and then extinguished with a loud thunder clap of color. The dome disappeared, but by now the rain had stopped falling.

Richard turned to Darius and whispered, "It worked this time, but don't think there won't be any more troubles." He smiled.

"I will take it one day at a time. Today I have acceptance." Darius shrugged his shoulders.

Darius dismissed the crowd with a wave of his hand and declared the next day a holiday full of festivities.

Christine clung to his arm and kissed his cheek. "I am so proud of you, my future husband."

Darius laughed and held her tightly. "You are worth more than the kingdom to me, dear Christine," he whispered into her ear. "I would defy them all for you!"

Mezar walked up to him and pulled him aside. After making sure no one else was around, he clasped his arm in a handshake. "Welcome to the ranks of wizards. It's been a long time since we have seen one declared openly in the leadership of the Realm."

Darius laughed. "And to think I thought you were my prisoner. With that show you just put on, Mezar, you could have destroyed me at any time, right?"

Mezar's smile was even bigger than Darius's was. "Yes. Yes, I could have."

The two of them laughed while the rain came down once more. Kelln motioned Darius over to the carriage.

"I have a lot of questions," Darius said to Mezar as they walked toward the carriage. "I hope you're not leaving too soon."

Mezar looked at Leandra, who just approached, and then back at Darius. "Even if I do, I will not be gone for long."

The rest of the day was filled with greetings and festivities. The people seemed to enjoy a new spirit of cooperation and hatreds between groups were starting to recede.

***

The next day Mezar stood with Darius outside of the castle doors. Darius was readying an honor guard to accompany the man south to his homeland.

"Do you think I need protection on the way through your Realm?" Mezar gave him a questioning look.

"No, my friend. I've only seen a small amount of what I am sure you could do with your power. It is my way of showing you my thanks and respect. I hope the Emperor will see the Realm as an ally and pull his troops back."

"You have my assurance there will be no attack. I am sure my grandfather is only anxious to see me again."

Darius looked down at the ground. "Mezar, what do I do about my power? I'm not really sure what the people think about it. Rumors are flying."

"Darius, you are a wizard. Never be ashamed of that fact. Even in Gildan, where the power is more accepted, it is still a rare and precious thing. The royal family seems to have more of its share of those who are strong in this power, and it has helped us many times."

"Maybe that is why I have it… as part of the royal family. Cray told me yesterday that my grandfather, Alric, had it."

Mezar lifted his eyebrows. "That is quite interesting. I wonder if all of the ruling families have been blessed with this power. I will do some research in the wizard's library."

"You have a wizard library?" Darius grew excited. "Did you have a teacher? How did you learn about it?"

"Yes, we have a small academy where they teach about it. You should come. It would do you well to learn from our masters."

"Would they let me?"

"I'll ask and let you know." Mezar looked behind him as he heard a boy bring up his horse. The honor guard was ready.

"Is there anything you can tell me now that would help me to understand my powers?" Darius asked.

Mezar looked thoughtful. "You have heard that there are different types of wizards?"

"I have heard. But it is not talked about much. The teachers gloss over it. All we mostly learn about is the wizard rebellion and how the powers of a wizard are evil and lead to destruction."

"Yes, that was unfortunate for us wizards." Mezar nodded his head in understanding. "Just like all men, there are good and bad ones, and those who misuse power, whether a wizard or not."

Darius agreed.

"Besides our school, there is the Wizard Conclave in Arc, the Wizard Sanctuary in Quentis, and rumors of a Wizard Citadel behind the barrier in Alaris. You would do well to meet with some of them." Mezar paused a moment sensing Darius was a bit overwhelmed by it all. Then he continued. "I think you are a wizard of the heart. One who gets his power from his feelings. You have noticed increased power through anger or love, I presume?"

"Much stronger through love than anger." Darius nodded. "A lesson I had to learn."

Mezar smiled. "The most powerful kind of wizard, but the most volatile one also."

"And what are you, Mezar?"

"I am a wizard of the mind. My power comes from what I learn and from my mind. It is usually more focused than an earth wizard and not as powerful as a wizard of the heart."

"I obviously have much to learn."

"You will do well."

"Take care, Mezar."

Mezar bowed low. "And you, my King."

They shook hands. Mezar turned toward his horse when Leandra came out from one of the structures of the castle compound. Darius watched them from a distance. He smiled as Mezar held her hand for a moment and kissed her cheek. Mezar proceeded to pull something out of his pocket and rubbed his hands over it. A golden light engulfed the trinket and then died down, leaving only a soft yellow gold. He slipped the gift over Leandra's neck. Darius could see a slight shade of blush on her face. She fingered the gift as Mezar mounted and rode off with his honor guard.

Mezar gave one last wave to all those who were gathered. Darius waved back.

* * *

Later that morning, Darius attended the funeral of Kelln's father. Even though the man had defected the previous year to fight with the Preacher, he had returned and saved Kelln's life in the end. Darius felt that he should show respect for that final act of bravery. He had brought an honor guard and organized a burial of the state.

The two friends now stood alone outside of the city cemetery after the funeral had ended. Pain filled Kelln's eyes as they walked away.

"Is your family all right?" asked Darius.

"My mother is strong. She will be fine. But my sisters are having a hard time. They, too, had been brought into the Preacher's dream of independence through fighting. Everything they have known for the last year has collapsed."

"A lot of people were hurt by the Preacher's need for power," Darius said. "And I have to tell you something important about him, Kelln."

Kelln looked confused.

He didn't want to tell Kelln earlier and spoil the funeral, but his friend deserved to know. "The Preacher and Sean escaped yesterday."

"What? How?" Kelln threw his hands in the air. "Have you found him yet?"

"No, we haven't." Darius paused. He hated to hurt his friend so close after the funeral, but he had to tell Kelln everything. "Kel, the guards say a young woman dressed in black tied them up and took their keys. She gave the Preacher a map to help him escape."

Kelln fell down onto a nearby bench. "Maybe it wasn't her," he whispered.

"They reported that the Preacher called her Alessandra."

"Why would she do this? Why?" Kelln put his face into his hands. "Why does she hate me so much?"

"I'm doing all I can. Cray has sent his men to scour the city and beyond. We are focusing our search on the roads leading to Mar. Stay here for a while with your family until they are doing better. You will be more protected here. There is no rush for you to leave Anikari immediately. And, if you need any help, let me know. There is nothing I will deny you, Kelln."

Darius sat down next to his friend and became more serious. "I want you to know that I was unfair to you, and I can never repay that, but—"

"But nothing." Kelln slapped his friend on the back, almost knocking Darius over. Some nearby guards took a step forward. "Is it against the rules to slap the King on the back?"

They both laughed in embarrassment, a welcome release to the day's events. Darius was amazed at how resilient his friend was. He knew he was worried about the Preacher and his daughter.

"I will take a few days to get my family settled—I owe them that—then I am going after them." Kelln's face grew stern. "I can't let him run free after all he has done. And I need to find Alessandra."

"I won't hold you back, if that is what you need to do. I gave you the position of ambassador for a reason, Kel. The councilors here have ignored what is going on around the Realm for too long. I will tour the land when I can, but in the meantime you will be part of my eyes and ears. The Preacher has caused enough trouble in Belor and for each of us personally. You will have permission and funds to go anywhere you need to in helping me maintain the peace of the Realm."

Not one to stay down for long, Kelln stood up and smiled weakly. "I can't believe you are the King, Darius."

"Our lives have sure changed haven't they?" Darius stood up next to his friend. "We still have a lot to do in catching the Preacher and restoring order to our borders, but I know we can do it."

"Personally, I think you will do a great job. I mean, it can't be any worse than what all those old cronies have done for years, right?"

"Kel! You can't say that." Darius looked around. "Someone might hear you."

"And do what? You *are* the King."

Darius smiled at the joke. "It really is nice to have you around again. I look forward to you being my ambassador. Maybe a councilor or governor later, but for now I want you to have the ability to do things a councilor might not be able to do."

"Like sneaking around?"

"Yes, like sneaking around. You up for it?" Darius whispered.

Kelln smiled big. Then the smile faded and grew stern once again. "That maniac still wants to kill me, I am sure. I will feel much better when he is behind bars again or dead."

"So would I. As far as I can tell, he has not returned to Anikari or Belor."

"From Alessandra's reactions, I will be traveling to Mar. That's where they will be."

A few moments later Kelln left to go back to his family, and Darius mounted his horse and joined his guard. He was needed back at the castle again for another meeting. Everyone wanted to speak to the King, and since he was new and young, they expected him to be everywhere. He hoped he would be able to meet Christine later. He smiled inside at the surprise he had waiting for her. It had taken a lot of late night planning.

As he walked through the courtyard on the way into the castle he heard his named being called.

"Darius... I mean King Darius."

Darius turned around. Coming from the direction of the stables, Jain sat on a new horse that Darius had given him. His sister Emily sat behind him. She waved shyly, and Darius waved and smiled back.

"Thank you," Jain added as they continued to ride out of the castle grounds.

Darius continued walking back inside the castle. He liked Jain a lot and intended to make good use of his services in the months and years to come. The Anderssn family would be considered royalty now, at least once Christine and he officially wed. He would give them the noble San title as soon as the wedding concluded. He wished Christine's father, Stefen, was still alive. Darius had never had a chance to say good-bye to him. He had been a good, strong man. Christine had told Darius her father's mother had been from the city. But then, Darius's own father's mother had been a farmer. If people could just understand that they really were all the same, peace could be found.

Richard already stood waiting for him at the castle. Darius wondered how he was so organized. *Maybe I can learn something from him.* They disagreed on policies and on ways of executing decisions sometimes, but Darius could finally admit many times his father was right.

His father smiled at him as he walked by his side into another meeting. Darius was about as big as his father now. Over the last year as he trained in the Superstition Mountains and marched to Denir and Belor, his body had become strong. His shoulders were broad and muscular. He smiled back at his father and realized they were indeed doing better.

The meeting was a short and simple one, and Darius soon found himself racing back to his rooms to prepare to meet Christine.

On his way there he stopped and said his good-byes to Leandra in person.

"I'm sorry Leandra, for everything you have been through. Where will you go now?"

"To visit family in Tean."

"Nor Mar then, where you are from?"

"No," she shook her head and blushed. Darius now understood. Tean was closer to Gildan than Mar was.

"I have set up an account for you to use," Darius said. "You and your family will be well cared for."

"Thank you, Sire," Leandra curtsied in her multi-colored skirt. "You really have been too kind."

Darius still felt bad at how he had treated her. He noticed her fingering the locket that sat against her neck. "From Mezar?" he asked with a smile, knowing full well the answer.

"None of your business," Leandra smiled, then quickly added, "Sire."

"No need for that Leandra," Darius said. "We've been through too much together. Call me Darius." He leaned forward and gave her a small peck on the cheek. "Good luck with everything. And please, know, the Realm will always be at your disposal for any help you need."

She smiled and Darius introduced her to her escort—a group of three riders that would bring her to Tean.

After leaving her, Darius returned to his rooms. He grabbed a few things, snuck away from his guards once again, and rode off on his horse. He knew he shouldn't use his power so, but he had one more thing to do that day. And it was a private affair.

Chapter Twenty Six

The day held warm, and the clouds from the previous day were long gone. The trees through the farmlands and forest were almost full. The emerging ferns and other undergrowth at the edge of the forest stood damp from the prior day's rain. Darius sucked in a deep breath, and excitement grew within him. His horse's hooves splashed up bits of dirt and mud as he rode faster. He emerged onto the field, looking around to make sure Christine hadn't arrived yet.

The sky overhead held a deep blue, and the lake reflected like a magnificent mirror. A small number of white clouds showed in its smooth ripples. He glanced toward the mountains and seemed to lose himself for a moment, thinking about his time there and how much had happened since first leaving Anikari the previous summer. The foothills of the mountains stood covered in mist as the sun warmed the grounds throughout the farmlands. It was still the most perfect spot he had ever seen.

Darius busied himself for a few minutes around the field. He kept looking up to see when Christine would arrive. Her Cremelino could be quiet and sneaky at times.

A short time later, Christine rode into the field. She had a quizzical look on her face.

Good day, Wizard.

Good day, Lightning. Darius sent the thoughts in his head toward the horse.

Your powers are getting stronger.

Why do you say that?

Because you are a shout in my head now instead of a whisper.

Sorry. I need to control a lot of things with the power.

Yes, you do. We need to have a long talk about that, but that will wait until later. Your lady seems to be perplexed.

Darius laughed out loud.

Christine looked over at him as she dismounted. Squares and circles of rope covered portions of the field. She looked around at them with no comprehension of what they meant.

"What is all of this?" Christine motioned as she approached him.

"All of what?" Darius tried not to smile, but it was difficult.

"All this rope." Christine jumped off of Lightning and joined Darius in the field.

"Oh, that." Darius shrugged.

"Darius!" She leaned over to give him a kiss but pulled away as he leaned into her. He almost lost his balance.

"Hey! Why did you do that?" He pretended to pout.

"Tell me about the rope, or I won't marry you." Christine folded her arms across her chest and stood in mock defiance with pouted red lips, her blond hair sparkling in the sun.

Darius laughed. "Well, you said you didn't know if you could stand living in the castle all the time, right? Too big and dark and old, I think you said."

"Yes." She unfolded her arms, squinted her eyes, and wrinkled her nose trying to figure it out.

"Well..." Darius spread his arms out toward the ropes. "Behold your new house. The Diamond Palace."

"My what?"

"We are going to build a house right here. Just for you and me."

"It looks bigger than a house."

Darius looked sheepish. "We will need to have room for some guards and servants, a few meeting rooms, but I promise to try and not bring too much business out here when we are here. We won't be able to be here all of the time, but you won't have to be at the castle all of the time either."

Her eyes lit up. "Here in the field?"

"Why not? Do you know of any place better?"

"No. No I don't." She leaned into him. "And you called this the Diamond Palace?"

"Yes. It will have a field of the greenest grass out front, with a large window we can look out from. And when the sun rises high during the day it will reflect off the lake and the grass and..."

"And we can put a swing in the big tree, just like my father had when we were young?" asked Christine. She ran to the tree and swung her arms around a lower branch, her gaze looking up into the tree.

Darius followed her over. "Anything for you, Christine!"

"And we'll still have our Field of Diamonds." She grabbed Darius tightly until he pleaded to breathe again. "Oh, thank you. Thank you, Darius."

"You're welcome, you're Highness." His laugh was deep and merry.

"Not just for the house, but for what it means. It means you were thinking about me. Even in the midst of all that has happened in the last few days, you were thinking about me."

"I won't ever forget to think about you." He gave her a kiss on the cheek. She smiled and returned it with a kiss on the lips. Darius felt as if he was being lifted off the ground. He had missed those lips so much over the past year.

"It's so beautiful here," whispered Christine, almost in reverence.

"What's that over there?" Darius pointed to a glitter in the grass.

"I don't know. Probably just a water drop sparkling in the sunshine."

"It looks like something else." Darius smiled a mischievous smile.

"All right, I'll go and investigate," said Christine with a laugh, knowing Darius was up to something else.

"Oh, Darius!" she yelled as she picked the ring up. "It's beautiful... and sparkles so much..."

"Just like you, Christine."

Darius took it softly from her and slid the brilliant diamond ring onto her slender fingers. "You did name this the Field of Diamonds, didn't you?" He laughed as happy tears rolled down Christine's face.

"I love you, Darius."

"I love you, too, my love."

They embraced and held each other for a moment. Darius lifted Christine's hand and put his hand over the ring. He tried to remember what Mezar had done. He called from deep inside him, and power rose from his fingertips and encircled both their hands. Darius projected a feeling of love into the power, and it flew up Christine's arm from the ring and into her heart.

She gasped, swaying on her feet. "Oh, Darius!"

Wizard! Lightning gasped also. *You are more powerful than we had ever imagined.*

A light circled around their hands and then settled back into the ring. It dimmed but left a small, glowing ember inside. "Now you can know how much I love you, Christine. No matter where you go, you will feel my love. Never doubt the power of love. I have learned this past year that above all other emotions, love is the strongest. It is the highest power there is. That is why the Preacher and his kind will never win. Hate and anger can never win."

A twig snapped. Darius drew his sword and brought forth his power without a moment's hesitation. It came to him almost effortlessly now.

"Darius, you aren't supposed to be out here alone. You are the King now." It was his father, Richard, with two of his personal guards.

"My Lord." Roald, one of the guards, bowed. "You should not escape our sight. We are here to protect you."

Darius looked chastised, but his father turned to the man. "Roald, remember whom you speak to."

Darius waved one hand in the air. "It's fine, Father. Roald is right in his protocol, and I have not been a good king."

"My King…" Roald stumbled for words. "I would never say that!"

Darius laughed merrily. "Roald, I am joking." Turning to his father, he said, "For one moment I just wanted to be only a young man in love."

Richard smiled as if he understood. "Just this once, Darius. After today, duty must rule the Realm. I will wait at the edge of the forest for you." He turned to leave with Roald and the other guard.

"You are wrong, Father," Darius said loudly in the crisp air. At that moment he was infused with joy.

Richard turned around. His eyebrows furrowed in confusion.

"You are wrong," Darius repeated for emphasis. "Starting today the power of love will rule the Realm." And with those words he brought his arms out in front of him and clapped.

Flowers bloomed around the field, and music filled the air… a song so sweet and soft it pierced the five of them. It lifted the heart and brought joy to the soul.

Tears came to Richard's eyes. He looked at the guards next to him. They, too, were smiling with memories of joy and happiness.

"I never imagined…" Richard said with a whisper, his faced transfixed with joy.

In a slow rotation, Darius brought his hands back down to his side and grabbed hold of Christine's hand again. The song faded, but the rapture lingered, almost sparkling in the air.

Christine stood in awe for a moment, then her knees buckled, and she knelt in front of him. Lightning, in all her pure white glory, knelt down on her two front legs. Richard approached and, with the two guards, knelt also.

Richard spoke first. The words were thick and difficult to bring forth through the emotion. "I never realized there was so much power in love."

Darius smiled. "Neither did I." He, too, was overwhelmed with what he had just done. He felt a love for his people that was without limit and condition. He knew he would make difficult decisions as king, but now he understood how to make those decisions. "It is truly how we are meant to rule."

All was quiet. Then Darius broke the silence with a soft but powerful whisper. "Father, I assume that I will be the first in many years to combine the powers of a wizard with the true power of the throne. I am a Wizard King!"

Richard looked up at his son, opened his eyes wider, and spoke. "I pledge my life and love to you, Darius DarSan Williams, King of the Realm, Protectorate of the People, and Wizard of the Heart. Your command is my wish. Your love is my desire. May you always rule in wisdom, judge in fairness, and serve in love."

Darius had a hard time seeing his father for the tears in his eyes. *He accepts me.* He pulled his father up into a strong embrace.

Christine, the two guards, and Lightning, now back standing, all bowed their heads in tribute to their new king. Darius motioned for them to rise. A glow surrounded him, and love engulfed him like never before.

Lastly, he reached out to touch Lightning, still not understanding his relationship with the Cremelino fully, but realizing it was meant to be.

Wizard, you have made us proud. The prophecy is beginning to be fulfilled:

Forgotten lines of ancient magic
and the power of the throne.
One will make them both his own
if his heart sees the true power.
He will bring light to fight darkness
and love to fight hate
if he reaches into the power of his heart.
He will find new allies, turn enemy to friend and
find the binding of all power on the path of peace. . .

You said beginning to be fulfilled? Darius asked the Cremelino of her cryptic prophecy.

Young Wizard King, you have found your heart and inherited the throne, but now you must establish peace. Only by binding together all of the power and light at your disposal can you defeat the darkness and triumph against your enemies once and for all.

Darius laughed. "Oh, that's all!"

EPILOGUE

The Preacher and Sean San Ghant huddled around some damp wood placed into a makeshift fire pit. The late spring rain still kept the distant Mountains of Gold shrouded in gray clouds. In the plains south of the Twin Cities sat a copse of trees surrounded by grassland. It was the only place offering some type of shelter in the area.

Sean sat on his haunches, trying to light the wood with flint and steel. The wetness of the wood restricted his ability. With a gruff growl, he threw the steel to the ground.

The Preacher walked over and, with a snap of his fingers, sparked a fire in the pit. He then proceeded to dry off a log to sit on using the same power.

"That would've been easier in the first place," snapped Sean.

"But not nearly as much fun as watching you struggle," said the Preacher with a large smile on his now red-bearded face.

"You should be a little nicer to me, Preacher, seeing I seem to be the only man around to help you."

"Others will come."

Using the map from Alessandra, the two men had wound their way through old tunnels and out the back of the castle walls and then eventually out of the city itself. The ceremony at the coliseum and the festivities following had allowed them the freedom to move around unnoticed. The Preacher surmised that the new King would be looking for him closer to Anikari or south toward Belor.

They had taken some horses and ridden together north from Anikari, traveling in the dark. They were to meet with some of the Preacher's other men south of the Twin Cities, far enough away from Anikari that they wouldn't be searched for there.

Sean sat back on a log and pulled some jerky out of his bag. They had stolen it from a small village on their way. "Why do they call you the Preacher? You don't look like a religious man to me."

"Religion comes in many different forms, Sean. I follow the tenants of the Eastern Kingdoms, one that teaches purity of thought and allows us to choose for ourselves. I attended their school of enlightenment and now I preach to people that they should decide for themselves what they want. People should not be held captive by others' ways of doing things."

"It sounds good in theory, I must admit. I've never liked others telling me what to do. But I believe someone needs to be in charge. Someone has to set the rules and hold people to them. Someone has to hold the power."

The Preacher turned a log over and dried the other side with his powers. "That is why I brought you along, Sean. You like power."

"I just want power over our new king." Sean stood up and threw a small branch off toward a tree. With his face reddening, he paced around. "I can't believe Darius's luck at being named the King. He didn't even want to be a noble."

"And you?"

"I've always wanted to be a noble. I always wanted power. If I had your power I would crush our new king and bring chaos to the throne."

"And what would chaos do, young noble?" The Preacher led his new student forward in his thoughts.

"Chaos brings opportunity. I would step in and take control. They would gladly give me power at that time. I will be their savior."

Chills ran down the Preacher's back. He had found an apt student. Sean would do nicely. He would listen to everything the Preacher would teach him. He was so gullible and full of revenge. It was almost too easy to lead him along, making the thoughts seem like his own, when in fact they were the Preacher's.

It was far easier than it had been with Darius. Darius wanted revenge and was confused, but deep down inside he had self-governing rules about how to act. Sean, on the other hand, had no scruples about getting his power any way he could.

"Darius betrayed us all, Sean. I, too, want to crush him and the royal family. I will bring him down and then hand over the land to my friends in the Eastern Kingdoms. Then they will reward us for our loyalty and shower us with praise and glory and power. We will rule the western land." He continued to poison the young noble's mind.

Sean sat mesmerized and only nodded his agreement.

The Preacher looked up. "I hear horses."

Sean got up and moved silently out of the blinding firelight to the edge of the trees. Three horses came into view.

The Preacher stood but stayed by the fire. "Welcome them in, Sean. These are my friends."

Three men in badly torn uniforms came into view. Sean motioned them to the fire.

"The others?" the Preacher asked.

The lead man shook his head from side to side.

"Oh well. The faithful will be rewarded. Come sit down. It is time to plan."

The five men planned late into the night, the Preacher sharing his vision and goals with them. They were convinced of his plans, and their eyes glowed with the fires of rebellion. A hatred of Darius and the royal family and the greed for power drove them forward.

After talking well into the night, the men all lay down to sleep. The rain cleared away, and although the night was cool, the air stayed dry.

In the morning they ate a ration of bread and cheese the three men had brought, fed their horses, and prepared to leave their separate ways.

"Sean, you are an important part in this plan." The Preacher stroked the young man's ego further. He had seen right away the usefulness of this greedy young noble boy. "While we are busy in Mar preparing for the Eastern Lords, you will travel to Sur and then make your way to the Kingdom of Arc. There is a contact who will meet you at Herro on the border. He is a spy in Arc. The kings there are weak politically and are mostly ruled by the Conclave of Wizards; however, the spy will have insight and opportunity inside their king's inner circle that we don't have. From there it will be up to you to convince them of the plan."

"I will convince them, Preacher. Don't worry about me," Sean said as he accepted a bag of coins from his new benefactor.

The gleam in his eye as he held the gold told the Preacher much about Sean's loyalties.

"Good," smiled the Preacher. "Don't spend the gold too quickly. I will provide a way for you to contact me later once the plans are in motion."

Sean smiled and nodded enthusiastically.

The Preacher stroked his newly formed beard in thoughtfulness. "I need to take care of a personal matter in Mar, and then I will be in contact with the Eastern Kingdom. By then your part of the plan should be in full motion. We will gain power and control from the chaos we create."

They all mounted their horses. The Preacher felt renewed in the morning sunshine and felt the early signs of summer already warming his fair skin.

"Sean." The Preacher grabbed the young noble's attention once last time. "Start thinking of what city you would like to rule. By this time next year, with the Eastern Kingdoms' blessings, I will rule the western lands, and you will have control of a city all your own. Sean San Ghant, Governor. How does that sound?"

Sean laughed and laughed. "Sounds perfect. I can't wait to see the look on Darius's face."

The two parties split, Sean going west and the Preacher and his men to the east. The Preacher spurred his horse on, sharing his power to increase the speed. His happy mood only slightly soured as he wondered what to do with Alessandra once he reached Mar. He was sure she would find him there eventually one way or another.

# # #

Read ***The Path Of Peace***,
Part 3 of The Cremelino Prophecy
to continue the adventures of Darius, Christine, Kelln, Mezar, and their friends...and find out The powerful secret of the Cremelinos.

A wizard King. An Evil influence. Powerful new magic.

Darius DarSan Williams, now newly crowned King of the Realm, is being pushed and tested on all sides by others vying for power.

His best friend Kelln is in Mar trying to find the escaped Preacher and his daughter.

Mezar discovers a plot in Gildan that could tear the Realm apart and put Christine in danger.

All are being watched over and guided by the mysterious Cremelino horses. They hold one final magical secret that could help Darius save those he loves and find the path of peace.

Can everyone come together in time and find a solution or will the Realm fall to a conquering foe?

With magic and wizardry abounding, and a race against time, the conclusion to The Cremelino Prophecy will not disappoint. Read it today!

Other Books By Mike Shelton
The Alaris Chronicles

A magical barrier. Civil war. Power-hungry Wizards.

The fate of a kingdom rests on the shoulders of three young wizards who couldn't be more different.

As the magical barrier protecting the kingdom of Alaris from dangerous outsiders begins to fail, and a fomenting rebellion threatens to divide the country in a civil war, the three wizards are thrust into the middle of a power struggle.

When the barrier comes down, the truth comes out. Was everything they were taught about their kingdom based on a lie?

Will they all choose to fight on the same side, or end up enemies in the battle over who should rule Alaris?

Sign up on Mike's website at www.MichaelSheltonBooks.com and get a copy of the prequel novella e-book to The Alaris Chronicles, Prophecy of the Dragon.

Protect the youngest heir of the Dragon King. That is the mission given to Imari in this prequel novella to The Alaris Chronicles.

The TruthSeer Archives

On an island far out in the Eastern Sea join a new adventure of magic through the stones of power.

The lies could kill her, but the truth could destroy a kingdom.

Given a rare TruthStone, Shaeleen suffers immense agony with every lie she hears or tells. While struggling to control her new power and curb the pain she learns a powerful truth that could thrust an entire continent into civil war.

The stones of power protect the five kingdoms of Wayland - and have done so for two hundred years. Now those stones are failing and a dark power threatens to take control. With the help of her brother, and a young thief, Shaeleen sets out on a dangerous journey to gather and restore the power of all the stones.

Shaeleen can either reveal the truths she finds and stop the physical torment or hold on to the lies and sacrifice her own well-being for the sake of the kingdom.

Will she succeed before the endless lies destroy her?

Readers of YA fantasy, unique magic, mighty wizards, reluctant heroes, and magnificent kingdoms will enjoy the TruthSeer Archives!

About the Author

Mike was born in California and has lived in multiple states from the west coast to the east coast. He cannot remember a time when he wasn't reading a book. At school, home, on vacation, at work at lunch time, and yes even a few pages in the car (at times when he just couldn't put that great book down). Though he has read all sorts of genres he has always been drawn to fantasy. It is his way of escaping to a simpler time filled with magic, wonders and heroics of young men and women.

Other than reading, Mike has always enjoyed the outdoors. From the beaches in Southern California to the warm waters of North Carolina. From the waterfalls in the Northwest to the Rocky Mountains in Utah. Mike has appreciated the beauty that God provides for us. He also enjoys hiking, discovering nature, playing a little basketball or volleyball, and most recently disc golf. He has a lovely wife who has always supported him, and three beautiful children who have been the center of his life.

Mike began writing stories in elementary school and moved on to larger novels in his early adult years. He has worked in corporate finance for most of his career. That, along with spending time with his wonderful family and obligations at church has made it difficult to find the time to truly dedicate to writing. In the last few years as his children have become older he has returned to doing what he truly enjoys – writing!

mikesheltonbooks@gmail.com
www.MichaelSheltonBooks.com
https://www.facebook.com/groups/MikeSheltonAuthor/
https://www.facebook.com/mikesheltonbooks/
http://www.Twitter.com/msheltonbooks
http://www.Instagram.com/mikesheltonbooks
https://www.pinterest.com/mikesheltonbooks/

9 780997 190038